The
Kew Gardens Girls

POSY LOVELL

PUTNAM
— EST. 1838 —

G. P. PUTNAM'S SONS
Publishers Since 1838
An imprint of Penguin Random House LLC
penguinrandomhouse.com

Text © The Orion Publishing Group Limited 2020
Trademark © The Board of Trustees of the Royal Botanic Gardens, Kew 2020
Kew is a registered trademark of The Board of Trustees of the Royal Botanic Gardens,
Kew Frontispiece © The Board of Trustees of the Royal Botanic Gardens, Kew
Published by arrangement with Orion Publishing Group Limited
First published in the United Kingdom in 2020

Library of Congress Cataloging-in-Publication Data

Names: Lovell, Posy, 1973– author.
Title: The Kew Gardens girls / Posy Lovell.
Description: New York : G. P. Putnam's Sons, [2021] |
Identifiers: LCCN 2020049810 (print) | LCCN 2020049811 (ebook) |
ISBN 9780593328231 (trade paperback) | ISBN 9780593328248 (ebook)
Subjects: LCSH: Royal Botanic Gardens, Kew—Fiction. | World War,
1914-1918—Women—England—Fiction. | GSAFD: Historical fiction.
Classification: LCC PR6102.A7748 K49 2021 (print) |
LCC PR6102.A7748 (ebook) | DDC 823/.92—dc23
LC record available at https://lccn.loc.gov/2020049810
LC ebook record available at https://lccn.loc.gov/2020049811
p.   cm.

Printed in the United States of America

☒   ☒

Book design by Laura K. Corless

Advance Praise for *The Kew Gardens Girls*

"An absolutely charming story about the strength and beauty of female friendship. *The Kew Gardens Girls* blossom from the pages as World War I changes their lives and they face the challenges of being the first women to work in the famous Kew Gardens. I loved the way Ivy, Louisa, and Win reveled in the many adventures they encountered and supported one another through the turmoil of wartime life. Settle into the story and be swept away!"

—Natasha Lester, *New York Times* bestselling author of *The Paris Secret*

"Utterly charming, The *Kew Garden Girls*, set in World War I London to the backdrop of the women's suffrage movement, is a tumbling bouquet of detail and dialogue that immediately transports the reader to one of the most famous city gardens in the world, a century in the past. Inspired by real events, Posy Lovell deftly explores issues of friendship, loss, class, equality, and freedom, weaving those serious topics into a beautiful story of women in wartime who find solace and meaning in tending the plants of Kew Gardens, coaxing new life from the soil even as they struggle to hold their own lives together. I'll never look at the sprawling, brilliant Kew Gardens—one of London's top tourist attractions and a World Heritage Site—the same way again."

—Kristin Harmel, international bestselling author of *The Book of Lost Names*

"*The Kew Gardens Girls* weaves an engaging, charming story of three women and their friendship while exploring the fascinating struggle for women's suffrage during World War I Britain. Lovell's story is just as layered and beautiful as the gardens she writes about. A delight!"

—Julia Kelly, international bestselling author of *The Light Over London*

"*The Kew Gardens Girls* is a delightful story about women from very different backgrounds who end up working together at London's Kew Gardens during World War I, taking on the jobs of the men who have gone to war. The 'girls' form fast friendships and something like a surrogate family. With beautifully well-drawn characters whom you root for from the beginning, and interesting historical details about both the Suffragette movement and Kew Gardens during World War I, this is a poignant, heartwarming read that I highly recommend!"   —Jane Healey, bestselling author of *The Beantown Girls*

G. P. PUTNAM'S SONS

NEW YORK

For the women gardeners
who have kept Kew blooming
for more than 100 years

The

Kew Gardens Girls

Prologue

Kew
1913

The bells seemed louder than usual this evening, Reverend Miller thought as he walked round the side of St. Anne's Church. Perhaps the bell ringers were feeling particularly energetic. He paused for a while, listening to the tuneful clanging with pleasure. He couldn't hear anything else but the bells, he noted. No shouts from the men working on the nearby river, no sound from the road or from the pub across the way. Just the bells. He nodded in satisfaction and continued on his twilight walk round the churchyard.

❧

Inside the bell tower, the noise was deafening as the bell ringers threw themselves into their practice, much to the delight of Ginny Walker, who was responsible for the loudest clanging. She pulled hard on the rope, feeling her shoulder muscles cry out in protest. But she didn't stop. She knew it was important to keep going, louder and louder. Glancing down, she saw the little silver hammer brooch she wore pinned to her lapel. The symbol that showed she was a Suffragette—and she would do anything to further the cause. She pulled on the rope once more, grunting with the exertion. She would do anything.

༺❈༻

The sound of the chiming bells rolled across the green, drowning out the noise made by three women who were standing by the wall.

"Go on, Olive," one of them hissed. "Hitch your skirt up if it's getting in the way."

With a grin, the woman hiked up her long dress round her waist and tucked it into her bloomers.

"Better?"

"Go on," the other one said again. "Look, she's up there already."

Above them, perched at the top of the wall, was another woman— younger than Olive and her friend Lilian. She'd scaled the barrier without hesitation and was now peering down over the other side.

"It's all quiet," she said. "Follow me."

There was a soft *thud* as she threw herself down from the wall and disappeared from view.

Olive and Lilian glanced at each other and then, with considerably less dexterity than their younger friend, began scaling the wall themselves.

Once they were on the other side, the young woman put her fingers to her lips.

"Sound travels strange inside Kew Gardens," she said under her breath. "Whispers carry through the trees and the bells won't cover everything. No more talking."

The women all nodded at one another and, after picking up the bags they'd thrown over the wall ahead of them, they silently crept through the trees toward the tea pavilion.

"Over there," the young woman said as they came to a clearing. The

2

building loomed up in front of them out of the gloom. "That's the tea pavilion."

She clutched Lilian's arm. "Just the pavilion, right?" she said. "Because what you did to the orchid house the other day, ruining all those plants? That wasn't right. They're living things, not bricks and mortar."

"Just the pavilion," Lilian agreed.

As one the women walked quietly to the front of the pavilion. Lilian pinned a note on the wall reading VOTES FOR WOMEN, and Olive pulled a pack of fabric from her bag—pads soaked in paraffin. She tucked a couple into the wooden slats by the door and another two by the steps. She doused the wooden slats by the door and threw it onto the pads by the steps. The smell rose up, making their nostrils tingle.

"Ready?" said Lilian.

Olive nodded, but the younger woman looked unsure.

"Is this the only way?" she asked. "Really?"

"Deeds, not words," said Lilian.

She struck a match and, with a flourish, threw it onto the steps behind the younger woman. Immediately, the rickety wooden structure burst into flames—higher and more powerful than any of them had expected.

"Ohh!" The young woman gasped in pain as the fire caught the wooden stair railing next to where she stood and licked her arm with its sharp orange tongue.

"Get back," Lilian cried. She pulled the teenager away from the flames and yanked her back toward the path, where Olive was already standing.

"It's too much," the young woman said, her face lit with the glow from the fire. "It's too much, this is wrong."

But Olive and Lilian simply shook their heads.

"We need them to pay attention," Olive said. "Perhaps this will help."

"I hope so," said the youngster. "I really hope you're right."

A noise from the bushes made them freeze.

"What was that?" Lilian breathed.

They all listened, senses on high alert. Was it footsteps?

"Keeper," said the teenager. "We need to go."

She pulled Olive's arm.

"This way," she said. "I know a way out. Follow me."

She vanished into the shadows and, with the sound of running footsteps echoing through the darkness, Olive and Lilian followed.

Chapter 1

Kew
June 1915

I'm really not sure about this," said Douglas MacMillan as he slowly walked down the line of potential new recruits. "Not sure about this at all."

He shook his head, pausing in his pacing.

"What do you think, Jim?"

His assistant, a younger man with a mop of dark hair and kind eyes, gave his boss an amused glance.

"I think you should give them a chance, Mac," he said. "We've lost more than half our gardeners already, and there are bound to be more that join up. We need them."

He sighed.

"We had this conversation when we put the ad in the *Times*, Mac. You agreed. We're lucky so many have turned up."

Mac huffed in disapproval.

"I'm just not sure they're up to the job," he muttered. "Bunch of namby-pamby lady poets and maiden aunts."

In the line, two of the recruits exchanged a look of solidarity—they were used to being underestimated by men—before standing to attention again as Mac continued his inspection. He paused by one of the women—tall and elegant, though a closer look would reveal her skirt had been mended many times and her coat was faded.

"What's your name?" he barked.

The woman winced, just a little, at his sharp tone, then straightened up and looked him straight in the eye.

"Louisa Taylor," she said.

"And you want to be a horticulturalist, do you? Fancy yourself as a gardener?"

"I'm already a gardener. But I'd like to work here, yes."

Mac huffed again. "Gardener, eh? What do you grow?"

"Vegetables, mostly, at the moment. But flowers, too. I only have window boxes because my flat is very small."

Mac nodded and the woman continued.

"I grew up in Kent," she said. "On a hops farm. I understand plants."

"Hops?" Mac's gruff Scottish voice sounded grudgingly impressed. "Not easy."

"No, sir."

Behind him, Jim grinned again.

"He'll come round eventually," he said in a low voice to the youngest woman in the line. "Don't worry."

She smiled at him. "Promise?" she said quietly.

"Promise."

A kerfuffle at the other end of the line made them both look up. A disheveled young man joined the group. His cap was askew, one trouser leg was half-tucked into his sock, and he was breathing heavily.

"Sorry I'm late," he panted. "Went to the wrong gate, and then it was difficult finding somewhere to lock up my bicycle."

Mac, looking relieved to see another male face, left his interrogation of Louisa Taylor and turned his attention to the man.

"What's your name?"

"Bernard," he said, still out of breath. "Bernie. Bernie Yorke."

"Well, Bernard Bernie Yorke," said Mac, "do you have any horticulture experience?"

Bernie chuckled. "Good heavens, no," he said. "None whatsoever. But I'm a fast learner, and I'm not frightened of hard work."

"Good," said Mac. "You're in. Go and give Jim your details."

The two women exchanged another glance and the younger woman, the one who'd been talking to Jim, raised an eyebrow. "Should have said your name was Louis, not Louisa," she said quietly.

Louisa stifled a laugh. She already liked this rather wild-looking girl beside her and hoped they'd both be chosen to work at Kew.

"Louisa?" Mac said, making her jump.

"Yes, sir?"

"Not one of those Suffragettes, are you?"

Louisa looked straight at him. "Absolutely not, sir."

"Good," said Mac. "They burned the tea pavilion, you know. And destroyed the orchid house. Terrible business."

"I heard," Louisa said.

Behind her back, she curled her fingers round the little silver hammer brooch she wore and which she'd removed just before Mac had reached her.

"Terrible."

"You're in," Mac said with a definite tinge of reluctance. "Give your details to Jim."

As Louisa went to leave the line, the younger woman next to her caught her hand and pushed something into it. It was another tiny hammer brooch.

Louisa looked at her and the younger woman pushed a strand of red hair out of her face and smiled. Giving her the tiniest of nods, Louisa headed over to where Jim sat on a tree trunk, meticulously writing down the names and addresses of all the new recruits. Bernie stood to one side, biting his lip nervously.

While she waited her turn to give Jim her information, she watched Mac interrogate the other women.

"He's not as bad as he seems," Jim said, watching her watching. "He's got a good heart."

Louisa raised an eyebrow and Jim chuckled.

"You'll see," he said.

Over in the line, Mac had reached the redheaded girl.

"Name," he barked.

"Ivy Adams," she said.

Beside Louisa, Jim raised his head, his kind eyes fixed on Ivy.

"Do you know her?" Louisa was intrigued by his interest.

"She's some girl," he said. "Some girl."

Ivy was small and wiry, with that unkempt red hair that kept whipping across her face as the breeze took it.

With an exasperated sigh, she gathered her locks up in her tiny hands, twisted, and tucked it into itself.

"Sorry," she said. "It's so annoying. I'd like to cut it all off one day. What was you saying?"

Louisa thought Mac would react badly to Ivy's inattention but, to her surprise, he smiled indulgently.

"You're Paddy Adams's oldest," he said.

Ivy smiled. "S'right."

"How's your dad?"

She shrugged. "Times are tough."

8

Mac looked sad. "He didn't want to come here? I'd give him a job any day of the week. Knowledge he has of flowers is second to none."

"Her dad worked at Columbia Road," Jim told Louisa. She looked at him curiously. How did he know that? "One of the best flower sellers down there, until . . ."

"He's drinking," Ivy said abruptly. "Too much. And we ain't seen him properly for weeks. You know what he's like. You don't want him here, sir."

"Shame," said Mac.

"He taught me everything."

Mac looked her up and down. "You might have the knowledge, but you're tiny. You're not built for physical work."

"I'm small, but I'm strong as an ox," she said. "Give me a chance and I'll prove it."

"I don't know, Ivy."

"Please," she said. "For my dad?"

There was a pause. Louisa silently urged Mac to give Ivy the chance she obviously wanted so desperately.

"Fine," he said eventually. "But if it's too much, you tell me?"

"I will," she said. "Thank you, sir."

"That's my girl," breathed Jim next to Louisa. Ahh, so they did know each other? Interesting.

Ivy appeared at Bernie's elbow.

"I'm in," she said happily. "One of the team."

Jim gave her a beaming smile. "You did well."

"Do you want my details?"

He showed her the form he was filling in with a stubby pencil. "Already wrote them down. See?"

A shadow drifted across Ivy's face, just for a second, and then vanished. She gazed at Jim and the pair seemed to lose sight of everyone else for a moment. Louisa felt a tiny stab of envy, remembering how lovely it once was to have someone look at her that way. Before things changed, of course. She pushed her shoulders back. She was far better off alone.

"Ahem," Bernie said, clearing his throat and interrupting Ivy and Jim's moment. "I was just wondering what will happen now?"

Jim blinked, as though he'd forgotten where he was for a second.

"Mac," he called. "What now?"

Mac looked over. "Give them a tour," he said. "Show them the palm house, and the temperate house first, I reckon. Then maybe take them over to the magnolias."

Jim grinned. "Right then," he said. "Follow me."

Obediently, Bernie, Louisa and Ivy fell into line behind him. Bernie began quizzing Jim about the plants they were passing, and Jim answered even the silliest questions good-naturedly.

"I'm glad we're going to get to work together," said Ivy to Louisa as they walked. "I think we've got a lot in common."

Realizing what she meant, Louisa dug around in the pocket of her coat for her brooch and held it out to her.

"Here," she said.

Ivy took it and pinned it on the underside of her lapel. Louisa followed her lead and the two women nodded to each other.

"I've never seen you before," Louisa said.

Ivy shook her head. "Nor me, you. Do you live nearby?"

"Wandsworth. You?"

Ivy rolled her eyes. "Hackney," she said.

"That's quite a journey."

The young woman nodded. "Worth it, though. I spend a lot of time round the Gardens. Always have done, since I was little. 'Cause of my dad and that."

"That how you know Jim?" Louisa asked.

Ivy flushed. "S'pose," she said. "Are you still going to meetings?"

With the change of subject, it was clear Ivy wasn't going to give anything else away about her and Jim. Amused at her reaction, Louisa decided to let it lie for now.

"Not really," she said. "We've all but stopped over in Wandsworth. Mrs. Pankhurst doesn't want anything interfering with the war effort."

"Us, too," Ivy agreed. "Nothing going on."

She paused.

"I miss it."

Louisa grinned at her, thrilled that someone understood.

"Me, too," she admitted. "So much. I miss the meetings and the women and the friendships. And I have to confess, I miss the thrill of the action, too."

The shadow crossed Ivy's face again and was gone in a flash.

"Mostly why I wanted to come and work here," she said. "So I could make some friends and feel useful again. Useful on my own terms, I mean. Not just doing what my dad tells me to do."

They were approaching the palm house. Its huge windows sparkled in the weak sunlight and Louisa felt a rush of excitement. Oh, to be given the chance to work here, in the most wonderful gardens in the world. She was lucky.

Impulsively, she looped her arm through Ivy's. The younger woman froze at first, then relaxed.

"Are you nervous?" Ivy said.

Louisa shrugged. "Nervous and excited, I suppose." She paused. "I've had a few ups and downs these last couple of years. More downs than ups, really. This feels like a new beginning for me."

"'New beginning,'" Ivy echoed. "I like that. Maybe it could be one for me, too."

"Tsk, you're a baby. Why would you need a new beginning?" Louisa chuckled. But that shadow wafted over Ivy's eyes once more and the younger woman shuddered.

"I reckon everyone could do with starting over, once in a while," she said mildly, gazing up at the palm house. "Shall we go in?"

Louisa nodded, and arm in arm, the two women followed Bernie and Jim into the palm house.

Chapter 2

Louisa was exhausted when she finally made it home to her tiny basement flat in Wandsworth after her first day at Kew. Exhausted but happy. She hadn't realized quite how much she had missed being outdoors.

As she crossed the threshold, though, her good mood wavered for a second as she saw the letter lying on the mat.

"Oh, Ma," she whispered as she bent down to pick it up. She looked at the envelope for a second or two. Her mother had written every week since Louisa left Kent, half a year ago. Louisa hadn't opened any of the letters. She didn't want to know what her mother had to say, because she wasn't sure she could ever forgive her for not supporting Louisa when she needed her most.

Louisa breathed in deeply, a long, shuddery breath. More importantly, if she wrote back, then that would confirm to everyone where she was. She'd given her address to her brother, Matthew, but she'd never expected him to share it with their parents—and if he'd told them where she was, who knew if he'd told anyone else? If he'd let it slip to Reg that she was in Wandsworth . . . She shivered at the idea of her husband finding her, remembering the hatred she'd seen in his eyes when he told her she was his forever.

Shaking her head to get rid of the unwelcome memory she dropped her mother's letter, unopened, into the wastepaper basket, feeling a wave of exhaustion. All she wanted to do was curl up in bed with a book, but she was completely filthy, she realized. So, instead, she peeled off her dirty skirt and stockings and banged her muddy boots together outside the door. Then, while she heated up water for a bath, she put on her dressing gown and wandered out into her little yard to look at her plants.

Her flat had its own entrance, with cast-iron stairs leading down from the street. And on either side of the steps, and outside her front window, was a small paved area. Some people in the other basement flats hung washing out in their little outdoor yard, but Louisa's was full of plants.

She'd been telling the truth to Mac. She did grow a lot of fruit and vegetables. She had lettuces in a window box, and peas growing up a pole. She had a pot where the tomatoes jostled for space, their sharp scent filling the evening air. She touched the leaves gently and admired the little green spheres that would soon turn red in the sunshine. She would get a good crop and she was pleased that she'd managed to grow so much so soon.

Next to the tomatoes she had strawberry plants in another pot, which were flourishing too.

There were a few sunflowers that were growing tall and strong, reaching up to the iron railings that edged the street. She hoped they would grow so tall that she would eventually be able to see them as she walked home, their large sunny faces welcoming her back to her house. And there were pots full of color—begonias and petunias and geraniums all blooming in the June sunshine.

Growing the plants had made Louisa feel at home when she'd first arrived in gray, wintery London all those months ago. She loved the anonymity of the big city and how she blended in with crowds of people—it made her feel safe from Reg to be among so many others—but she missed the outdoors and the feeling of the earth between her fingers. Growing her plants gave her a taste of Kent while still keeping her away. It was the best of both worlds, she thought. Or rather, a way of making the best of a situation that she'd never imagined she'd find herself in.

She pottered about happily for a few minutes, watering the pots that were dry and picking a few of the strawberries, warm from the sun, and popping them into her mouth. Then she went back inside and filled the bath and sank gratefully into the water.

Her legs ached from the physical work—she was out of practice after spending the last few months working behind the counter in a shop—and she was more tired than she'd been since she'd come to London, but she was content. Possibly the most content she'd felt since, well, since all the trouble.

She closed her eyes as the memories flooded back. Of the fear she felt when Reg would come home. Would he be in a good mood or a bad one? Would he want to kiss and cuddle her, or would one wrong word from her send her sprawling to the floor as he took out his anger on her?

Under the water, she let her hand drift down to her flat stomach. Her belly would never swell with pregnancy, thanks to Reg's punches. She still felt vaguely unsettled after receiving her mother's letter, but for the first time she found she could think about her past without feeling so utterly wretched.

"I've done it," she murmured to herself. "I've built myself a new life just as I dreamed."

She smiled as she started to scrub the mud from under her fingernails. It hadn't been easy—a nighttime flit from Kent, and the first train into London in the morning with the milk. Hiding out in one of the luggage compartments in case she was spotted and word got back to Reg. And then the sheer, terrifying size of London. And the noise. And the people.

But she'd found first this little flat, and then her job in a hat shop. Her Suffragette friends in Kent—a whole bunch of women who felt the same helplessness and frustration that she did and who'd helped her more than they could ever know—had put her in touch with like-minded women nearby.

She stood up, water dripping, and reached for a towel. Thinking of her friends in the Suffragettes made her think of Ivy. Ivy, with her wild hair, the glint in her eye, and her hammer brooch hidden in her fist. Ivy, who seemed tough but whose voice had shaken when she talked about her father, and who looked so desperately hopeful when Mac was questioning her.

Louisa nodded to herself as she dried her legs and put on her nightgown. She felt a pull toward the unkempt teenager and she thought Ivy had felt it too. As though they were two lost souls who'd found each other. Perhaps, she thought, there was more than one way to be a mother.

❦

Across London, in Hackney, Ivy was thinking about Louisa, too, as she dragged a comb through her straggly hair and tried to tame it into some sort of twist.

"Why do you need to go?"

She turned and grinned at Jim, who was sitting on the single bed in the room she shared with her younger sister.

"I need to go to a meeting and you just need to go," she said "Ma will be back soon, with the littl'uns. She can't see you here."

Jim looked sulky. "We've not done anything wrong."

"I know that, and you know that, but what do you reckon she'll think if she sees you in my bedroom, eh? She's not going to think you've been teaching me about plants. It'll be straight to birds and bees, for her filthy mind."

Jim chuckled. "Fair enough."

He slid off the bed and stood up, stretching his arms above his head like a cat. "Where's your dad?"

Ivy shrugged. "Not seen hide nor hair of him for weeks. Might turn up, might not."

Not wanting to think about her father, or the tiredness that was obvious on her mother's skinny face, Ivy turned her attention to her hair again, groaning as she tried in vain to make it look neat, and then pinned on her hammer brooch.

"She was nice, weren't she? Louisa?"

Jim had finished his stretching. "They were all nice, I reckoned."

Ivy thought for a minute. "What about Mac?"

"Told you, his bark's worse than his bite. Once he sees you all getting on with it, he'll come round. We need you, Ivy."

He came over to where she stood, looking in the blotchy mirror, and wrapped his strong arms round her.

"I need you," he said. He kissed her neck and she shivered with pleasure as he ran a hand down her back. But she pulled away as he tried to stroke her bare arm.

"Jim, give it a rest," she said affectionately, reaching for her jacket and pulling it on over the arm he'd touched. "You need to go."

"Oh, all right, I know when I'm not wanted," he teased. "Maybe I'll join up. Would you miss me?"

Ivy felt a lurch of fear at his jokes.

"Please don't," she said, serious all of a sudden. "Please don't. Not even when you're eighteen. I couldn't bear it. You're all I have."

Jim kissed her very gently on her lips. "Let's see what happens, shall we? No point worrying about it now."

Ivy bit her lip, still fretting, then caught a glimpse of the time on the clock on the mantelpiece.

"It's after seven," she said in horror. "Go, Jim!"

"Come with me."

"I can't, you know that. I've got to go to the meeting."

"I think you love those women more than me."

She grinned at him, and shoved him in the direction of the window. "They're my family," she said. "Go."

With a cheeky wink, Jim threw one long leg over the window ledge. "See you tomorrow," he said. "At work."

Then he clambered down the trellis on the side of the house and disappeared, just in the nick of time, because downstairs Ivy heard the sound of her mother and younger siblings arriving home.

She thought for a second about going down, greeting them, helping Ma with bedtime and telling her about her new job. Then she thought of the endless questions from the littl'uns, the haunted look in Ma's eyes as she slumped on a chair, aching with fatigue, and changed her mind. Today had been perfect, she thought. Getting the chance to work with Jim at her most favorite place in London and having the opportunity to make amends for what she had done. Meeting Louisa, too, had been fun—and funny Bernie, with the glasses and his mop of hair. She didn't want anything to spoil that now.

She hitched her skirt up, and clambered over the windowsill and out into the street, just as Jim had done.

⁜

Bernie took his glasses off and laid them on his bedside table. He wasn't shortsighted. In fact, he didn't need spectacles at all—the ones he wore had clear glass lenses. He had picked them up at a gentleman's outfitters store when he bought a new hat, in the hope that people who saw he wore glasses wouldn't question why he hadn't yet joined up.

He heard his landlady, Mrs. Spencer, moving around downstairs, cooking dinner, and nodded. She'd never asked why he was still in England when hundreds of men were fighting in the trenches in France and Belgium, so it was obviously working.

But for how long? he wondered, picking up today's newspaper. There was talk of the government introducing a new law to force all men to join up and Bernie did not want to go to war.

It wasn't that he was a coward, though of course the very thought of the brutality of war made his blood run cold. But rather, he was a Quaker. A pacifist. He firmly believed that nothing good would come from this war and he didn't want to be a part of it. He sighed, looking at the newspaper once more. But what would he do if the law was passed and he was forced to enlist? He had no idea.

"Dinner will be in ten minutes," Mrs. Spencer called up the stairs. She was a rather fearsome woman whose husband had enlisted almost as soon as war had been declared. She was passionate about supporting the troops and spent her time knitting socks for soldiers and raising money for war bonds. Her two sullen children were dragged along to her efforts collecting tinned food for refugees or gifts for the troops on a weekly basis.

"I'll be right there," he called back. He picked up his glasses and put them back on.

He was hoping his work at Kew would be considered essential, should the conscription bill be passed. That was largely why he'd applied. He'd thought, briefly, about going back to teaching, but just the thought broke him out in a cold sweat. He'd found peace within himself, after the torment of everything that had happened with Vivienne—a music teacher at his old school—though it had taken a long time for him to get over the humiliation he'd suffered when she'd turned down his proposal so cruelly. And so publicly.

He felt his shoulders hunching as he remembered the cold realization that Vivienne had merely been playing with his feelings, as a cat played with a mouse. Using him as a source of help with lesson planning, of paying for theater tickets, drinks and dinners, and more often than not of hard cash. And all the while laughing at him behind his back—and, as it turned out, to his face. It had been a dark time for him.

No, he wasn't sure his mind would recover if he had to go back to the classroom. But he didn't have the skills or knowledge to take up any other work that could help him avoid conscription. Then he'd seen the advert in the back of the *Times* for Kew and thought it could be the answer to his prayers.

Today, though, had been hard work for a man like him, unaccustomed as he was to physical labor. He looked at the blisters on his palm in mild disgust, hoping he'd toughen up before too long. He'd felt out of his depth and—unusual for him—a bit stupid, listening to the apprentice gardener, Jim, explain what they should be doing in the herbaceous border.

Still, if there was one thing Bernie was good at, it was learning. He scanned the bookshelves lining his room and found what he was looking for—a copy of a book called *A Year in My Garden*. His mother, who'd been a keen gardener before arthritis twisted her hands, had passed it to him, but he'd never had much cause to read it before now.

Nodding in satisfaction, he laid it on his chair to read after dinner. He wasn't beaten yet.

Chapter 3

The first few weeks at Kew passed in a blur for Louisa. She worked hard all day and then fell into bed at night and slept until her alarm clock woke her with a start and she saw the sunshine peeking round her curtains each morning.

She and the other women recruits—and Bernie—were certainly earning their pay at Kew. It was as though Mac wanted to test them to make sure they were up to the job. Louisa thought they'd more than proved themselves already, but Mac worked them harder every day. He didn't let the female gardeners do much—not yet. For now they were limited to working in the herbaceous borders and in the rock and flower gardens. It was good enough for Louisa, though. She loved every moment.

It was a glorious summer. Louisa's face had turned brown in the sun, and her nose was sprinkled with freckles. But today was more overcast, with a hint of rain in the air. Louisa smiled. That was good for the flowers, she thought, as she walked along the river to work. A shout behind her made her stop and look round. Ivy was hurrying along the path behind her.

"I thought I wasn't going to catch you," she said, red-faced. "You don't half walk at a cracking pace, Lou."

Louisa smiled. "It's because I'm so keen to get to work."

Ivy rolled her eyes and tucked her hand into Louisa's arm.

"Come on, then, you old swot," she said. "Let's see what you can impress Mac with today."

Louisa enjoyed Ivy's teasing. She was right, in a way. Louisa was keen to impress Mac. Partly because she loved the work so much and wanted to stay at Kew, and partly because she was desperate to prove wrong his initial misgivings about employing female gardeners.

"We're doing the rock gardens today," Louisa said. "Heavy work."

Ivy nodded. "Jim said that Mac wants to extend them a bit. We'll be lugging rocks all day." Her eyes gleamed with mischief. "Reckon he's testing us?"

"Almost certainly."

"Reckon we're up to it?"

"Definitely."

Laughing together, the women went through the huge Victorian iron gate and headed off to find Mac.

She had been right, Louisa thought as she wiped sweat from her dripping brow later. It was heavy work, probably the most difficult physical labor they'd done in the weeks they'd been working at Kew. She and Ivy were moving rocks from a pile that had been dumped by the path and arranging them on the new patch that would become the extension to the rock garden. Some of the rocks were small, but most of them were as big as footballs, or even larger, and heavy. The women carried them in their arms, cradling them like a baby, or sometimes sharing the load between them.

THE KEW GARDENS GIRLS

After an hour or so, Mac came over. He stood watching them work for a moment and then cast his eyes over the arrangement of stones.

"You've done well, there," he said eventually. "Good work."

Louisa exchanged a quick glance with Ivy. Maybe they had impressed him at last.

"I'll get Bernie to come and help with this last bit," Mac said.

"We're fine on our own," Louisa said, disappointed he obviously thought they needed a man to help.

The corners of Mac's mouth twitched.

"Not because I don't think you're fine on your own," he said, a hint of amusement in his gruff Scottish tone. "Because I reckon you're hungry, and with a bit of help you'll get it finished before lunch."

He wandered off to find Bernie, and Louisa grinned at Ivy.

"He's softening," she said.

Ivy nodded. "Jim says he's a nice bloke and Jim's a great judge of character."

Louisa braced herself to pick up another rock. "You're close, are you? You and Jim?" she said, grunting as she heaved it up, feeling the muscles in her shoulders protesting.

Ivy's cheeks flushed pink. "Bit," she said.

"You knew each other before?" Louisa dropped the rock into position and stretched out her arms in relief.

"Help me with this one," Ivy said, choosing a bigger one to go at the back of the garden. Louisa took one end of the stone and together they lugged it over the soft earth.

"I used to come to Kew with my dad," Ivy said. "I got talking to Jim one day and we hit it off. Down here?"

They lowered the rock carefully onto the earth and stood back to admire their handiwork.

"Couple more, I reckon," Ivy said. Louisa nodded.

23

"Jim's the nicest person I've ever met," Ivy said. She paused. "Wasn't always easy at home, when I was little."

She sat down on the biggest rock and wiped her brow.

"My dad was . . ." She searched for the right word. "What is it when you're not sure if they'll be nice or nasty?"

Louisa felt a rush of recognition as she remembered life with her Reg.

"Unpredictable," she said.

"That's it. Dad was—is—unpredictable. He's not always around. Sometimes he's brilliant, working hard and doing right by Ma. Other times he's drinking, disappearing for weeks on end. You know what it's like?"

"I do."

"When he was good, he used to come down here to meet the gardeners. Chat about flowers and that. Like I said, I'd come with him because I've always liked all that stuff. And I met Jim. And now he's my family."

She said it so simply, that Louisa couldn't help but smile. "He's your sweetheart."

Ivy nodded. "And I'm his."

Oh, to be young and in love, Louisa thought. Before the reality of life sets in.

"What about you?"

She blinked at Ivy. "What about me?"

"Do you have a sweetheart?"

Louisa laughed. "I'm thirty-five years old, Ivy."

The younger woman shrugged. "So, never say never." She looked mischievous. "What about Mac?"

"No thank you," Louisa said firmly. "Even if he does have a good heart deep down."

"Bernie, then? He's a nice-looking chap."

"And ten years younger than me," Louisa said in mock horror. "Thank you, Ivy, but I'm fine by myself."

She felt Ivy's curious eyes on her.

"Were you married before?"

Louisa froze. "Why do you ask?"

"Good-looking woman like you, nice accent, you said your parents have a farm? Bound to be snapped up." She narrowed her eyes. "So why are you here in London, single, and spending all your time with Suffragettes?"

Louisa felt exhausted suddenly. She sat down next to Ivy on the rock. "Really want to know?"

Ivy nodded.

"It's not pretty."

"We're friends, ain't we? Whatever you say won't change that."

Louisa took a breath. "I was married, you're right. Still am, I guess."

Ivy raised her eyebrows, but she didn't speak.

"His name is Reggie. Reggie Taylor. He was the son of the people who farmed the land next to ours and I'd known him since school." She sighed. "He was nice enough back then. My father encouraged our romance because he thought it would mean merging our farms."

"It didn't work out?"

Louisa shook her head. "Farming is tough. Really tough. Reg lost both his parents young, so he took over the farm before he was ready, really. He was out in the fields all hours, worrying about money..."

She stopped, swallowing a sob.

"He took it out on you?" Ivy finished for her.

"He had such a temper," Louisa said. "Unpredictable, like you said. Some evenings he'd come home and be all sweetness and light. Some he'd be raging at something that'd gone wrong, or something I'd said that he'd been stewing over all day."

She took a breath. She didn't talk about Reg much. Not ever, really. But it seemed now that she'd started she couldn't stop.

"The first time he hit me, he was sorry afterward. The next time, he didn't seem sorry. Or the next."

Ivy took her hand and Louisa kept going.

"He broke my arm," she said. "I told the doctor I'd tripped feeding the chickens. I had more black eyes than I had hot dinners. He split my lip three times? Maybe four. And the worst . . ."

She paused.

"The worst was when I was pregnant. Twice it was early on. Maybe I wasn't pregnant, who knows? There was just a lot of blood. More than normal."

Ivy squeezed Louisa's hand, and the older woman carried on, trying to keep her voice steady.

"And then, after I'd thought I'd never have a baby, that I was too old to be a mother, I found I was expecting again. But Reg pushed me down the stairs and I lost the baby."

"How far along was you?" Ivy said, her voice almost a whisper.

Louisa pinched her lips together. "Quite far," she said. "Far enough for me to know that the baby had stopped moving. Far enough for me to give birth."

"Oh, Louisa," Ivy said. "What happened?"

"I went to my mother," Louisa said, gathering herself as memories of her lost baby threatened to overwhelm her. "And I told her what Reg had done."

"What did she say?"

"She said I'd made my bed and I had to lie in it."

"Christ," said Ivy. "Really? My ma has a lot on her plate, but I don't doubt she'd deck a fella who laid a hand on me."

Louisa gave her a small smile. "So I ran away," she said. "I came to London."

"By yourself?"

"Yes and no. I was a Suffragette already, down in Kent, though I never talked about it much to my family or to Reg. When I was desperate it was my friends there who helped me. One of them put me in touch with the Women's Social and Political Union, the WSPU, in Wandsworth, and they helped me find my flat." She smiled and then frowned. "Reg was furious when I said I was going. I ran away at night. But I was scared he'd find me. London seemed the best place to go so I could disappear. The best place to find a job and start again."

"Did you?"

Louisa nodded. "I got a job as an assistant in a hat shop. Deathly dull. I was thrilled when I saw the Gardens ad in the *Times*."

"How long ago was that?"

"Six months I've been in London now."

"All alone?"

"I found a whole new family with the Suffragettes here."

Ivy beamed at her. "That's how I feel, too," she said. "Those women are like my sisters and my mothers and my friends all rolled into one. They've been so good to me—and Ma. When Dad does one of his disappearing acts, they're always on hand. Especially now, when we're not really active anymore."

Louisa nodded. "Did you do much?" she said, curious about how young Ivy was and wondering how involved she had been. "When things were happening?"

Ivy looked awkward for a second. "Bits and pieces," she said. "I was only a kid, really. You?"

Louisa grinned. "Oh yes. I was in every march I could get to. I often traveled into London by train to take part. I smashed windows. I threw potatoes at Mr. Churchill."

"You never did," breathed Ivy. "You don't seem the type."

"I was very angry with men," Louisa said. "Not men individually, you understand, though trust me, I've had my moments of sheer fury at Reg. But more the world of men. The world being built for men, by men. You see?"

"I do see," Ivy said.

"Sometimes things went too far, though," Louisa went on. "They burned the tea pavilion here, you know? And destroyed the orchid house."

Ivy shifted on the hard rock. "I heard."

"Course, two of them went to jail for it. Olive Wharry and Lilian Lenton."

"Yes, that's right. They weren't inside for long, though, I heard."

Louisa lowered her voice. "They said there was someone else with them that night who got away with it." Her eyes gleamed with the thrill of it. "They never found the other person."

"Need a hand, ladies?"

Ivy and Louisa jumped as Bernie approached.

"Good Lord, I'm sorry. I didn't mean to startle you."

"Heavens, Bernie, we were chatting and didn't notice you coming," said Louisa. She hoped he'd not heard their talk of arson and jail and throwing things at politicians.

"Mac said I should come and help you out," Bernie said. He looked miserable, Louisa noticed now. As though he had the weight of the world on his shoulders. "I think he's annoyed with me, because I pushed the mower over some seedlings this morning and then I dug up the wrong flower bed."

Louisa and Ivy both stared at him. The jobs they were doing were so simple a child could do them. They were both feeling frustrated they weren't being entrusted with more complicated tasks, while Bernie was struggling with the easy ones?

"I'm worried he's going to sack me," Bernie carried on, running his fingers through his mop of hair. "And I need this job, I really need it."

Louisa took pity on him. "Come on, then," she said. "Let's get shifting the last of these rocks. It's not hard and we'll be done quicker with you helping."

Bernie looked grateful. "Thanks so much," he said.

Chapter 4

Bernie hadn't been exaggerating when he told the women he was worried about his job. He seemed to be making endless mistakes every day and while Mac was being tolerant for now, he wasn't sure how long it was going to last.

He'd read and reread *A Year in My Garden* and asked all the right questions about flowers and plants, but somehow there seemed to be a disconnect between his brain and his body when it came to physical work. He'd always been clumsy, even as a child, but it had never mattered in the classroom as a pupil or when he'd been teaching. Dropping the occasional book or breaking a piece of chalk was nothing compared to mowing down some carefully cultivated seedlings or digging up the wrong patch of a flower bed.

He sighed. He was devouring the newspapers every day, checking for any mention of the proposed conscription act. It was said that some jobs would be considered essential and the people doing those roles would be exempt from being enlisted. It was ironic, he thought, that teaching was almost certain to be considered essential. He just had to hope that when push came to shove, gardening at Kew would be, too. Though he doubted it would be.

"Are you with us?" Ivy's voice snapped him out of his self-pity. "There are more rocks to shift."

"Sorry," he said. "Point me in the right direction then."

He followed Ivy's lead and, with some effort, lifted one of the rocks, staggering slightly under its weight. He looked at the women with a certain amount of admiration. Ivy was tiny but wiry and her slight frame obviously hid strong muscles. And Louisa was more sturdily built but still smaller than he. He would never have imagined women capable of such physical work. Though, he admitted to himself, he had never really spent much time with women. Other than his mother when he was very young, of course, and then Vivienne.

He shook his head. This was no time to be thinking of Vivienne. Not when he should be concentrating.

With a grunt, he dropped the rock onto the flower bed. Across the garden, Mac—who'd been watching Bernie's efforts—straightened up.

"Careful there," he called. "Place the rocks down. You'll know about it if it lands on your toes."

Bernie closed his eyes briefly and Louisa nudged him.

"Don't worry," she said. "Honestly, we're all just learning."

"You're both so much more capable than I am."

She grinned. "We both grew up around gardens and farms," she pointed out. "I was working in the hops fields and in the orchards as soon as I could walk. And Ivy's tagged along with her dad since she was tiny."

"I've been reading a book," Bernie said, eager to please these kind women. "About gardens. I want to know more."

Ivy put down the last rock and stood back, wiping the earth from her palms.

"Not sure what books can teach you about gardening," she said. "You have to feel it. Get your hands in the dirt."

There was a glint in her eye that Bernie liked. He'd seen it occasionally when he'd been teaching, when boys had really grasped the beauty of the language in the *Iliad* or the *Odyssey*, or when they'd understood how wonderful the poetry of Catullus could be. He'd never seen it with regards to something so physical, though. Something so . . . he sought the word . . . so real.

"What plants will go in here?" he asked. "I can look them up."

Ivy thought for a moment. "Probably won't plant most things until the spring," she said. "But they needed those rocks shifting."

"Where did they come from?"

Ivy's cheeks flushed, but Bernie didn't know why.

"Some are from the tea pavilion. It burned down a while back."

"Shame."

"Good that they're making use of the rubble," Louisa said quickly. Bernie looked at her. She seemed awkward, too. Was it something he'd said? He shifted on his feet, which were beginning to ache.

"Will it stay empty, then? The rock garden?"

Ivy shrugged. "Not completely. For now, maybe Mac will put in a few shrubs. Alpines, you know?"

Bernie didn't know really, but he nodded as though he did.

"Think Mac wants to put a couple of conifers in at the back, too. Just little ones. They'll need keeping an eye on, though, because they grow like buggers."

Bernie tried not to look surprised at Ivy's language but obviously failed because she laughed at his expression, and the tension that had fallen over their little group lifted, like the sun coming out from behind a cloud.

"Got your lunch?" she said.

Bernie nodded.

"Let's eat."

They all cleaned their hands and sat down in the shade of a tree to eat.

"What books have you been reading?" Louisa asked politely.

"*A Year in My Garden*," Bernie said. "It goes through the seasons. It's a wonderful book. I'm learning so much."

Ivy snorted. "You can't learn gardening from books," she said again, more adamantly than she'd said it before.

"I've picked up a few bits," Bernie said, but Ivy glared at him in defiance.

"Oh really? Tell me what you know."

Once again he was transported back to the classroom, the smell of chalk dust in his nostrils and a mouthy pupil arguing that there was no point in learning the classics.

Feeling his heart begin to beat faster, he breathed in deeply and blinked, and forced himself to feel the grass beneath his legs and the sun on his face and smell the deep earthy scent of Kew. He was fine. He was safe.

Louisa was watching him, her brow etched with concern. "Are you all right?" she asked. "You disappeared there for a moment."

"I'm fine," he said, looking down at the sandwich his landlady had made him that morning. "Just some bad memories, is all."

Ivy looked distraught. "Was it me?" she said. "Did I say something wrong? Sorry, Bernie."

He smiled at her, eager to reassure her that the problem was with him, not her.

"I had a bit of trouble in my old job," he said, choosing his words with care. "I got ill and then I couldn't work there anymore."

"What did you do?" Louisa's eyes were sharp.

"I taught classics," he said. "At a rather old and serious boys' school called St. Richard's."

"That's why you love books so much," Ivy said, as though she'd cracked a code, and Bernie found himself chuckling at her triumphant expression. It was the first time he'd laughed properly for months and months.

"It is," he agreed. He reached over and grabbed his bag. "Let me show you my garden book. You can have a look for yourself and see if you think it's useful."

He opened his bag and as he did, a gust of wind swept through the trees and lifted a bundle of paper that was inside, scattering the pages across the rock garden and the lawn beyond.

"Oh bloody hell," Bernie said in horror, leaping to his feet. Across the way, Mac was sitting with some of the regular gardeners, and he got up, too.

"For heaven's sake, Bernie," he shouted. "Catch those papers."

Bernie looked round in despair. There were pages everywhere—scattered so widely and still dancing around in the wind that he didn't know which direction to run in first. Then Ivy appeared at his elbow and squeezed his arm.

"I'll go that way," she said, pointing toward Mac and the other gardeners. "You get the ones in the rock garden and, Lou, you head for the rhododendrons."

Bernie smiled in gratitude, and veered off toward the rocks, catching pages as he went. He hoped Louisa and Ivy wouldn't read any of his writing. He fancied himself as something of a poet, but his work wouldn't stand up to being read. Not yet.

"Got them," Louisa sang from the bushes. "Oof, no, here's another one." She was laughing as she chased the pages. Her cheeks were flushed; her hair was escaping from its bun. Her forehead had lost the worried frown she often wore and she looked younger than her years. Bernie smiled as he watched her and then mimicked her dancing steps to catch the pages in the rock garden, darting this way and that.

"My fault, Mac," Ivy said gleefully. She was enjoying this unexpected exercise, too, Bernie thought. "I knocked over Bernie's bag."

That's not true at all, Bernie thought, watching as Mac—who was obviously very fond of Ivy, despite his feelings about female gardeners—tutted at her in an indulgent fashion and caught one of the runaway pages himself.

"Here you go," Ivy said, appearing in front of him. "Got them all." She thrust the pages at him all higgledy-piggledy.

"Thank you," he said. "And thank you for taking the blame with Mac."

She shrugged. "Wasn't your fault, and I didn't want him getting the hump with you."

"It was nice," Bernie said.

Louisa arrived, her pages more neatly arranged in her hands.

"Here," she said, her bright eyes looking at the words scrawled across the paper. "Are you a writer?"

Bernie felt himself flush with embarrassment.

"I write poetry," he said, stammering over his words. "I find it helps. When I have troubling thoughts."

Louisa nodded. "Did you write when you were having a difficult time at work?"

Bernie winced, thinking of the love poems he'd written to Vivi. The poems where he'd opened his heart and told her how he felt about her. And which she'd left in the staff room for everyone to see. His ears started to thunder with the sound of the laughter that had followed him round school for weeks.

"Sorry," Louisa said, thankfully stopping the noise in his head and clearly realizing he didn't want to talk about it—couldn't talk about it, not really.

"S'all right," Bernie muttered.

"Show me the book," Louisa said, changing the subject. "Let's finish lunch and you can show us the book you've been learning from. I'm sure Ivy will have some opinions she wants to share."

Relieved that the moment had passed, Bernie sat down again and carefully pushed the papers into his bag. He took out *A Year in My Garden* and then fastened the straps so his pages couldn't escape again.

"It's a lovely read," he said. "I had it on my shelf before I even visited Kew. Wonderful descriptions of the flowers."

"We're going to be doing the herbaceous borders later," Louisa said. "Only weeding, but they're looking glorious at the moment. What does it say about those?"

Bernie was aware Louisa was being kind, trying to get him to chat about things he was comfortable with instead of asking questions about school, but instead of being embarrassed he found he was pleased. Grateful for her kindness. And, to his surprise, keen to talk.

He found the right page in the book and read out a small passage describing some of the flowers. Ivy was sitting a little way away from them and stayed quiet, but she was clearly listening carefully.

"That's right, actually," she said. "Peonies are like that. I love the way they disappear over winter and then sneak up on you. They're crafty. It's good."

Bernie held out the book. "Do you want to see?"

Ivy shook her head.

"Honestly, have a look. There are even some photographs. And a whole section on peonies, for you to read."

"I don't want to."

"Have a look."

Ivy glowered at him. "Leave it, Bernie," she snapped.

There was a pause and they all looked at one another.

"What's wrong, Ivy?" Louisa asked.

Ivy looked away, suddenly seeming very young and once more reminding Bernie of his sulkiest pupils. "I just don't want to look at the book."

Louisa and Bernie exchanged a glance. Louisa's eyes were full of understanding while Bernie was fairly sure his just looked confused. What was happening here?

"Ivy," Louisa said gently, "can you read?"

"What?" Ivy said. "Course."

"Really?"

There was another pause. Bernie could hear the shouts of the gardeners across the way, but everything seemed quiet where they were.

Ivy looked up at the blue sky. "No," she said. "I can't read."

෴

Ivy hugged her knees into her chest and waited for Bernie or Louisa to say something. She couldn't believe she'd just blurted out her secret. It wasn't quite the thing she was most ashamed of in the whole world, that was something different, but it wasn't anything to be proud of. She couldn't bring herself to meet their eyes in case they were looking disgusted.

"Ivy?" Louisa said gently. She touched Ivy's arm. "Ivy, it's all right."

Slowly, Ivy looked up.

"Tisn't all right," she said. "It just makes me feel so stupid. Even my little brothers and sisters can read, but I just never went to school enough. I was always with Dad at the market. Or running wild down on the Hackney Marshes."

She looked straight at Louisa. "I never let on to the Suffragettes," she said. "Not once. I just avoided all the banners and placards and all that stuff. Made myself useful in other ways."

Louisa nodded. "I bet you were more than useful," she said. "They're lucky to have you."

Ivy gave her a small smile.

"You're a Suffragette?" Bernie said, startled.

Ivy shushed him. "Don't tell Mac. He hates us."

Bernie looked at Louisa, his eyebrows raised. "You, too?"

"Shh."

He smiled. "None of my business."

Looking relieved, Louisa turned back to Ivy. "Does Jim know?"

Ivy was still thinking of the Suffragettes, so when Louisa mentioned Jim, she winced and wrapped her arms around herself. Louisa was still looking at her, though, and she realized with a start that she meant did Jim know about her not being able to read. Not the other thing.

"Jim knows. He showed me the ad in the paper and I couldn't read it and he twigged, like you did, Lou."

"What did he say?"

Ivy remembered how awful she'd felt when Jim had worked out why she avoided certain situations and then how relieved and loved she'd felt when he'd simply shrugged.

"He says some things are harder for some people," she said. "He read out the ad, and he wrote the application letter for me. He's got lovely writing, Jim has."

"You're bright as a button, Ivy," Louisa said. "I don't believe for one minute that reading is harder for you than it is for anyone else. I imagine you've simply not had a proper chance to learn."

Ivy was chuffed with Louisa's praise, which she felt she didn't deserve. She felt her cheeks flush with pride.

"Nah, don't count on it," she said, embarrassed. "I'm slow as anything."

"Ladies," said Mac, coming up behind them and ignoring the fact that Bernie was there, too. "I need you weeding the borders. Let's get on, shall we?"

Pleased to have an excuse to abandon the awkward conversation, Ivy jumped up and brushed off her skirt.

"Come on, then," she said.

Weeding the borders was boring and hot, kneeling down in the earth in the summer sun, being careful not to squash any of the flowers that were in full bloom. But Ivy enjoyed it. She had meant what she said to

Bernie before—she did think gardening was about getting your hands in the dirt, smelling the earth and feeling part of something.

The three of them worked in contented silence for most of the afternoon, sharing observations with one another when they felt like it, but mostly happily getting on with the job, listening to the birdsong.

"It's so nice to be quiet," Louisa said eventually. "When I first came to London it was the noise that I couldn't bear. All the people and the horses and the shouting; it was too much for a country girl like me. I sometimes find it hard to believe we're still in the city when we're here."

Ivy raised an eyebrow. "You want to come to our house if you want to hear noise," she said. "All the kids playing, and Ma shouting, and Dad grumbling about something."

Bernie was standing, a faraway look in his eye.

"When I had my trouble I had a constant noise in my head. A voice telling me how stupid I'd been. How everyone was laughing at me."

Ivy glanced at Louisa. She wasn't quite sure what to make of Bernie, who seemed both fragile and strong at the same time. She wondered what kind of trouble he'd been in.

"My school was in East Sussex, you know. Close to the sea."

"Nice."

He grimaced. "Not once the fighting began. We could hear it. Hear the guns rumbling. It was like a constant reminder that there were men just across the Channel dying. Boys I'd taught, even. People's brothers, sons, husbands. I hated that I couldn't get away from the noise."

Louisa was busy weeding a patch of delphiniums, her brisk fingers pulling out the tiny strands before they took hold. Now she looked up at Bernie. "Do you still hear it? The noise?"

Bernie shook his head. "One day, I wandered into a Quaker meeting. Do you know what that is?"

Both women murmured that they did not.

"It's silence," said Bernie in satisfaction. "It's quiet and still and some-times someone speaks, but often they don't. It felt like coming home." He looked embarrassed suddenly. "It helped."

"Do you still go? Are you a Quaker?" Ivy was glad Louisa had asked, because the way Bernie described his meetings as being like home sounded like the way she felt about her WSPU meetings. Perhaps they had more in common than she'd first thought.

"I do," Bernie said. "I am."

Louisa nodded. "Good."

There was a pause.

"These are pretty," Bernie said, changing the subject and gesturing to a small plant with pink flowers.

Ivy shuddered. "Begonia," she said.

"Don't you like them?" Louisa looked up, interested.

"They're pretty enough, but they mean danger, beware."

Bernie scoffed. "What?" he said. "How could a pretty little pink flower like this have a meaning like that?"

"Dunno," Ivy said. "But it does. Makes me think of the war, Bernie, like you said. Lads I grew up with have gone to fight. My oldest brother is fourteen—he's already talking about enlisting when he can. Don't bear thinking about."

Bernie looked at the bright blooms with curiosity while Louisa straightened up, rubbing the small of her back.

"It used to be a thing, didn't it? The language of flowers," she said. "I remember my mother and her friends talking about it—how their sweet-hearts would give them little posies with secret meanings."

Ivy was thrilled. "Yes, that's it. My dad used to tell me about it. And Jim knows so much. He's been teaching me."

"I'd like to learn." Louisa and Bernie both spoke at once, and they all laughed.

"Do you think he would teach us?" Louisa added.

"Course," said Ivy.

"What else do you know?" Bernie looked round at the glorious double-width border they were working on. The scent of the flowers was heavy in the air, and bees buzzed round the blooms. "What does this all mean except for a lot of hard work?"

Ivy chuckled. "Peonies, my favorites, they mean happy marriage," she said. "I always reckon it's because there's stuff going on with a marriage, under the surface, that you don't know about. Like with peonies in winter."

Louisa grimaced, obviously thinking of the things that went on in her marriage that no one knew about, and feeling bad about reminding her, Ivy hurriedly carried on.

"Snapdragons mean deception," she said. "Imagine giving someone those."

"What about ivy? What does that mean?" Bernie was smiling.

Ivy felt her cheeks reddening again, and not just because of the sun.

"Jim says it means fidelity," she said. "And love."

"Maybe it means something completely different and Jim just said it means love to woo you," teased Louisa.

Ivy laughed properly this time, a loud guffaw that sent a butterfly circling up in the air. "Sounds like Jim," she said. "He's got the gift of the gab, all right."

"What else?" Bernie said eagerly.

"If you give someone daisies it means you'll keep their secret." Ivy fixed Bernie and Louisa with a stern glare. "So imagine you're giving me them now and you won't ever tell no one about my reading and writing."

Louisa nodded, smiling, but Bernie looked thoughtful.

"I could teach you," he said.

Ivy looked at him. "What?"

"Teach you how to read."

She waved his suggestion away with a dirty hand. "Nah," she said. "You couldn't."

Bernie lifted his chin. "I'm a good teacher. At least, I was."

"I'm sure you are, Bern. But I'm sixteen years old. I reckon if I was going to learn, I'd have done it by now."

"You're a baby, Ivy," Louisa said. "I think this is a marvelous idea."

"I owe you a favor, for taking the blame for my runaway pages," Bernie said.

"That was nothing compared with teaching someone like me how to read."

"Oh, come on, Ivy. It's important."

She fixed Bernie with a hard stare. "I've done all right up until now."

"What if Jim hadn't been around to read that ad for you? Where would you be now?"

Ivy thought for a moment. She'd probably be scratching a living selling flowers on Columbia Road, trying to keep her dad's business ticking away while he disappeared again. Or working in a munitions factory like some of her mates, spending long days indoors and never feeling the earth between her fingers.

"I wouldn't be here," she admitted.

"Let Bernie teach you how to read," Louisa urged. "And you and Jim can teach Bernie and me about the language of flowers."

Ivy knew when she was beaten. "Fine," she said. "You can have a go, but I'm warning you. I won't get it."

Bernie looked excited. "I'll start with the letters," he began, but Ivy gave him a nudge that was perhaps a bit harder than it needed to be.

"I know my letters," she said. "Well, most of them anyway. I'm not a baby. It's just putting them all together that I struggle with."

Bernie chuckled. It was a nice sound and Ivy and Louisa couldn't help but laugh, too.

"I'll teach you from *A Year in My Garden*," he said. "And you can tell me all the bits they've got wrong."

Suddenly, learning how to read with Bernie sounded like the nicest thing Ivy could do with her time—apart from spending it with Jim, of course. She grinned. "You're on."

But Bernie looked worried. "Where should we do our lessons, though? I'd say come to my digs, but my landlady is a stickler for propriety and I don't think she'd take kindly to me inviting a young woman in."

Ivy made a face. "No room at ours. Not with all the littl'uns running round."

"What about my flat?" Louisa said. "It's not big, but there's a table for you to use, and I won't get in your way. You'd be very welcome."

"Really?" Ivy wasn't sure. "Thought you liked having your own space?"

"I do, I love it. But not all the time. It would be nice having some company a couple of times a week."

She looked at Bernie. "I'm in Wandsworth, so it's not far."

"I'm in Battersea, so that's perfect. I could even walk home if I was feeling energetic."

"Ivy?" Louisa asked. "I know it's much farther for you."

Ivy wasn't bothered by the prospect of traipsing across London to work at Kew, to find flowers for her dad's stall, for WSPU meetings, or to spend time with these new friends. She grinned. "Suits me."

"Then that's settled," said Louisa briskly. "We'll start tomorrow after work. I'll make tea."

"I could bring a cake," Bernie said.

"Even better."

"In my experience, pupils are always more willing to listen, and lessons are always easier, when one has something sweet to nibble on."

Ivy suddenly felt nervous at the prospect of dear Bernie realizing how little she knew.

"I'm really not clever," she said, trying to joke but not sounding very convincing. "You'll probably get fed up once you see just how stupid I am."

Bernie smiled at her. "I am frightened of many things, Ivy," he said. "But one thing I'm never afraid of is a challenge."

Ivy rolled her eyes. "Yeah?" she said. "I just hope you're right."

Chapter 5

Ivy was nervous before the first reading lesson.

"It's a really good idea," Jim said, trying to calm her nerves. "You can't go through your whole life not being able to read or write."

"Why not?" said Ivy. They were sneaking a half hour together under the trees in Kew. "Got you to do it for me, ain't I?"

She leaned against the thick bark of a sycamore tree and looked at him defiantly.

"You do," Jim said sweetly. He gave her a kiss. "But what if I'm not here?"

Ivy felt her stomach turn over in fear at the thought of his not being around. "Where are you going?"

"Nowhere, yet. But what if they do pass this conscription bill? I could get called up."

"You're too young."

"At the moment. I'll be eighteen next year. And people say it's better to volunteer because you get more choice."

Ivy thought she might vomit with the sheer horror that Jim's words made her feel. She pushed him away from her with two hands.

"Don't," she said. "Don't talk like that. You need to stay here, with me."

Jim was calm. "All I mean is, it's important for you to learn."

Ivy knew he was right, but she was still cross about him mentioning the war. She hated any talk of his being called up or—worse—enlisting himself. She wasn't sure she believed in God, not really, but every night when she got into the bed she shared with her sister, she prayed that the war would be over soon. The stories she heard, though, made it sound like it was actually getting worse rather than ending. Bernie's tale about listening to the guns in France when he was at his school made her shudder.

"I have to go," she said to Jim. "Louisa will be waiting for me."

He grabbed her round her waist and pulled her close. "Don't fret, Ivy," he said. "What will be will be."

He kissed her and, for a moment, she forgot all her fears.

They came flooding back, however, later on when she was sitting at Louisa's little table, in her basement flat, ready to begin the lesson.

Ivy was very taken with Louisa's home. It was small, that was true, but she'd made it so nice. She'd covered the drab settee with a pretty crocheted blanket, and even though it was below ground there was enough light that it wasn't gloomy. She had lots of plants, too, and proudly showed Ivy and Bernie what she was growing in the pots she had.

"You've got green fingers, that's for sure," said Ivy admiringly. She rubbed the leaves of the sunflowers that were reaching up to the sky. "These will be taller than the wall in a couple of weeks."

"That's what I'm hoping. I want to see their glorious faces peeping out through the railings when I come home."

"Like when the sun comes out on a cloudy day," said Ivy. "Nice."

"You ladies are very talented." Bernie was looking at Louisa's plants in awe. "I've no idea how you make things grow so beautifully. The knowledge you both have of flowers and plants is wonderful. I'm looking forward to sharing it."

"Just stuff I've picked up over the years." Ivy shrugged. "Like breathing."

"Well, I think it's very impressive."

She smiled at him. He was such a sweet man, she thought. Gentle and kind. It occurred to her that if there were more men in the world like him perhaps the war wouldn't have started at all. She wondered if Bernie would get called up and how he would fare if he did. Not well, she thought. She couldn't imagine him with a gun in his hand.

"Ready?" he said, snapping her out of her horrible daydream.

She nodded. "As I'll ever be."

Bernie was, predictably, a patient and thoughtful teacher. Ivy had been worried he would use baby books and make her feel silly, but of course he didn't. He'd brought along his *A Year in My Garden* book and had written out simple words for her to try, all plant-related. She was so interested in the words he'd chosen, and how they fit in with the story of the year in flowers that the book told, that she almost forgot she was stumbling over the letters.

When Bernie asked her to do some writing, she was nervous again.

He'd written out some simple names of flowers and plants and asked her to copy them. Worried she was going to make a fool of herself she picked up a pencil.

"That's ivy," she said, recognizing the first word. "I know that one."

Bernie grinned. "Thought you would."

Carefully, Ivy wrote the word out in her notepad, and then next to the letters, she drew a small ivy leaf.

"Lovely," said Bernie. "That's going to help you remember the words. Now the next one."

Ivy carried on, writing out the botanical words he'd given her and drawing leaves or flowers next to the words.

"That's wonderful." Louisa had been sitting, reading quietly while Bernie gave the lesson, but now she came over and looked at what Ivy had been doing. "I didn't know you were an artist, too."

Ivy beamed at her. "I've always drawn plants," she said. Then she looked sheepish. "Probably because I couldn't write."

"I hate to interrupt, but we're going to have to get going, Ivy, if we want to make it in time."

Bernie began clearing the books away. "Of course, ladies. I don't want to take up too much of your evening."

Ivy reached out and squeezed his hand. "Don't be a silly sod," she said. "It's been lovely. And I'm really thankful you're taking time out of your life to teach me."

Bernie gave her fingers a squeeze in return. "It's helping me, too. And I'm looking forward to learning about the meaning of all the flowers when your Jim can spare five minutes."

"Me, too," said Louisa. "I've been doing a bit of reading about it already, actually."

Ivy sighed. "Maybe I'll do some reading about it one day."

"You most certainly will." Bernie was adamant. "I've never failed a pupil yet. Now, take the page you wrote the words on and read it every night before bed."

Obediently, Ivy took the paper and put it into her bag. Then she stood up.

"I'm ready to go," she told Louisa.

"Where are you off to?" Bernie asked.

Louisa and Ivy exchanged a look. They'd agreed not to mention their Suffragette activities to anyone at Kew because they knew how badly thought of they were at the Gardens. And rightly so, Ivy thought with a shudder. Even Jim didn't know everything about Ivy's involvement with the WSPU. But Bernie was their friend, wasn't he? And they'd already told him they were Suffragettes.

"We're just meeting some women," Louisa said vaguely. "It's a church thing."

Ivy blinked at her. They were indeed meeting in a church hall, but claiming it was related to religion was a bit of a stretch.

Bernie's face lit up, though. "Suffragettes?"

Louisa grinned. "Yes," she admitted. "Suffragettes."

"How nice. I have found such comfort in my meetings. I'm actually going to one myself this evening."

"Is it a service?" Ivy asked. She'd never been one for church and wasn't sure what the Quakers did, exactly.

"Not this evening. We're talking about the war, actually . . ." Bernie trailed off, and Ivy was glad.

"I don't want to hurry you, but we really should get on," Louisa said.

Together, they all followed her out of the flat, and Bernie and Ivy stood at the top of the iron staircase to wait for her to lock the door.

"Which way are you going, Bernie?"

He pointed down the street toward the river.

"Then we'll have to say good-bye now, because we're off in the other direction," said Louisa, appearing at the top of the steps.

"Thanks so much for my lesson," Ivy said. On impulse, she stood on tiptoes and kissed his cheek.

Bernie looked pleased. "I look forward to our next one," he said. "See you tomorrow."

He gave them a cheery wave and headed off down the road. Ivy tucked her hand into Louisa's arm.

"Where are we off to, then?"

Louisa had invited her to meet up with some women from the Wandsworth branch of the WSPU, as it was handy for after her lesson with Bernie, and Ivy had agreed. Ivy had been feeling rather unenthusiastic about her local Suffragette meetings recently. Since the fighting had begun, Emmeline Pankhurst had called for the women to stop their activities and instead throw themselves into supporting the war. But Ivy had mixed feelings about the war altogether. She wasn't completely sure she understood why they were fighting in the first place, and the cries of patriotism and doing it for king and country sounded hollow as she watched boys she'd grown up with head to the trenches. She found she couldn't summon up the enthusiasm required to encourage men to enlist, as Mrs. Pankhurst wanted, and so she'd started to avoid her local meetings. She was hoping Louisa's branch might feel more like home.

Louisa was proudly filling her in on the women she was going to meet at the church hall close to Wandsworth Bridge.

"And there's Ethel, who's an absolute card," she was saying. "She's seventy if she's a day, but she's one of the fiercest women you'll ever meet. The stories she tells of her time in Holloway will have your toes curling."

Ivy chuckled. "I can't believe she went to prison at her age."

"Lots of women did," Louisa said, her expression darkening. "We've all done all sorts of things we would never have thought possible once upon a time. I just hope it was worth it."

Despite the warmth in the summer evening, Ivy cradled her arm. "I hope so, too," she said.

But the meeting was a disappointment—for Ivy, at least. There was a woman speaking who was passionately in favor of conscription. She explained that more men were needed to fight and the government would be voting to force all those of a certain age to sign up. Ivy felt sick at the prospect of her brother Jack or her Jim being sent to the awful trenches in France or Belgium and coming back changed, or worse, not coming back at all.

"What about the men who won't want to fight?" she asked. "Surely some men won't go?"

The woman looked disgusted. "Well, they shall have to go," she said. "This is for Britain. For the king. Why should they sit idly by while our brothers, our fathers, our husbands, are dying?"

There was a ripple of applause.

"And what if they refuse?" Ivy said, not giving up yet.

"Prison?" the woman said, her face growing red with anger. "Or, frankly, I think prison would be too good for the cowards. I think anyone who refuses to go should be shot."

The silence that greeted her declaration reassured Ivy that she wasn't the only one who thought that idea was going way too far. But these were the Suffragettes, who'd once been her family. Who'd cared for her when she was a young girl running wild in the streets of East London, and who'd made her feel less alone, less hungry, less scared. But they'd changed. Ivy didn't feel like they were all part of the same fight anymore.

She said as much to Louisa as they all piled out of the church hall and Ivy prepared for the long trek to Hackney.

"I just don't see why everything's stopped when women still don't have the vote," she complained. "And everyone is already doing all they can to support the war effort, even though our boys are being sent to fight for something we don't really understand."

"I'm not sure that's entirely true, Ivy," Louisa said mildly.

"It is true." Ivy was riled by the woman's speech. "I don't see how conscription can be a good thing."

Louisa shrugged. "We have to do what's necessary," she said.

Ivy glared at her. "But that's exactly it," she said. "We don't have to do anything, do we? It's fine for us. Great, in fact. We'd never have been allowed to work at Kew if so many male gardeners hadn't gone to war. But for the lads . . ." She swallowed a sob. "I'm just scared of losing Jim."

Distraught, Louisa threw her arms round Ivy and pulled her close. "Oh, my girl," she said. "Don't you worry one bit. Jim's not old enough to sign up and I'm sure this blasted war will be over before it comes to that."

"I hope so," Ivy said. But over Louisa's shoulder she caught a glimpse of some bright begonias, dancing in the evening breeze in a window box of a nearby house, and suddenly she felt very scared.

Chapter 6

The lessons were a success, Louisa thought a couple of weeks later, as she was watering one of the herbaceous borders. Slow-going, admittedly, but a success nonetheless. She liked having Bernie and Ivy around her flat a couple of times a week, and though she stayed out of the way while they were working, she enjoyed hearing the murmur of their conversation in the background and seeing Ivy's progress. She was reading better now, though she was still finding writing difficult.

"It's harder to learn the older you get," Bernie commented to Louisa one evening, as she made tea for everyone. Ivy had gone outside for some fresh air, needing a break from her books. "Children are like sponges and soak up everything you throw at them, but it's more difficult when they're older."

"Ivy's only sixteen," Louisa had pointed out. It was hard to remember sometimes how young Ivy was. She seemed much older—jaded, even— and Louisa guessed it was because of looking after her family when her father did his disappearing acts. Worry aged a person; Louisa knew that from her own experiences. Sometimes she looked at herself in the mirror, at the lines on her forehead and around her eyes, and the scattering of gray hairs appearing at her temples almost daily, and couldn't believe she was the same person who'd stood next to Reg in the village church and dreamed of raising a family with him as she vowed happily to obey. If only she'd known then what she knew now.

Summer was in its last days and the women gardeners, and Bernie, had been at Kew Gardens for a whole season. Louisa's sunflowers were blooming beautifully and she never got tired of seeing their joyful yellow faces turned to the sky as she hurried home from Kew each evening. And the Gardens themselves were heavy with blooms; you could smell the scents mingling as soon as you stepped through the iron gates. It was really something to behold. Louisa found herself sniffing the air as she walked toward work, trying to catch the scent as early as she could, and Ivy and Bernie had both confessed to doing the same.

They were an odd group, the three new recruits—Ivy, Bernie and Louisa—along with Jim, but they were getting along rather well. Ivy's prickliness and defiant nature seemed to soften when Jim was there, and when she was digging in the earth or taking cuttings from a plant. Bernie was still clumsy and cack-handed most of the time but took correction in good spirit and was learning fast. Jim was a lovely lad, kind and patient with Bernie, gently teasing with Ivy, and sweetly respectful of Louisa.

We make a good team, Louisa thought as she drained the last of the watering can onto the flowers below. As though Ivy is the flower, Jim the earth, and Bernie the water helping her grow. And then she laughed at herself for coming up with such a ridiculous idea and went to refill the can.

Jim was by the water barrel and he greeted her warmly.

"Working hard?" he asked. It was early September but the sun was still hot and his friendly face was ruddy.

Louisa nodded. "Watering," she said. "The ground is so dry. I'm hoping for rain soon."

Jim paused and looked up toward the west.

"It's coming. I can smell it."

Louisa looked in the direction he did but saw only blue sky.

"Really?" she said doubtfully.

He nodded. "Not today. But tomorrow, perhaps."

Louisa raised an eyebrow and Jim laughed.

"You'll see. I'll give you a hand with the watering cans. Be quicker if you take a couple over."

Together they filled four cans and heaved them across to the herbaceous border. Ivy and Bernie were both there, too, Ivy carefully explaining to Bernie why the small plants he'd just weeded had to be replanted.

"They're not weeds, Bernie," she said. "I watched Mac plant them just the other day."

Bernie was looking aghast. "Crumbs," he said. "I really thought I was getting better."

Louisa and Jim both chuckled.

"Easy enough mistake to make, Bern," Jim said. "Let's get them back in before Mac spots us, eh?"

They worked on together, with Bernie huffing and puffing and checking behind himself to make sure Mac wasn't approaching.

"Jim, tell us more flower language," Ivy said.

"Oh yes, please." Louisa was enjoying learning what the different blooms meant.

Jim leaned on his spade, looking more like the farmers Louisa had grown up around than the seventeen-year-old lad he was. "What do you want to know?"

"What's courage?" asked Bernie.

Jim shot him an amused glance.

"Mac's really not so bad," he said. "He's ever so pleased with you lot, you know. He calls you his girls."

"Even me?" Bernie said wryly. Jim laughed.

"He's a grumpy old thing, but he's sweet as anything," Ivy agreed. "He used to look out for me when I came with Dad. There weren't many that did that."

Louisa found she was absurdly proud that Mac was pleased with their work.

"What did he say exactly?" she asked Jim, but he only shrugged.

"Just that."

"But we're doing all right?"

He grinned at her. "Better than all right," he said. "I can't hardly remember what it was like without you."

Ivy nudged him roughly. "Courage," she said.

"Oh right. Come with me."

Obediently, they all downed their tools and traipsed obediently after Jim as he led down the path beside the border and over toward the rock garden.

Carefully, he clambered over the stones until he found a large patch of tiny white flowers, shaped like the most beautiful stars.

"Edelweiss," he said. "For courage."

Bernie peered down at the pretty stellar display. "They're so delicate."

"But strong," Jim said. "They grow in the Alps."

"German?" Louisa said with distaste. Jim gave her a look that was heavy with disappointment, and immediately she felt ashamed. What did it matter? These pretty little flowers weren't part of the war.

"They grow all over," Jim said carefully. "Austria, Germany, Switzerland."

He bent down and touched one of the flowers with a gently finger.

"They flourish in rocky ground in pretty tough conditions. They're sturdy little plants. I reckon we could all learn a thing or two from them about hanging on when things are difficult."

"Indeed," said Louisa, wanting to make up for her misguided comment about Germany.

"Thinking of the war, Bernie?" Ivy asked. Bernie nodded but didn't speak.

"There are a few plants that could hold messages about the war," Jim said thoughtfully. "How about this one?"

He led them back to the border, farther down than where they'd been working earlier, to a small purple plant that bore a passing resemblance to lavender.

Ivy frowned. "Hyssop," she said. "Good for coughs, ain't it?"

Jim nodded. "It's good for all sorts of things, tummy ache and that. But it also means sacrifice."

"That's a message for the war, all right," said Bernie. "Sacrifice."

Louisa wondered if he was thinking about his former pupils who'd gone to fight and been lost. Men he'd known as boys just a few years before.

Jim, sensing the mood had dropped, bounded over to another patch and pointed. "These," he said.

"Nasturtiums?" Louisa said. She was fond of the bright orange flowers and had several in her pots at home.

"Patriotism," Jim said. "That's what they mean."

Louisa was delighted and immediately decided to tell the women at her next meeting about the meaning of the bright plants. Believing in Great Britain was such an important message during times like these.

"Lovely," she said.

Ivy frowned again. She looked unsure, but Louisa wasn't sure why.

"You should draw them," she said hurriedly, wanting to cheer up the younger woman, whose earlier happiness seemed to have deserted her.

"That's a wonderful idea," Bernie said. "You've got a lovely eye for flowers and plants and your drawings are beautifully delicate."

Ivy flushed with pride.

"I agree," Jim said. "You could keep cuttings, too, and press flowers. I've seen you do that at home anyway. But you could make it like a real journal of the year at Kew. It's a good time to start with everything in full bloom."

"And you can add the meanings of the plants in your notes," Louisa said. "It'll be good writing practice, too."

Ivy shrugged. "I've not got the stuff I'd need," she said.

Bernie had been gazing at the nasturtiums, but now he stood up and raised his chin.

"I shall get you a pad," he declared. "And pencils. Talent like yours should be nurtured, Ivy."

Ivy giggled at his determination and then squeezed his arm. "Thanks, Bernie," she said. "I'd like that a lot. Will you help me with the writing?"

"Of course I will."

"Wherever will you start?" Louisa said, gazing round at the riches on offer.

"With whatever is easiest to spell," Ivy joked. Bernie laughed loudly and Louisa's spirits lifted at the sound. He didn't laugh often, Bernie. He seemed to be worried most of the time, fretting about something he didn't want to share. So she was pleased he seemed happier now—if only for a moment.

"Having fun?" Mac's voice boomed out over the flowers and they all jumped. But he was smiling, much to Louisa's relief.

"I heard what you were saying," he told them. "Ivy, I didn't know you were an artist?"

Ivy waved her hand at him, as if to say he'd got it all wrong. "I'm no artist, but I like messing around and drawing plants."

"And you're planning a diary of the year at Kew?"

She nodded. "Can I?"

He smiled again. Louisa wasn't sure she'd ever seen him looking so happy. It seemed Jim was right and he was pleased with their work.

As if he'd read her mind, Mac turned to her. "You're doing well, Miss Taylor," he said.

"Louisa, please."

"Louisa." He nodded. "Glad to have you all here."

There was a pause as they all smiled at one another, pleased with themselves. And then Mac coughed.

"But there's too much lazing about going on here for my liking," he said, clapping his hands. "Bernie, Ivy, I need you digging out the border at the end, separating those delphiniums and making room for the asters."

He nudged Ivy. "Take some of the delphs if you like, to press for your diary."

Ivy looked pleased as she and Bernie picked up the spades and headed toward the end of the border, and Mac wandered back over to where he'd been working on the lawn.

"What do delphiniums symbolize?" Louisa asked Jim with interest. She was intrigued by the language of flowers and eager to learn more. "Is it something awful? They're terribly poisonous, aren't they?"

Jim looked over at the blue blooms and thought. "I can't remember exactly, but I don't think it's horrible. I'll have to look it up, but I think it's having an open heart, being cheerful."

Bernie paused as they were talking.

"I know this one," he said, chuffed with himself. "I believe the name comes from *delphis*, which means *dolphin*."

Louisa smiled, pleased with the explanation.

"I suppose you could say the buds look a bit like dolphins," she said, with the confident knowledge of one who'd only ever seen a picture of the exotic mammal in a book. "But it's a bit of a stretch. Though the blue is like the sea."

But Bernie wasn't finished.

"Legend has it, the flowers bloomed in the blood of the mighty warrior Ajax, who fought in the Trojan War," he said. Louisa watched in pleasure as his face lit up while he talked of his favorite subject. "He went mad after Achilles died, and killed himself. And the blue flowers sprung up where his blood spilled."

Louisa made a face. "That's a bit gruesome," she said.

Bernie spread his arms out wide. "No, it's wonderful," he said. "Wonderful storytellers, the ancient Greeks. Each delphinium petal bears the letters *ai*. It means *alas* in Greek."

Jim screwed his face up. "No they don't," he said. "At least, not that I've noticed."

Louisa and Bernie both laughed.

"Maybe you just need to look more carefully," Bernie said, and Jim laughed, too.

Ivy was bored of waiting.

"Come on, Bern," she grumbled. "I can't do this on my own."

She glanced over to the others and flashed them her infectious smile.

"I'll take a cutting to press, and I'll draw the petals," she said. "We'll see who's right about these letters."

The sound of their chuckles echoed across the Gardens as they all got back to work.

Chapter 7

Ivy was so thrilled with the sketchbook and pencils Bernie gave her that she couldn't speak for a moment.

"Oh, Bern," she said eventually, putting her hand to her chest. "Oh, Bernie."

"I chose it because the paper is quite thick and I thought it would work for drawings and pressed flowers," he explained, pleased with her reaction. He always worried about not getting things right, not judging a situation correctly—heaven knows he'd made a big enough mistake with Vivienne—but this time, it seemed, he'd done well.

"This is honestly the nicest thing anyone's ever given me," Ivy said, her eyes filled with tears. She squeezed his arm tightly, which in Ivy's world showed enormous affection, and Bernie felt quite tearful himself.

"Pleasure," he muttered. "I think you've really got something here, Ivy."

She gazed at her haul for a moment, stroking the pages of the book, and then a thought struck her and her expression darkened.

"This will be ruined if I take it home. I can't trust the littl'uns with anything nice. They'll be scribbling all over it. Can I leave it here, Lou?"

As always they were in Louisa's basement flat for the lesson. Louisa was sitting on the sofa reading, as she usually did while Bernie was teaching. Today, though, she was reading the newspaper instead of her customary novels and huffing and puffing, tutting and exclaiming, as she turned the pages. Bernie had carefully ignored her. He had a feeling he and Louisa wouldn't see eye to eye when it came to current affairs and the war especially, and he didn't want to ruin a blossoming friendship.

Now Louisa looked up. "What's that?"

"Can I leave my sketchbook here? I'm worried if I take it home it'll be spoiled by my stupid siblings."

"Of course you can," Louisa said. She turned her attention back to the newspaper and tapped the page she'd been reading.

"Things happening in Greece," she said to Bernie. She often did this, speaking to him of the war. He thought she assumed he'd share her interest in what was going on, when in reality the mention of the conflict sent him into a deep spiraling gloom. He'd heard rumors the British troops were planning to use poison gas and felt sick even thinking about it. What an awful thing to do. How could something so brutal ever be right?

He shook his head to dislodge the worries and spoke up. "I have to go, I'm afraid," he said, interrupting Louisa before she could fill him in on this week's casualties in France. "Ivy, shall I walk you to the bus stop?"

"That would be great, Bernie," she said.

"Not seeing Jim this evening?" Louisa asked.

Ivy shrugged. "Got something on." She looked a bit shifty, like she was hiding something, so Bernie was glad Louisa was absorbed in her newspaper.

When they were out in the street, he looked at Ivy. "What are you up to?"

She pulled her shawl round her shoulders. Summer was definitely on its way out and the evenings had a chill now.

"Nothing," she said.

Bernie chuckled. "You're a terrible liar, Ivy Adams," he said. "What's going on?"

She sighed and tugged his hand to get him to sit down on a wooden bench close to the bus stop.

"Promise you won't tell?"

"Depends what it is," said Bernie honestly. He hated being asked to keep secrets before he knew what those secrets were.

Ivy gave him an exasperated look, but she took a breath and spoke quickly. "I'm not sure how I feel about the war, is all," she said in a hurry.

Bernie realized he'd been holding his breath. "Me neither," he admitted.

They both looked at each other in slight shock about what they'd admitted.

"I'm so frightened that Jim will enlist," Ivy went on. "I lie in bed at night, just trembling at the thought. He's the best thing that ever happened to me."

Bernie managed a small smile. "I thought that was the sketchbook," he said.

Ivy thumped him on his arm with a grin. "You know what I mean," she said. Suddenly serious again, she added: "I know boys from school, or from the market, that have gone to France and not come back and it's awful, Bernie. I see their mums round our way, and they're changed, you know? They're kind of folded in on themselves because they're so sad. I don't want that. Not for me, not for my mum. Not for anyone."

Bernie nodded. "I understand," he said. "I've got pupils—former pupils—who have gone. I think about them as small boys because that's what they were when I was teaching them. I simply can't imagine their eager little faces, covered in mud and blood and Christ knows what else." He shuddered. "It's unbearable."

He pushed his shoulders back, getting the courage up to speak more. If they were sharing confidences, perhaps now was the time to share his deepest thoughts?

"I am a Quaker, as you know," he said. "And Quakers are pacifists."

Ivy looked blank. "I don't know what that is."

"We don't believe that war is ever the right course of action."

She looked up to the sky, her lips pinched together, thinking. "Seems a sensible way of thinking."

"Not everyone agrees."

"Well, lots of people are getting their knickers in a twist about it, ain't they?" Ivy said. Bernie chuckled at the supreme understatement. "Louisa and I . . ." She stopped talking for a second, then gathered herself and started again. "We've got some friends who are all over it. Going on about fighting for the king, and how all we women should be doing our bit."

She paused again. "There's a woman round our way, you might know her name? Sylvia Pankhurst?"

Bernie was surprised but tried to hide it. To hear Ivy talk of herself you'd think she was just another urchin running wild on the London streets, but then you'd catch a glimpse of her incredible knowledge of plants and flowers, her talent for drawing, her passion for nature, her deep thinking about the war, and now her casually dropping the name of one of—in Bernie's opinion—the most interesting social reformers of their time. He blinked.

"I do know her name, indeed I do."

"She's got this group going, the East London Federation of Suffragettes."

Bernie nodded slowly. He wasn't entirely sure how he felt about Suffragettes generally, but he adored Ivy and Louisa, and he'd heard many good things about Sylvia Pankhurst and her breakaway group.

Ivy went on: "When the war started, it got really rough round our way, really quick. Lots of the factories closed, almost straightaway. Men lost their jobs, or the ones on the reserves list just got called up and had to go. There were families with little kids, starving, Bernie. I saw it."

"Terrible business."

"And Sylvia got her women together and started giving out milk to the littl'uns. And food and that. And now they've got a factory making toys—I know a few people who have got themselves jobs there. My mum's even talking about giving it a go and I reckon she should, because it's got to be better than doing munitions."

She was looking animated now, waving her hands in the air as she talked.

"It just seems more . . ." She searched for the word. "More real."

"More real than . . . ?"

She paused again.

"More real than talking about the glory of the war," she said eventually.

Bernie was astonished. He looked at Ivy and nodded. "You're absolutely right," he said. "Absolutely. But as I said, not everyone sees it that way and we must respect the beliefs of others."

Ivy tutted but she smiled, too.

"I'm going to a meeting," she said. "This evening. A Federation meeting."

"Excellent."

"I want to see what it's all about. See if I can help, when I'm not at Kew."

"You are really something, Ivy," Bernie said. "A force of nature."

She thumped him on the arm again. "Shut up."

They smiled at each other for a moment.

"Don't tell Louisa, will you?" Ivy said. "I think she's lovely. She's so clever and quick-witted, and what she doesn't know about politics isn't worth knowing. And she's had enough troubles of her own to fill a book. Two books. And she's built herself back up again ..." She bit her lip. "I'm just not sure we agree about this, that's all."

Bernie nodded. "I think you're right, Ivy," he said. "And could I ask you to do the same? Of course, it's no secret that the Quakers are pacifists, but I don't want to make a thing of it at Kew."

Ivy nodded. "No big deal, though, is it? Who cares if you don't think war is the right thing to do? Won't stop those bigwigs sending a load more boys to the trenches, will it? They're not going to say, 'Ooh, Bernie from Battersea thinks we should stop, so let's call a halt, shall we?' Are they?"

Bernie laughed at what Ivy obviously considered a posh voice and wished with all his heart that she was right. Because he knew deep down people would care. Perhaps not at the moment, when enlisting was still voluntary, but conscription was coming; he felt it like a gathering storm. When Louisa had mentioned Greece earlier, he'd gone cold, knowing Britain had promised the Greeks they would send more troops. Where would they all come from?

Nervously, he pushed his clear spectacles up his nose. Would pretending to be shortsighted be enough to avoid being forced to join up? He feared not. Nor, he suspected, would it be enough to convince others that he had a reason not to fight. He thought about the mothers Ivy had talked of, bowed with grief, and how they would feel seeing him— a young, healthy man with four strong limbs and a sharp mind— refusing to go to face the Germans in France or Germany, and he felt sick.

"Bernie," Ivy said, concern in her voice. "Are you all right?"

He snapped out of his musings and looked at her. "Sorry, Ivy, I was miles away there."

She patted his hand affectionately. "Lots on your mind?"

"Exactly."

She studied him carefully. "Are your thoughts bothering you?" she asked astutely. "Why not go to one of your Quaker meetings? Could you get to one this evening? Might help calm things down."

Touched by her concern, he smiled.

"I think I will," he said. "Or perhaps I shall sit quietly and write my thoughts down in my journal."

Ivy nodded. "Do you think I'll ever be able to write like you?"

He gave a small laugh. "I think you'll be able to do whatever you want, Ivy," he said.

"I'm rubbish at writing, though."

"It's hard to learn when you're older; you should be kinder to yourself. It's not easy starting again."

"Slow going, ain't it?"

"It'll be worth it in the end."

Along the street, he could see the bus approaching, its engine pumping out clouds of smoke.

"At last," Ivy said. "I've been waiting longer and longer for the bus recently. Someone told me all the conductors and drivers have gone off to fight. I reckon they want to get some women in to do the jobs instead."

"Enjoy your meeting," Bernie said. "I'd like to hear more about the Federation."

"I'll tell you all about it tomorrow."

She had stood up, ready to jump on the bus when it arrived, but now she bent down and kissed him on the cheek.

"You're a good man, Bernie," she said, then she picked up her bag, swung it onto her back, and waved to the bus driver to get him to stop.

Bernie watched as she clambered up the stairs to the top deck and lifted his hand to wave good-bye. A good man? He'd never been called that before. A foolish man, certainly. A weak man. A clever man. But never good. He rather liked it. He waited for the bus to pull away and then he stood up and made his way back home.

Chapter 8

March 1916

Spring was late that year. March arrived like a lion, with blustery showers and nightly frosts. At Kew, the gardeners worked on, regardless. Louisa had been surprised by just how much there was to do during winter but had enjoyed being outside whatever the weather. The cold didn't bother her, but the relentless rain was getting her down and she was longing for a break in the gloom.

News from the Front didn't help. The conflict was spreading to more countries and it seemed for every gain the British troops made, there were more losses. Sometimes Louisa wondered if Reg had joined up. She couldn't imagine him in the army, but it was possible. Of course, now that the conscription act had passed, things were different. Reg was still young enough—just—to be forced to enlist. Farming could be one of the scheduled occupations, but Louisa had read that applying to be exempt took some work and she doubted Reg would put in the effort. Mind you, she thought, legally she and Reg were still married and at the moment it was only single men who were being drafted. How ironic if it was their marriage, which had almost destroyed her, was the thing that saved Reg.

Lost in thought, she stared out the window of the small break room at Kew, watching the rain running down the glass. She was the only one there for now, as she'd arrived early today. The buses were running better now that women were allowed to drive and Louisa had made it to work in no time. She was enjoying the silence and the time alone with her thoughts and, to be quite honest, she didn't really want to have to head outside into the wet.

Bernie will be here soon, she thought. He was an early bird normally. She smiled fondly as she thought of him with his disheveled hair and the specs perched on the end of his nose. He'd learned so much in their months at Kew, working hard to listen and understand everything Jim or Mac taught them, and reading everything he could about flowers and plants when he wasn't in the Gardens. He was really rather knowledge-able about botany now, which had impressed Louisa.

It was astonishing how quickly these people had become so impor-tant to her. They'd not even been at Kew for a year—hadn't seen how all four seasons changed the Gardens—and yet, Bernie, Ivy, Jim, and even Mac were like her family now. And, she thought, they'd arrived just at the right time. Since she'd moved to London it was her Suffragette family who'd bolstered her and welcomed her, and she'd missed the regular meetings and actions when the war started. But now she had her Kew family and the occasional WSPU meeting, too. There was one this eve-ning, in fact.

"Penny for them?"

Louisa turned, startled out of her thoughts by Ivy's arrival.

"It's horrible out there. I've only walked from the bus stop and I'm soaked through." Ivy started peeling off her wet outer layers and hanging them up.

Louisa smiled at her. "Good morning," she said. "I was just having a moment to myself before the day begins."

"Sorry to interrupt," Ivy said, but Louisa waved her apology away.

"Nonsense, now we can have a moment together. Do you have new pictures to show me?"

"I do," said Ivy. She opened her locker and pulled out the sketchbook Bernie had bought her. It was looking a bit battered now and was bulging so much Ivy kept it fastened with string. Now she pulled the string off and passed the book to Louisa, who sat down on one of the wooden chairs in the break room so she could open the book carefully.

Ivy had excelled with this book. Bernie had been so right to give her the tools she needed for her project, because it was something wonderful. She'd charted the changing scenery of Kew as the months passed. She'd collected cuttings from plants, pressed flowers, picked up seedpods and pasted them into the pages. In her childlike handwriting she had carefully copied out the names of the months and written the names of the plants, too. Alongside the cuttings, she'd also drawn the whole plant. A wonderful, detailed sketch of a conifer, delicately drawn in shades of green, took up a whole page, next to a pressed cutting from its branches. A glorious black-and-white drawing of a snowdrop, breaking through the icy ground, was next to the pasted-in flower from the same plant. *Snowdrop Febrary 1916* was printed carefully in Ivy's handwriting. Louisa didn't point out the spelling mistake. Why would she, when Ivy was working so hard?

"Look at the new stuff," Ivy said eagerly. She was always keen to get Louisa's opinion on her work. "I found some cyclamen in among the snowdrops. They're such a gorgeous color."

Louisa flicked to the end of the book and discovered vivid pink drawings of the small plants, next to another pressed flower and a small drawing of an ant.

"These are lovely, Ivy," she said. "Why the ant?"

"Ants carry the cyclamen seeds on their backs," she explained. "I thought I should include them."

Delighted, Louisa gazed at the pages. "What does cyclamen mean?" she asked. "I can't remember."

Ivy winced. "It's not nice," she said. "I almost thought about not drawing it because of its meaning."

"Really?"

She nodded. "It means resignation and good-bye," she said, her voice catching. Immediately, Louisa got up and went to the younger woman, wrapping her arms round her.

"Don't fret," she said into Ivy's hair. "Jim's too young to be enlisted."

"He's too young for now, but he'll be eighteen at the end of the year. And what if they change the ages?"

Louisa soothed her friend, stroking her hair.

"We'll worry about that if it happens," she said. "For now, it's not worth the mental toil."

Ivy nodded, but she didn't look too sure.

"What about Bernie?" she whispered. "He's such a peaceful bloke, but he's only twenty-eight. He'll be snapped up."

Louisa frowned. She'd not thought about Bernie.

"I'm not sure," she said. "He's shortsighted, isn't he? Perhaps that's why he's not been called up? Or perhaps it's to do with his teaching? Maybe he'll be told he has to go back to a school."

"I hope not," said Ivy. "I like having him here."

"So do I, but we all have to do our bit, Ivy."

Ivy grimaced and Louisa decided it was best to change the subject.

"You need to keep busy," she said, releasing Ivy from her embrace. "There's a meeting tonight. In Caxton Hall."

"A central meeting?" Ivy said, looking interested. "There haven't been many of those lately."

"No, indeed. I'm looking forward to it. Will you come along? You've not been to the few meetings we've had in Wandsworth."

"I've mostly been doing some things with Suffragettes locally," Ivy said vaguely. "East London way."

Louisa frowned. She had a feeling that Ivy had been avoiding the usual WSPU meetings recently, but she wasn't sure why. She'd wondered if she was spending every minute she had with Jim, given that he could soon be off to the Front, but now she was claiming to have been going to local meetings. Were there even any? Things had been very quiet for months, with Mrs. Pankhurst urging the women to instead focus on what they could do for the country. Louisa wasn't quite as ardent as their leader, but she did believe her approach was correct. After all, the question of women's suffrage wasn't going to be addressed while the war was going on—there simply wasn't enough time for parliament to consider it with all the other things happening. And Louisa had a hope that while women were stepping up to fill the shoes of the men who'd gone to war, they were showing the lawmakers and parliamentarians just how capable they were. How could they deny them the vote, she thought, when they'd proved they could make weapons, drive buses, keep the factories running, and even play football, as well as the men?

"So will you come?" she asked Ivy. "Mrs. Pankhurst is going to be speaking."

The younger woman nodded. "Yes, I'll come," she said. "I'd like to hear what she's got to say."

Ivy sounded slightly defiant, to Louisa's surprise. Perhaps she'd just misheard. She was going to ask what she meant, but the break room began filling up with other gardeners ready to start their day and the moment was lost.

After work, the two women met at the same spot.

"I'm so fed up with this rain," Louisa said, beginning the slow process of taking off her gardening clothes and putting on her wet-weather gear. "I am longing for summer."

"And then it will be a year since we came to Kew," Ivy said. "I can't believe how fast these last few months have gone."

"Time always goes quickly when you're absorbed in a task. I think we've all been learning so much, the hours have flown. Especially you, Ivy, with your writing and reading."

Ivy made a sound like a sigh mixed with a grunt. "I'm not getting on very well," she said. "Bernie's so patient with me, bless him, but all I can really do is copy letters. And my reading still isn't good. I think I'm better off sticking with drawing."

"You do it beautifully," Louisa said. She offered her arm to Ivy and together they walked out of the Gardens toward the train station.

It only took them an hour or so to get to Caxton Hall, where the meeting was being held. There were many women hurrying inside out of the rain, and then milling around chatting and catching up with friends. As always the atmosphere was friendly and welcoming and Louisa and Ivy were soon enveloped into the throng of smiling women.

"It's nice to see everyone," Louisa said, shaking the rain off her mac. "Hello, Beatrice, how's your mother doing?"

"Better, thank you so much," said Beatrice as she passed. "Oh, there's Helen. I must catch her, but let's talk later. I want to speak to you about the white feather campaign."

Louisa watched her bustle away, amused. Beatrice was nothing if not passionate, about Suffrage, about the war, about everything, really.

"Ivy, we've not seen you for a while," another woman said, kissing Ivy on both cheeks and then doing the same to Louisa. "Hello, Lou."

"Hello, Mary," Louisa said. Mary Clark was one of the leaders of the Wandsworth branch of the WSPU. She'd been so good to Louisa when she first moved to London, holding out the hand of friendship, offering support and a shoulder to cry on, helping Louisa find work and encouraging her to apply for the job at Kew, that Louisa sometimes thought she'd never be able to repay her debt. "Ivy's been mostly going to meetings locally, in East London."

Mary gave Ivy a sharp look, curiosity gleaming in her sharp eyes.

"Is that right," she said. "Federation?"

Ivy looked at her feet, which were wet from the rain. "Sometimes," she muttered.

"Hmm."

Louisa watched the two women with interest: Mary, gray-haired and with the weight of experience on her shoulders—and Ivy, fresh-faced and eager, yet being coy and evasive. What was going on here?

Ivy lifted her gaze and met Mary's stare and relaxed as she saw her smile.

"My mum's working at the toy factory," Ivy said, and Mary's grin widened.

"Wonderful stuff," she said.

"Sylvia's toy factory," Louisa said. "Sylvia Pankhurst?" She'd read about the Federation, of course, and heard talk of it. It seemed the women in the East End were doing some marvelous things, giving food to children and employment to mothers. But she hadn't known Ivy was involved. With a slight feeling of discomfort she realized Ivy probably hadn't told her in case she didn't approve. She knew some Suffragettes didn't like Sylvia's focus on working-class issues and her left-wing leanings, but while Louisa was in full agreement with Emmeline's opinions on the war, she also found it impossible to find anything wrong with what her daughter was doing. Perhaps, she thought, in the future, she should listen to others and talk about issues before being so strident with her own views. She did have a tendency to assume everyone agreed with her without even asking.

Feeling mildly ashamed, she followed Mary and Ivy to a row of empty chairs and sat down, just as Mrs. Pankhurst got up onstage.

"Today I want to talk to you about something new that is damaging the British war effort," Mrs. Pankhurst began. "Conscientious objectors."

Chapter 9

It all sounds a bit much, if you ask me," Jim said to Ivy the following day. The rain had finally stopped and so they'd sneaked away from the others to share their lunch on a bench by a crowd of daffodils, their golden heads bobbing in the breeze.

Ivy made a face. "It's definitely too much."

She opened up her sandwich and peered inside at the unappetizing gray meat on dry bread.

"Not hungry?" Jim asked.

"Not for this."

Jim shrugged. "I'll have it."

He took a huge bite and Ivy grinned.

"So tell me more about these feathers. Like I say, it's a bit much," he said through a mouthful of stale crumbs.

Ivy sighed. "Mrs. Pankhurst and some of her hangers-on have been doing it for a while, giving white feathers to any lads they see not in uniform."

"Because they think they're cowards?"

She nodded, grim-faced. She wasn't impressed with this approach at all. "They keep a load in their pockets and give them to anyone and everyone."

"But they could be home on leave or injured or doing a job that's vital to the war effort here," Jim pointed out.

"Exactly. But they just brand them all as cowards, without stopping to think about it."

"Nasty."

"It is. I don't like it at all."

"Will they stop now? Now there's conscription?"

Ivy shuddered at the word and laced her fingers into Jim's. "Well, that's the thing. No, they're not going to stop. In fact, they want us all to get involved. Because obviously now there's these conscientious objectors."

Jim finished Ivy's sandwich and screwed his nose up. "That was horrible."

She rolled her eyes. "I can't believe you ate it."

"I was hungry."

They smiled at each other for a moment, enjoying this time together, and then Ivy sighed.

"They don't believe anyone has a good reason for not going to fight. They have no time for conscientious objectors, and they want them exposed and shamed for not doing their bit."

"Well, really, everyone should be stepping up," Jim said, frowning. "It's not fair, is it, that some lads have to go and fight and be injured or killed, and others don't."

Ivy threw her head back.

"I know," she said. "It's not fair. But why should these boys be fighting? The people in charge aren't doing it. They're just making decisions in an office in London, safe and warm and dry, and sending another load of lads to Belgium to be shot at."

"Ivy, that's just how things work."

"Makes me sick. That some old posh bloke can just decide what happens to you."

Jim winced. "I don't want to go, either, but if I get called up, then I will. I won't say no, not when lads I know have gone before me."

Ivy squeezed his hand. "You're too young," she said. "You have to be eighteen."

"I'll be eighteen in November. The war won't be over by then."

Ivy felt ill just thinking about it.

"There are some jobs that if you do them, you don't have to fight," she said. "Someone asked about those blokes at the meeting. It's teachers and that. Vicars, I think. Few others."

"Gardeners?" said Jim hopefully.

"Don't think so." Ivy snorted. "It is useful, though, isn't it? What we're doing here. We've got that veg patch going now, and the allotments and that. We're helping people feed their families."

"Guess you could argue everyone's important in a way. Train drivers, and plumbers, and all sorts. We're no different from them and they've all gone."

"S'pose." Ivy wasn't enjoying this conversation at all.

"What about Bernie?" Jim sat up straighter as the thought struck him.

"What about him?"

"Mac's married, so he won't be called up, but just about everyone else has gone. And Bernie's the right age, and he's single. Why's he not been called up yet?"

Ivy didn't answer and Jim carried on.

"Has he said anything to you? You spend more time with him than anyone else."

Ivy shifted on the bench. She and Bernie hadn't really discussed the war since they'd both opened up that time last summer. It was as though they both knew they were in agreement and they didn't need to chat about it. She occasionally told him bits and pieces about the Federation and what was happening in the East End and he'd actually given her donations of food, milk, and even toys for the children. She remembered what he'd said about Quakers being pacifists, but she knew that it didn't matter what he thought about the war; he'd have to go anyway. No one was interested in what the Tommies' opinions were. They were just there to kill the enemy. Kill or be killed. She shuddered again and Jim looked at her, brow furrowed.

"Chilly?"

"Goose walked over my grave," she said. "Thinking about poor Bernie going to fight."

Jim was thoughtful. "He's quite posh. Nicely spoken. Maybe he'll be an officer?"

"I can't imagine that at all. He's so quiet. I can't picture him giving orders."

"He must have done when he was teaching. He must have had control of a whole load of rowdy schoolboys."

Ivy shook her head. "Not by shouting at them, though. He's so interested in what he's telling you, it's like you can't help but listen. You find yourself really trying hard just to impress him, and he's so pleased when you get something right, it's lovely."

Jim grinned. "And yet, your writing is still awful."

She thumped his arm. "Oi!" she said. "It's better than it was. I couldn't write anything at all before Bernie got hold of me. Now I'm writing names of flowers and all sorts. And reading stuff."

"You're doing so well," Jim said fondly. "I never thought you'd stick at it."

Ivy flushed with pleasure.

"I don't want anyone thinking I'm stupid, or thinking badly of you because of me," she admitted. "I don't want your family thinking, 'What's he doing with a girl like her, that can't read nor write?' And I don't want people turning up their noses at you for choosing me."

Jim put his arm round her and pulled her close and she snuggled into his chest for a moment.

"Ivy Adams, I don't think anyone who spent more than two minutes in your company could ever think you were stupid," he said. "Some people just have trouble with letters. I knew a couple of boys at school like that. Doesn't mean nothing at all. Not when your brain's as sharp as yours is and you're as talented an artist as you are."

Ivy sat up. "Bugger, I was going to draw those daffs this lunchtime while they're at their best. You've distracted me, Jim."

Jim grinned. "Do it now. I won't bother you."

Ivy stood up and dropped a kiss onto his forehead. "Stay here. I'll be back in a minute."

She ran off to find her sketchbook, waving at Louisa and Bernie as she passed. They were deep in conversation about something. It was nice that they were such good friends. Ivy had wondered if there might be a hint of romance there, at first, but Louisa was a good bit older than Bernie and he seemed to have sworn off women. He'd not told Ivy much about what had happened, but she'd gathered he'd got involved with a woman at the school he taught in—she was a musician who took choir rehearsals. Ivy got the impression she was rather glamorous and thought herself above the normal teachers. From what Bernie had said, it seemed he had fallen in love with this Vivienne, but she'd used him. She'd asked for favors and borrowed money. When he'd given in to his passion and proposed to her, she'd first laughed, then turned him down flat and then—worst of all— told everyone at school what had happened. The other staff had thought it hilarious and even the boys got wind of it and teased him mercilessly. Poor Bernie. Ivy couldn't bear the thought of anyone being mean to him; he was such a sweet, good-hearted, kind man.

She grabbed her sketchbook and pencils from the locker and raced back to Jim, out of breath slightly.

"Might be his glasses," she said, as she opened her book to a fresh, clean page.

Jim blinked at her. "What's that?"

"Bernie," she said. "I just saw him and I thought it might be his glasses, why he's not been called up."

Jim nodded. "I'd agree with you there if it wasn't for one thing."

"Go on." Ivy was only half listening as she drew the outline of the daffodil bloom.

"I don't reckon they're real specs."

"What?" Ivy scoffed. "Course they're real specs. Why wouldn't they be?"

"My little brothers both wear glasses, right?"

Jim had twin brothers who were twelve years old and blind as bats without their specs.

"Right."

"And when they put them on, their eyes look different because of the lenses. They go big, don't they? Like they're magnified."

Ivy thought about the boys. Jim was right, their eyes looked funny behind their specs.

"Like little frogs."

"Exactly. Bernie's eyes stay exactly the same. His specs have clear lenses."

"Really?" Ivy was still not convinced.

"I'm sure of it."

"Even if you're right, why would he do that? Wear specs if he doesn't need to?"

Jim shrugged. "No idea," he said. "But whatever the reason is for him not being called up, it's not his eyesight. Trust me."

Ivy didn't answer for a moment, as she shaded the daffodil flower in shades of yellow in her book.

"Well, there must be a reason and I suppose it's none of our business."

Jim gave her a sharp look. "You're not on board with this white feather thing, then?"

"Definitely not. We don't know anything about people, do we? We shouldn't be judging them. Maybe Bernie's got a disease. Or perhaps his legs don't work properly. Or he's got a dicky heart."

Jim looked dubious, but Ivy glowered at him.

"The point is, it doesn't matter," she said. "It doesn't matter because it's none of our business. He'll tell us when he's ready. Just like all the men who've not gone to fight. Maybe they're too young, or too old, or they're married or ill or something. How would we know just from seeing them in the street? It doesn't matter what Mrs. Pankhurst says, I ain't putting white feathers in no one's pockets."

She sat back on the bench, satisfied she'd made her point, and examined her sketch. She was rather pleased with it. She had wanted to draw the whole bunch of daffodils, nestling for space among one another, and she thought she'd captured it quite well.

"What do you think?" she said, showing Jim. "I'll cut one, too, and press it."

Jim looked at the picture in admiration and then at Ivy.

"I think, Ivy Adams, that you're the most incredible girl I've ever met."

Ivy gave him a shove. "Shut up."

"It's true. I think you're wonderful and I think one day, you're going to be my wife."

Ivy felt her cheeks flame. "Well, maybe I will," she said. "But you're going to have to talk me into it."

Jim laughed out loud. "Maybe I will," he echoed.

They kissed, quickly, before Mac saw. Everyone knew about Ivy and Jim—their romance was impossible to keep secret and, really, why should they? They were doing nothing wrong. But they felt Mac wouldn't be impressed to see them kissing at work or gazing into each other's eyes when they should be digging over a flower bed or planting bulbs, so they kept things professional at Kew. Most of the time.

Ivy slid off the bench and bent down to pick one of the daffodils to press later.

"Do you know what they mean?" Jim asked, and she looked up at him, wanting to know the answer.

"It's not something awful, like casualties of war, is it?"

Jim smiled, looking right at her. "Not even close," he said. "They mean the sun is always shining when I'm with you."

Ivy was delighted. "That's the loveliest meaning yet," she said. "Will you help me write it in my sketchbook?"

Jim smiled. "Course I will," he said. "I'll do anything for you, Ivy Adams. Anything at all."

Chapter 10

Bernie was nervous. Constantly on edge. He wasn't sleeping properly, or eating really. He was making silly mistakes at work—the sort of mistakes he'd made in his early days at Kew. Mac had been tolerant then, but now he was less willing to overlook Bernie's mishaps.

"For crying out loud, Bernie," he kept saying, which wasn't helping Bernie's anxiety in the slightest.

The conscription act was in full force now. Bernie had been called up but had burned the papers, feeling rebellious and terrified at the same time. He knew he wasn't alone; there were a few men at his Quaker meeting who'd done as he'd done, but that didn't make him feel less nervous. Nothing had happened so far. He'd not had another letter. He was sure another would arrive, though. Sooner rather than later.

The rain had stopped, which was good. Spring was on the way. The spirits of the other gardeners had all improved with the weather, but Bernie's had not. He had a sense of impending doom and he knew it was only a matter of time until someone found out he should be on his way to the Front but wasn't.

Despite the fears of being found out, Bernie was, oddly, entirely at peace with his decision. He had never wavered in his conviction that this war—like all wars—was wrong. He did not want to kill German men, who were the same as he was under their uniforms. He did not want to kill anyone, ever. He did not want to kill and he would not kill. Not for the king, not for his country, not for anyone.

The rain had given all the spring plants at Kew a boost and the herbaceous border was overgrown with weeds.

"Bernie, get cracking on that patch, can you?" Mac said. "I know it's dull, but the girls are all busy deadheading the daffs." Mac may have been becoming prouder of his female gardeners with each day that passed, but that didn't stop him apologizing when he gave Bernie what he considered a "girlie" task to do, even though Louisa, Ivy, and the rest were far more skilled than Bernie.

Bernie waved to let Mac know he was on it, and got to work. As he knelt on the grass, he let the smell of the earth and the spring blooms soothe his worried mind. Ivy swore that being close—physically close—to nature made her feel better and Bernie believed she might be on to something there. He dug out some stubborn weeds with his trowel and plucked others with his long fingers and felt the soft spring air on his face.

The sound of voices made him look up. Along the path a little way, Louisa was standing talking to a visitor to the Gardens. She was a well-dressed woman wearing a bonnet, which the wind was tugging. Frustrated with the breeze, she untied her ribbon and pulled the hat from her head, laughing as she did so. But Bernie wasn't laughing. He looked in surprise at the woman he recognized as one of Vivienne's friends. He couldn't remember her name. Adele? Ada? Something like that.

He hoped she wouldn't see him; his nerves were so frayed at the moment that he couldn't bear the thought of having to replay everything that had happened at St. Richard's and with Vivienne. Like a cat watching a mouse, he crouched down behind a shrub and pretended to be deeply involved with his weeding.

"Bernie?" Oh Lord, she'd seen him. "Is that you? Bernie Yorke?"

Reluctantly, Bernie stood up and she clapped her hands delightedly.

"Do you remember me?" she sang. "It's Adelaide. Adelaide Marks. Friend of Vivi's."

Bernie took a deep breath. "I do remember," he said. "Hello, Adelaide. How nice to see you."

Adelaide rushed over to greet him, kissing him on both cheeks.

"Love the specs," she said. "Bookworm like you was always going to end up losing his eyesight."

Bernie smiled half-heartedly. This was painful.

"So sorry to hear what happened with Vivi," Adelaide said. "She's always been a handful."

Bernie felt sick. He hated remembering how Vivienne had used him and mocked him. The way Adelaide was talking made it sound like it had just been a big old lark. It certainly hadn't felt like it.

Adelaide was looking around her at Bernie's overalls, his trowel, the pile of weeds by his feet.

"Do you work here?"

He nodded. "I do."

"But you're a teacher. Classics, wasn't it?"

Bernie winced.

"Not anymore," he said. Vivi put an end to all that, he wanted to add, but didn't.

"So why aren't you . . . ?"

In uniform, she meant. Bernie froze, not knowing what to say. This was the first time he'd been asked outright.

"Ah, well," he began, desperately thinking of an excuse. "The thing is . . ."

But Adelaide was already moving on.

"The war is all-consuming, isn't it? It is simply taking up my every waking moment. In fact, that's how I know your colleague Louisa," she said. "We've met through mutual friends at some Red Cross meetings."

"Lovely," muttered Bernie.

"Must dash," Adelaide said, realizing she wasn't going to get much response from him on anything. "I'm due to wind bandages this afternoon. It's all-consuming, Bernie."

She waved gaily at him and bounced across the lawn to say her good-byes to Louisa. After a quick but earnest chat, Adelaide walked away. Louisa watched her go and then turned and stared at Bernie. Her face was expressionless, but her eyes bored into him and he felt a flicker of unease. He didn't like his two lives colliding in this way.

"Old friend," he called. Louisa didn't speak, simply nodded and bent down to her daffodils again.

"Come on, Bernie," he murmured to himself as he knelt back down at the border. "Come on, old chap. Keep going. It's all going to be fine."

As he picked up his trowel he noticed he'd laid it on the grass next to a patch of daisies. The symbolism of the cheerful little flowers had never seemed so apt.

"Keep my secret," he whispered. "Keep my secret."

✤

Louisa looked at where Adelaide was virtually skipping down the path. She'd met her once or twice before at fund-raising events for the war and had always been astonished by her energy and vigor. Today had been no different, though this time she'd left Louisa feeling as though the stuffing had been knocked out of her. Because she knew Bernie.

"Lovely chap," she'd told Louisa when she'd been to say hello to her old friend. "Always felt bad about the way Vivi treated him. She's got a cruel streak, that one. Mind you, he seems to be over it now."

Louisa hadn't responded, hadn't wanted to betray Bernie's confidence by saying he'd given up teaching and come to work at Kew, all because of his humiliation at Vivienne's hands.

Adelaide had eyed Bernie across the plants and then lowered her voice.

"I had heard he'd joined the church," she said. "But clearly I was wrong."

"I think he is fairly religious. Quaker, I believe," Louisa said. She was keen to get back to the daffodils, and having suffered through idle gossip when she was married, she didn't like discussing other people's business.

"Quaker, of course." Adelaide nodded. "That explains it."

Louisa raised a questioning eyebrow. "Explains?"

"Why he's here and not off at the Front. They're pacifists, aren't they? The Quakers."

She'd bounced on her tiptoes as though she couldn't spend another moment in one place.

"I have to go, Louisa. I really just popped in for some fresh air, as I'm spending the entire afternoon winding bandages with my very dull aunt for company. Lovely to see you."

She blew Louisa a kiss and hurried off, leaving Louisa as she was now, staring after her in shock.

"Pacifists," she breathed. She found herself meeting Bernie's gaze. Was she imagining it or did he look worried? Louisa couldn't lie. She'd been thinking about Bernie a lot recently, wondering why he'd not enlisted or been called up since conscription began. He was single, unlike Mac, and neither too young, like Jim, nor too old. He was no longer a teacher—one of the protected professions—nor was he a clergyman, no matter what Adelaide had thought. And being a gardener was certainly not a vital job in times of war. In fact, the only reason she and the other women were at Kew was because all the male gardeners had joined up so there was no excuse there.

Bernie broke the gaze first, and Louisa bent down again to tend to the daffodils.

Why Bernie was still at Kew had been a niggle in the back of her mind, probably since she and Ivy went to the meeting where Mrs. Pankhurst had talked so passionately about conscientious objectors. She could have asked him outright, she supposed, but he seemed so fragile, she hadn't wanted to hurt him. The evidence, though, was mounting. She felt a small spark of anger deep inside. Did he really think it was acceptable to avoid the war just because he was a pacifist? Weren't they all pacifists on some level? She most certainly was, deep down. After all, she knew more than most how violence didn't solve anything. She was confident, though, that the government and the king knew what they were doing. They'd never have gone to war if it wasn't completely necessary. Because, after all, no one liked conflict, no one wanted to go and fight. But the sad truth was that was what was happening now. Men and boys were joining up and facing their fears. So why should men like Bernie, healthy, single, strong men, avoid the Front just because they were scared?

"Coward," she breathed.

Next to her, Ivy looked up. "What's that you're saying?"

Louisa took her arm and turned her away from Bernie so he couldn't work out what they were saying if he happened to look in their direction.

"Ivy, I need to tell you something awful. About Bernie."

Ivy's face went white. "What's happened? Is he ill? Is it his nerves again?"

Louisa shook her head, pinching her lips together. "He's a pacifist. A conscientious objector."

Ivy covered her mouth with her hand.

"I know," Louisa said.

"Are you sure?"

"Almost certain. He's not at the Front. He's not ill, or married, so there's no reason for him to be here." She took a breath, trying to keep her annoyance under control. "He's just decided that his life is worth more than the other men's."

"Oh, Lou, I don't think that's it. He just doesn't believe the war is the best way to sort things."

Ivy looked straight at her friend. "You should know that fighting is never the answer. Never did you no good, did it?"

Louisa bristled at Ivy using her own awful experiences against her. "That's different."

"Is it? Doubt Bernie would think so."

Louisa stared at her. "Did you know? Have you spoken about this?"

"No," Ivy said. "Least, not recently. But I knew the Quakers were pacifists."

"We need to ask him."

"Do we?"

"Of course we do. We need to be sure. Mrs. Pankhurst says . . ."

"Mrs. Pankhurst is not always right," Ivy said firmly.

Shocked, Louisa stopped talking.

"The white feather campaign is not good," Ivy said. "Of course I support women's suffrage, of course I bloody do. But this is something different. Attacking men who could have a reason not to be fighting isn't right, Lou."

Louisa looked at Ivy as though she was a stranger. She'd thought they were friends. Partners in the fight for women's rights, working hard for the war effort. But perhaps she'd been wrong.

"I agree that we need to be sure," she said coldly. "Which is why I think we should ask him."

She turned back to face the herbaceous border, where Bernie was weeding diligently.

"Bernie!" she called.

"Don't," Ivy said. "Don't ask him."

"Bernie!"

With slow, deliberate movements, Bernie put his trowel down and stood up.

"Could we have a quick word?" Louisa called.

Like he was wading through treacle, Bernie plodded toward them, his head hanging. Louisa glanced at Ivy, who looked wretched, and for a moment she thought of ignoring this. Of pretending Adelaide had never popped into Kew, had never recognized Bernie or let slip enough information for these suspicions to surface. Then they could all just carry on gardening, and Bernie could continue Ivy's lessons, and everything could go back to how it was. But then she thought of the troops she'd seen getting on the trains in town, heading off to the Front. Just young lads, with their whole lives ahead of them, looking ashen and scared but going all the same. Why should they go if Bernie didn't? She thought of her brother, Matthew, who was safe at home in Kent because he was a farmer, and wondered how she'd feel if she knew he was in the mud on a battle-field. She'd feel awful, she thought. Terrified for him. Again she felt that bubble of anger and she spun on her heel to face Bernie as he approached.

"What can I do for you?" he asked, his forced joviality at odds with the stricken expression on his face.

Louisa took a breath.

"Bernie," she said, raising her chin. "Are you a conscientious objector?"

Chapter 11

Bernie didn't speak for what seemed like an age. Ivy stood stock-still, looking from him to Louisa and back again. She didn't know what to say to make things better. Perhaps there was nothing she could say.

Eventually Bernie nodded slowly.

"I am a Quaker," he said. "We're committed to peace."

"But this isn't peace, Bernie," Louisa said. "It's war. And we all need to do our bit."

Ivy half expected Bernie to crumple. He always seemed so unsure of himself, so fragile. But now he looked more confident than she'd ever seen him.

"It's war, and it's wrong. I will not be a part of it."

"Why should you stay safe while others go and risk their lives?" Louisa was growing red in the face, but her voice was still calm. Ivy could see the truth in what she was saying, even though she herself didn't think the war was a good thing, either. She felt conflicted, torn between her two friends.

Bernie opened his mouth to speak but shut it again as Mac approached.

"Everything all right?" he said, looking at them all and frowning. Ivy thought he must be able to feel the atmosphere between them. Bernie was almost quivering with tension as he stood, staring at Louisa. Louisa herself looked furious, with red spots on both cheeks.

"Fine," Ivy said, forcing a smile. "Just saying how quickly the daffs come and go."

Mac nodded. "There's no better reminder of the passage of time than working in a garden." He put his hand on Bernie's shoulder. "I need to have a quick word with you all. Can you join the others in the break room?"

Ivy glanced at Louisa to see if she knew what this was about, but she remained stony-faced as they followed Mac across the lawn to where the rest of the gardeners were gathering.

Ivy perched on the wall beside Jim. Bernie hovered at the back of the group, and Louisa, pointedly, made her way to the opposite side to him and glowered at him from where she stood.

"It's all falling apart," Ivy muttered out of the side of her mouth so Jim could hear her but no one else. "Bernie's a conchie and Lou's got her knickers in a twist about it."

Jim looked shocked. "What? When did this all happen?"

"Just now. One of his old friends . . ."

She stopped talking as Mac clapped his hands for attention.

"I wanted to say thank you to all of you for stepping up and becoming a valuable part of Kew Gardens," Mac said. Ivy made a face. This was very out of character for their normally gruff and unappreciative boss. "With the men gone, we're left to rely on you girls . . ."

"Oi," said Dennis, another junior gardener who'd been too young to enlist, like Jim. Everyone chuckled, and Mac rolled his eyes.

"Thank you, Dennis," he said. "As I was saying, we're relying on you to keep things going while the men are away."

He took a breath.

"And that's going to include me, I'm afraid. It seems conscription for old married chaps like me is just around the corner, so after a bit of chat with my missus, I've decided to get in early and enlist."

There was a stunned silence among the women—and Dennis, Jim and Bernie.

"Did you know about this?" Ivy hissed at Jim.

"Didn't have a clue," he said, looking as surprised as she did.

Louisa was the first to speak.

"I can't say we won't miss you," she said. "But you're doing the right thing, Mac."

She went over to him and took his hands in hers.

"You're a brave, good, kind man and you've taught me—all of us—so much in our time at Kew. You can be sure we'll keep things going while you're away and I promise you'll be impressed with what we've done when you get back."

Mac looked chuffed to bits by Louisa's little speech and gave her a brief hug to show it. Ivy was less pleased. She felt as though Lou had really been talking to Bernie. But she joined the throng of gardeners gathering round Mac to wish him luck and ask questions about who'd be in charge and what was going to happen while he was away.

"I'm not sure, exactly," Mac was saying. "Let me get myself down to the recruitment office and find out when I'll be off and then we can plan."

"It'll be soon, right?" Ivy asked Jim, who still looked surprised. "They don't hang about."

"Dunno," he said with a shrug. "I guess we'll find out soon enough, eh, Den?"

Dennis grimaced. "Guess so."

"Ivy, could I have a quick word?"

Louisa was there, looking pale and worried. She led Ivy away from the group. Over her shoulder, Ivy could see Bernie watching them. He seemed resigned rather than concerned as he watched them talk.

"There's a meeting tonight," Louisa said. "I wasn't going to go because I think it's just a few people, but we should. Given what's happened."

Ivy blinked at her. "What's happened?"

"With Bernie."

"Why do we need to go to a meeting about Bernie?" Ivy was bewildered.

"To find out what we should do, now we know he's a conchie."

Ivy glared at her. "Why should we do anything?"

"In a few months' time, Ivy, men we care about could be fighting the Germans in the trenches," Louisa said. "Your Jim could be going over the top, running toward death."

Ivy felt dizzy at the thought. "Don't, Lou," she said. "I don't want to hear it."

But Lou wasn't stopping.

"And Mac will be there first. Grumpy, funny Mac, who really prefers plants to people and who's been so kind to us. He'll be there in the mud. Frightened."

Ivy winced.

"But Bernie will be tucked up, safe and sound in his warm bed in Battersea, Ivy. Snuggled up under his blanket, reading his precious books and not troubled by gunshots or mortar fire. Do you think that's right?"

"No," Ivy whispered. "But . . ."

"But, nothing. We need to tell someone."

"I don't want to." Ivy felt wretched. There was no right way as far as she could see it. The war was absolutely wrong in her opinion. She didn't think anyone should have to fight. But they were fighting and Louisa had a point. Why should lads like her Jim go to the Front, if Bernie stayed behind? Nothing made sense anymore.

"Will Mrs. Pankhurst help?" she said hopefully. "Will she know what we should do?"

"I have no doubt," Louisa said.

"Then I'll come."

❧

As it turned out, Mrs. Pankhurst did have a very clear idea about what they should do, but it was not what Ivy had wanted.

"White feather," she said as soon as Louisa had explained their predicament at the meeting that evening. "Cowards like him should be exposed and then enlisted. He can't hide behind your flowers much longer."

Ivy closed her eyes for a second, hoping that when she opened them again everything would be different. But it wasn't.

"As many as you can," another woman said, handing Louisa a bunch of the delicate feathers. Ivy wondered how something so pretty could hold such a nasty meaning. It was like the flowers, she supposed. Marigolds symbolizing despair, or a pretty petunia standing for anger.

"Put them in his bag, his pockets, wherever you can. We need him to be ashamed of himself and his actions."

Ivy felt ashamed of her own actions, but she didn't speak up until they were out of the hall where the meeting had been held and along the street.

"You're very quiet," said Louisa.

"I don't want to do this. Bernie's our friend. It's a betrayal."

"He's betraying every Tommy that's out there already and all the ones who'll be going soon," Louisa said. "Not to mention his king and his country."

"He's helped me so much."

Louisa shrugged. "I think this is helping him in a way. He should be doing his bit, just like everyone else. In twenty or thirty years' time, how will he feel knowing all those men died and he stood idly by?"

"'Daddy, what did you do in the Great War?'" said Ivy, quoting the poster that adorned the side of every bus and all the escalators in the tube stations.

"Exactly," said Louisa. She sat down on a bench and pulled Ivy's hand so she sat down, too.

"I know it's difficult, Ivy. I understand how you must be feeling. But this is wrong. Lord knows, I hate violence of any kind but . . ." She trailed off.

"It's all wrong," Ivy said bleakly. "The war, the feathers, conscription, everything."

"I know," Louisa said. She reached for Ivy's hand.

They sat there together for a moment, hand in hand, both feeling awful about everything. Ivy took comfort from the feeling of Lou's fingers in hers. Louisa was a good person who understood better than lots of people how humans made others suffer. Surely she wouldn't expose Bernie as a conchie and lead him to deal with the consequences?

But no. Louisa was actually quiet because she was making plans.

"I'll get to Kew early tomorrow morning," she said, almost to herself. "I can put one in his gardening bag, and his overalls, and wherever else I can sneak them."

"Louisa, no," Ivy said. "No."

"I have to."

"Why?"

Louisa shrugged. "Because he's doing something wrong and I want him to understand that. And because I trust Mrs. Pankhurst, and if she says this is the right thing to do, then I believe her."

Ivy snorted. "Not everything she does is right," she said. "Not everything the Suffragettes do is perfect."

Louisa raised an eyebrow at Ivy. "Is that so?" she said, her voice like ice.

"Course it is. They make mistakes like anyone. Mrs. Pankhurst's been awful to Sylvia, and the Suffragettes burned down the tea pavilion at Kew, don't forget. And they smashed up the orchid house."

"That was years ago," Louisa said. "Things have changed."

"Nothing's changed," Ivy said. "Nothing at all."

Louisa stood up. "We're at war, Ivy," she said. "And that changes everything. People's priorities change. Their jobs change. Their lives change."

She glared down at Ivy, who was still sitting on the bench, her fight having deserted her.

"I'm going to do this, whether you want to help me or not. And if you don't . . ." She stopped and suddenly Ivy felt a rush of adrenaline and anger. She sprang to her feet and met Louisa's defiant stare.

"What?" she said. "If I don't help you, then what?"

The two women were inches apart, staring into each other's eyes like boxers squaring up before a match.

Louisa took a breath. "Then you're not the person I thought you were, Ivy Adams."

Ivy pushed her hair away from her face and laughed joylessly.

"Or maybe you were wrong about me all along," she said. "You do this if it makes you feel better, Louisa, and I look forward to you coming to apologize when you realize it was wrong. And in case I've not made it clear, no, I'm not going to help you. When it comes to humiliating a man who I'm proud to call a friend, then you're on your own."

She felt her heart thumping in her chest so wildly she looked down to check it wasn't bursting through her rib cage. Ivy had never been a wallflower, never been afraid to stand up for herself at the market with her dad, with her siblings, arguing with her mum, or even with Mac when he was being difficult. But squaring up to an older woman over such an emotional matter was something new. She didn't like it.

"I'm doing this," Louisa said with a defiant nod. "You'll see."

She tossed her hair, spun on her heel and marched off down the road without looking back.

Chapter 12

Bernie was late for work the next day, which didn't help his nervy, flustered mood.

"Sorry, sorry, sorry," he muttered as he dashed into the break room to ditch his bag and put on his overalls.

Around him, the gardeners were drifting off to start work. Bernie looked round, but he couldn't see Louisa, much to his relief. Ivy, though, was tying a scarf round her hair and she gave him a small, cautious smile.

"All right, Bern?" she said.

He nodded. "Not bad."

"Mac's not here," Ivy said. "No one's sure what's happening. He can't have enlisted already, surely? And he'd have made sure everything was fine before he went."

Bernie glanced over to where Jim was standing with Mac's battered notebook, trying to decipher his scrawled writing and work out what he had planned for the gardeners to work on that day.

"Definitely doesn't sound like Mac," Bernie agreed. "Even if he has enlisted . . ." The word stuck in his throat and he had to swallow a couple of times before he carried on. "Even if he has, they won't send him off straightaway."

Ivy looked pale and tired.

"Lord, I hope he's all right," she said. "I can't cope with anything else going wrong. Not with . . ." She trailed off and Bernie looked at his feet, embarrassed. He knew she meant him.

"Ivy," he began, but as he spoke, Mac arrived in the break room, throwing open the door so violently that it slammed against the wall. His face was like thunder and he glowered at the gathered gardeners.

"Why the bloody hell are you all still in here?" he shouted. "It's ten past, you should be outside. Go on, go."

Like obedient mice, the gardeners all scurried away.

"Ivy, can you and Bernie go and check on the allotments and our veg patch first?" Jim said under his breath to them as they passed. "I'm going to stay here and see what's up with Mac."

Bernie nodded and Ivy touched Jim gently on the arm. Then, in silence, they both headed out to the Gardens, leaving poor Jim to deal with Mac's rage.

"Christ," said Ivy as they wandered over toward the vegetable gardens. "What was all that about? Think he's scared about going away?"

"Almost certainly," Bernie agreed. "But this seemed more, don't you think?"

"More what? Oh, look, those lettuces are doing nicely already. That's because of all the rain, I reckon."

Bernie thought for a minute. "Not sure," he said. "But I've seen lads ready to go and they normally go quiet. They're not angry." He took a breath. "Not yet."

There was an awkward pause.

"We need to thin out those carrots," Ivy said.

Bernie looked at where she was pointing and nodded. "Let's start there, then. And then I think the spring cabbages could be ready."

Ivy looked impressed.

"You've worked so hard on learning about the plants," she said. "I hope Mac appreciates your effort."

Bernie winced. "He did. I'm not sure how much longer he'll appreciate it."

Ivy had been crouched over the carrots. Now she looked up.

"Louisa's been through a lot and that's made her the way she is," she said.

For the hundredth time Bernie was taken aback by Ivy's astute way of seeing the world. One day she would stop surprising him, but it didn't seem like happening any time soon.

"Her husband sounds like a right bad'un," Ivy was saying. "He beat her badly, you know?"

Bernie didn't know the full story, but he'd heard bits and pieces. He nodded. "I know some."

"When she asked her mum for help, her mum told her she just had to put up with it. But she didn't. She got herself together and she left him and came to London, all by herself. Do you have any idea how brave that was?"

Feeling as though she was telling him off, Bernie nodded again. "She's very brave."

"She is," Ivy said. "And she's got a very clear sense of what's right and what's wrong." She took a breath. "Even if she's not always correct."

"What are you trying to tell me, Ivy?" Bernie said, anxiety never far from the surface.

"I'm trying to tell you that Louisa is angry about you being a conchie now, but she's a good person and I don't think she'll do anything to hurt you."

"Really?"

"Really."

Feeling a tiny bit better, Bernie got on with thinning the carrots. He hoped Ivy was right. He wanted to stay quietly at Kew, helping the war effort in his own way. If Louisa exposed him, if she told everyone he should have enlisted, then he'd be forced to leave and no doubt marched down to the recruitment office and signed up on the spot. He'd have a rifle in his hand and some burly sergeant major teaching him how to use it to kill in a matter of weeks. He felt sick at the thought.

After about an hour's hard work in the vegetable patch, a shout from over the path made them both look up.

"Ivy!" Jim was waving.

He jogged over to where they both stood looking expectantly at him.

"Have you been with Mac this whole time?" Ivy asked. "Is he doing all right?"

"Yes, I've been with him," Jim said. He sat down on the grass round the vegetable patch with a *thud*. "And no, he's not doing all right."

Ivy sank down onto the grass, too. Bernie followed.

"What's happened?" he asked.

"Mac enlisted," Jim began. "At least, he tried to. They turned him down."

"What?" Ivy said. "That must be a mistake. Mac's strong as an ox."

"He's deaf."

Bernie and Ivy stared at Jim.

"Really?" Bernie said. "Are you sure?"

Jim nodded. "He failed the hearing test, so they gave him another one to be sure and he failed that, too."

"And he didn't know?"

"He says he's always had to ask people to speak up, and he often misses part of conversations," Jim said.

"He's not ignoring us when he doesn't answer our questions," Ivy said, realization dawning on her face. "He's not being grumpy. He just can't hear us."

"Bugger," said Bernie, feeling genuine sympathy for the man, even though he was relieved it meant Mac wouldn't be facing the Germans anytime soon.

"Poor sod's in bits," said Jim. "I told him I'd spread the word to the gardeners. I reckon he'd appreciate it if no one mentions it for a while."

"Course." Ivy and Bernie spoke in unison.

"He said the recruiting officer was ever so nice. Told him he was doing important work here and not to be downhearted. But Mac says he just feels awful about all the lads who've gone when he can't do his bit."

Bernie shuffled uncomfortably from foot to foot. "You don't have to fight to make a difference," he said.

Jim gave him a sharp look and Bernie realized Ivy had clearly been discussing his objections to the war with her boyfriend.

"That's just how he feels," Jim snapped. He looked at Bernie. "You might want to keep quiet about your pacifism shit," he said, spitting out the ugly word and making both Bernie and Ivy wince. "Mac won't want to hear it."

"Right," muttered Bernie. Desperate to get away, he turned to Ivy. "I'm going to get going on those cabbages."

"Great," she said, giving him a small smile.

He worked on the cabbages until lunchtime and then ate alone. Ivy had gone off somewhere with Jim and there was still no sign of Louisa. Mac was deep in conversation with Dennis and two of the female gardeners outside the break room, and Bernie was glad of the opportunity to sneak past him to collect his lunch without having to speak.

The afternoon passed quietly, too. Jim asked Bernie to dig some manure into the beds, which was an unpleasant job, but Bernie didn't argue. He worked hard, trying to ignore the knot of anxiety in his stomach. He was concerned about Mac and so worried about what Louisa might do that he found it hard to think of anything else. He thought perhaps he might feel better if he spoke to her—take a leaf out of her book, in fact, and face his fears. Stand up for himself, instead of running away. And so he decided, uncharacteristically, he would go to Louisa's flat after work and speak to her, try to make her understand his argument, even if she didn't completely agree with it.

Feeling more at peace, at six o'clock—later than he normally worked—he put away his fork and spade and went into the break room to take off his manure-stained overalls. As he was unbuttoning them, Mac appeared.

"Bernie," he said.

"Mac."

There was a pause and then Mac added: "You've heard?"

"I have." Bernie turned round so he was facing Mac directly. He'd been thinking about his condition as he worked and realized the man often missed conversations if he wasn't looking at the speaker. Perhaps he'd learned to lip-read without realizing. "Sorry things didn't work out the way you wanted."

Mac gave Bernie a small smile. "Things rarely do, I find."

"I agree."

Bernie took a breath. "I don't expect you'll want to hear it, not yet, but I'm pleased you'll still be here at Kew."

Mac didn't speak, simply nodded. He pulled out a chair and sat down, weary. The men looked at each other for a second, then Bernie turned back to his locker and carried on unbuttoning his overalls. He peeled them off and put them in the dirty laundry basket, pulled on his trousers and tucked in his shirt. Then he took his raincoat from the coat stand and went to put that on, too.

But as he put his arm in, a white feather floated out. It must have been stuffed down the sleeve and he'd dislodged it with his fingers. Bernie froze, watching the delicate plume drift down to the floor. Slowly it danced downward, Bernie's eyes never leaving it until it settled gently on the tiles. Heart pounding, he raised his gaze and saw, to his despair, Mac had seen it, too. Neither of them spoke. Could he brazen this one out? It was possible. Carefully, he put his other arm through the other sleeve. Nothing. But as he pulled his bag from his locker a whole load of feathers tumbled out, each one spinning and twisting in the breeze from the open door as they fell to the ground.

Bernie didn't move, but he felt Mac's eyes boring into his back, and as the feathers fell, he forced himself to turn round and face the older man's stare.

"What is this?" Mac said. He sounded calm, which frightened Bernie more than if he'd been angry. "What does this mean?"

Bernie's mouth was dry. He tried to swallow but couldn't. He cleared his throat.

"Someone," he began.

"Speak. Up," Mac said, his calm voice beginning to simmer with rage. "Speak the hell up."

Bernie tried again.

"Someone thinks I should have enlisted," he said. The words quivered as he spoke, like the fronds of the feathers floating around him.

"Should you have enlisted?"

Bernie licked his dry lips.

"Yes, sir," he said. He'd never called Mac "sir" before. "I should have enlisted."

Mac nodded, as though that was the answer he had been expecting.

"And why haven't you?"

Memories of the humiliation he'd felt when he'd proposed to Vivienne and she'd laughed began to surface. Bernie felt dizzy. He didn't speak.

"Why haven't you enlisted, Yorke?"

"Because I'm a Quaker, sir," he said. "A pacifist."

Mac glared at him and he tried again.

"I'm a conscientious objector."

Mac grimaced. "Get. Out," he said.

"Sir?"

"Get out of the Gardens," Mac said. "I never want to see you again." He nodded and then carried on, as though they were having an amiable conversation. "In fact, if I do catch sight of your sniveling, cowardly face, Yorke, I'll consider it my contribution to the war effort to smack it so hard your nose comes out the back of your head. Understood?"

Bernie understood, all right. Gibbering apologies and aware there were tears beginning to brim in his eyes, he gathered his bag to his chest and ran away.

He ran all the way to the bus stop, and his heart didn't stop thumping even when he'd got to Battersea. What a thing to happen. What an awful, dreadful thing.

Still in a state of shock and upset, he reached the front door of his digs. But as he patted his pockets frantically, he realized he'd left his keys in his locker. Mrs. Spencer wouldn't be impressed, but what could he do? He couldn't go back and get them. Instead he yanked on the doorbell, hoping she was in and feeling in a kindly mood.

For once, his luck was in. She flung open the door and her stern face softened immediately as she saw him hunched on the doorstep.

"Jesus Christ, what's happened to you?" she said, bustling him inside and into the lounge. "Come in, come in. You're in a right old state."

With her kind words, Bernie fell apart. He started trembling so violently that Mrs. Spencer thought he was ill.

"Are you having an attack?" she said. "Are you going to be sick? Should I fetch a doctor?"

He waved her worries away.

"I just need to sit down," he croaked. "Could I sit down?"

"Here. Lie down on the sofa. Let's get your coat off first," she said. Like a child, Bernie let her peel his mackintosh from his shoulders and then watched in shock as another feather—how could there be so many of them?—appeared. Mrs. Spencer watched it float down to the floor and then reached out a swift hand and caught it.

"Conchie," she said. Her concerned look had vanished, replaced with disgust.

Bernie threw his head back in despair. There was no point in trying to lie.

"Yes," he said. "Conchie."

"Then you're not welcome in my house," said Mrs. Spencer. "Pack your bags. You've got ten minutes, or I'll call a policeman."

Bernie nodded, bewildered by how his life had fallen apart so thoroughly in less than a day. Still, it wasn't the first time and he was beginning to think it wouldn't be the last.

Wearily he made his way to the lounge door.

"Ten minutes?" he said. "I'll be gone in five."

Chapter 13

Ivy was one of the first at work the next day and the break room was deserted when she went in to drop off her bag. She felt uneasy, uncomfortable, as though everything she'd thought was solid was shifting. She'd not seen Louisa properly since they'd been to the meeting; she was worried about seeing Mac and hadn't yet decided if she should bring up his hearing problem or leave it unsaid. And Bernie. Well, the knowledge that Louisa felt obliged to act about him being a conscientious objector was hanging over Ivy like a rain cloud. She was still hoping Louisa might see sense and change her mind and let Bernie be.

But as Ivy went to her locker she noticed, on the floor of the room, a small heap of white feathers. Right below Bernie's cubbyhole.

"Ohhh bugger," she breathed. "Bugger."

Quick as a flash, and hoping no one else had spotted them, she got down on her knees and scooped up all the feathers together, bunching them in her hands.

As she stood up again, she realized Mac was there, looking at her. He often came in early and made himself a cup of tea that he drank outside, watching the Gardens wake up. Stupid Ivy not to remember that. She met his stare, still cupping her hands round the feathers.

"White feathers," Mac said quietly.

Ivy forced herself to laugh.

"No idea where they've come from," she said casually. "I thought at first a bird had got in here, but I can't see anything."

"Don't, Ivy," Mac said. "I know."

Ivy's stomach dropped into her work boots. "You know?"

"I know Bernie's a conchie."

Mac was known to have a bad temper that flared up unpredictably, and often violently. Ivy felt sick now as she looked at him. "Did you see him?"

"Yes."

"What happened? Where is he? Is he all right?"

Mac took a breath. Frantic, Ivy scanned the floor for signs of a fight. Was there any blood?

"I don't know where he is."

"What did you do?"

"I threw him out," Mac said. "I told him I never want to see his face in here again."

Ivy was dizzy with relief. She steadied herself against the lockers. "But you didn't hit him? He's not hurt?"

"No." Mac almost seemed indignant at the suggestion. "Not hurt."

He took a step toward her. His eyes were sad, which unsettled Ivy more than him being angry would have.

"I was upset, Ivy, about my hearing. It was bad timing, is all. I was angry at the world and I took it out on Bernie. It was a mistake and I'm sorry."

THE KEW GARDENS GIRLS

Ivy gripped the feathers in her hand a bit tighter, their spines digging into her fingers.

"So he can come back? You can give him his job back?"

He sighed. "No."

"But if you made a mistake . . . ?"

"I've reported him."

Ivy leaned against the lockers again.

"So that's it?" she said. "Someone will be knocking on his door and sending him down to the recruitment office any minute?"

Mac looked at the floor. "I suppose so."

"I need to warn him," Ivy said in a hurry. "I need to tell him what's happening and warn him."

She shoved the feathers at Mac. "Throw these away," she said. "I'm taking the day off."

Without waiting to hear if he agreed, she headed back out into the Gardens toward the gate. In the distance she saw Louisa, chatting to one of the other gardeners and briefly she thought about going to confront her. But time was of the essence here. She had no idea how long Bernie would have before he was forced to enlist, and she wanted to get to him first. To say good-bye. She swallowed a sob as she thought about her reading and writing lessons, about Bernie buying her the sketchbook, about everything. But she carried on, almost running to the bus stop to get to Battersea and Bernie's digs.

She made good time, but when she arrived, Bernie's sour-faced landlady was nasty and unhelpful.

"What are you, his fancy woman?" she said, when Ivy asked to see Bernie. She looked Ivy up and down, her nose wrinkled as though Ivy smelled bad.

"I work with him," Ivy said firmly. "He's my friend."

The woman snorted. "Right."

"Can I come in?"

"He's not here."

"Where is he?"

She shrugged, folding her arms. "How should I know?"

"He didn't say he was going out, or mention where he was going?"

Ivy's questions were obviously annoying the woman and she'd lost patience.

"I don't know," she said, beginning to shut the door.

Ivy stuck her foot out and, grateful for her heavy work boots, kept the woman from closing it. "Where is he?"

The woman glowered at Ivy. "Threw him out, didn't I? He's a bloody conchie. Despicable, if you ask me."

"I didn't ask you."

They stared at each other for a moment and Ivy eventually, reluctantly, removed her boot from the doorstep.

"If you see him," she began, but the door slammed shut in her face. "Tell him Ivy's looking for him," she finished to the wooden panel in front of her.

She felt hopeless. Where was Bernie? Despite his being more than a decade older than her, and her teacher, Ivy felt protective of Bernie. She always thought of him as being fragile. In need of a bit of looking after. She couldn't let him wander the streets of London with no home and no job without at least checking he was all right.

She thought for a moment. Where could he go? Up to Wandsworth Common? Possible, but there were rain clouds gathering overhead. To a hotel? Did he have enough money? Where else could he go that was dry and where he wouldn't be bothered . . .

"The library," she muttered. "I bet he's gone to the bloody library."

Quick on her feet, she darted across the road and started striding up Lavender Hill toward the imposing redbrick building that housed Battersea Library. She pushed open the heavy door and dashed inside where it was quiet and still and caught her breath for a minute, looking round.

It was quiet inside. A few readers sat at tables in the center of the room, in silence. Ivy could hear her own breathing and tried to quieten it as she searched for Bernie. No, he was nowhere to be seen. Disappointed, she turned to go and there, behind her, was the man she'd been looking for.

"Ivy?" he said in surprise. His arms were full of books. Books about plants, if the picture on the cover of the one on top was anything to go by. The thought of Bernie hiding out in the library, reading about flowers instead of working at Kew, broke Ivy's heart.

She took his arm and led him a little way away from the readers in the center and the librarian.

"Why are you here?" he whispered.

"To see you."

He raised an eyebrow. "Why?"

"Because Mac told me what happened, and I went to your digs and your landlady said she'd thrown you out, too."

Bernie went pale. "You spoke to Mac?"

"I did." She clutched his hand. "He's sorry, Bernie. He knows he went off on one. He said it was more to do with him than it was you."

Hope flared, just a tiny bit, in Bernie's eyes and Ivy's heart broke all over again.

"Can I come back?" he said. "To Kew?"

Slowly, Ivy shook her head.

" 'Fraid not," she said.

"But if Mac's sorry?"

"He reported you, Bernie. They'll be coming to find you."

Bernie dropped the pile of books he was holding with a clatter. The readers and the librarian all looked up, and the librarian frowned.

"Sorry," Ivy said in a loud whisper. "Sorry."

She steered Bernie to a chair and he sat down with a thump as Ivy bent down to pick up the books.

"What will I do?" Bernie said under his breath, over and over, as Ivy collected the heavy tomes that were scattered around her. "What will I do?"

Ivy was still on the floor. She reached up and put the last book on the table beside Bernie, then got to her feet.

"Looks like you'll go and fight," she said.

If Bernie was pale before, he looked positively ashen now.

"I can't," he said. "I can't. I can't take a gun and use it against other men. Human beings. Boys younger than the ones I used to teach. I can't do it, Ivy."

"Then go back to St. Richard's. They won't make you fight if you're teaching."

Bernie closed his eyes.

"I fear I burned all my bridges when I had my troubles," he said. "It's a small world, that of teaching, and there's not a school in the country would have me back now. And rightly so." He lifted his hands and showed them to Ivy. They were shaking vigorously. He tucked them back into his lap, trying to control the shaking. "This is how I react when I just think about going back into a classroom. Imagine how I'd cope with a roomful of twenty or thirty boys?"

Overwhelmed with sympathy, Ivy perched on the side of Bernie's chair and put her arm round his shoulders.

"There, there," she said. "We'll sort it out, don't you worry. We just need to find somewhere for you to go, while we come up with a plan. Somewhere no one will know to look."

The librarian looked over at them and made a loud "ahem" as she saw them so close together. Ivy got up again. She was at a loss. She couldn't take Bernie home, because there was just no room. Same went for Jim's house. And she could hardly ask Louisa to hide him.

She opened her mouth to ask if Bernie had any friends who might help, knowing the answer would be no, but her speech was drowned out by the sound of nearby church bells tolling.

"Funeral," said Bernie, slumping down farther in his chair. "Suits my mood."

But the noise awoke a memory for Ivy, and despite the somber sound she suddenly felt more positive.

"I've got an idea," she said. "Come on."

Obediently, Bernie followed her out of the library, leaving the botany books strewn across the table, much to the librarian's annoyance. He had all his possessions—which wasn't much—in two canvas bags. Ivy carried one and Bernie the other, as they made their way back to Kew.

"I don't like this," Bernie kept saying. "I wish you'd tell me where we're going."

But Ivy didn't want to say anything until she knew if she could pull this off. She couldn't bear to see hope in Bernie's eyes again.

When they got to Kew Green, Ivy got Bernie to sit down on a bench across from the gates to the Gardens.

"Stay here for a little while," she said. "I've just got to check something."

She dashed off in the opposite direction to the Gardens, toward St. Anne's Church. She paused for a moment at the entrance to the churchyard, next to the imposing stone pillars, steeling herself.

"Come on, Ivy," she said out loud. "You've got this."

With a burst of determination, she ducked inside the graveyard and followed the path round to the back of the church. And there, just as she'd remembered, were three stone steps leading down to a wooden door.

Crossing her fingers, Ivy jumped down the steps and tried the door. It was locked. But she reached up and felt along the top of the frame and gasped in relief as her fingers closed round a large iron key.

She stuck it into the hole and, using both hands, started to unlock the door. It was stiff and heavy, but the metal handle eventually turned and she could push open the entrance. It creaked loudly as she shoved it, sending shivers down her spine.

"You're lucky I love you, Bernie," she muttered, peering into the gloom behind the door. As her eyes adjusted she could see more steps leading downward into the crypt of the church. No one used it anymore. Everyone had their funerals up in the churchyard now, instead of down in the depths. As far as Ivy knew, no one ever came down there. And that was why it was so perfect.

She took a deep breath, building up her courage, and then crept down the steps to the bottom. So far, so good. She crouched down and felt with her hands round the side of the stairs and there, just as she'd hoped, was a bundle of candles and some matches.

"Thank bloody God," she breathed. Obviously no one had been down there for years. Well, not since that night . . .

She shook her head. Now was not the time to get lost in memories. She had to get Bernie. She left the candles where they were and bounded back up the stairs, pulling the door to behind her but not locking it. She retraced her steps round the churchyard and found Bernie where she'd left him, anxiously watching the gates of Kew in case he spotted anyone familiar.

"Quickly," she said. "Let's go."

Once again not questioning her, Bernie got up and followed Ivy into the churchyard once more.

"Round here," she said. "Come on."

She led the way to the back of the church and down the stone steps, pulling the key from the lock as she went.

"What is this place?" Bernie said, pausing at the top and looking alarmed.

"It's somewhere safe."

She felt for a candle and lit it. As the light flared, she saw Bernie's frightened face looking down.

"It's fine," she reassured him. "Come down."

Cautiously, Bernie descended the stairs.

"It's a crypt," he said, half-scared, half-interested.

"It's somewhere you can stay."

"Really?"

"No one ever comes down here," Ivy said. "You can stay here for a few days. A couple of weeks, even. While we come up with a new plan to get you out of enlisting. You can lock the door behind me when I go and then you'll be sure no one will bother you. And if you're careful, you can have a wander in the churchyard when you want some fresh air. Just don't let anyone see you."

"What about food?"

Ivy had thought of that. "I'll bring you veg and that from the Gardens. I'll tell Jim. He'll help us."

Bernie looked astonished. "Jim's not on my side. He said—"

"I know what he said, but he'll be fine. He was just upset for Mac, is all. I'll talk to him."

"Are you sure?"

"Positive."

"But you could get into trouble yourself."

Ivy shrugged.

"Not for the first time," she said. "I don't think you should have to go and fight if you don't believe in war, Bernie. I want to help."

She paused. "Maybe we could even carry on our lessons. If you wouldn't mind?"

Bernie smiled. It was the first time Ivy had seen him smile since she'd found him in the library, and the sight pleased her.

"I wouldn't mind at all."

"Good, then that's settled."

She looked round. The crypt was just as she remembered. Stone floor and vaulted ceiling. Several large tombs on either side of a main walkway, and some smaller ones at the end. It was creepy, that was sure, but it was quiet and dry and no one would ever know he was there.

"I'll find you some blankets and you can make yourself a little sleeping area," she said. "I'll bring down books for you and something to eat and drink. If you need the toilet, go outside."

"How did you know this place existed?" Bernie looked curious.

"Oh, some women I used to know used it for a while," Ivy said, deliberately vague. "We left some bits and pieces down here."

Bernie frowned, but to Ivy's relief, he didn't pursue it.

"It's spooky," he said. "All these dead people."

Ivy nodded.

"At least you know they won't hurt you," she said. "Unlike the living."

Chapter 14

July 1916

It was strange, Bernie thought, how quickly the new and strange became the everyday. He'd never imagined for one moment that he'd still be spending his nights in the crypt at St. Anne's months after Ivy suggested it, but there he was.

And though it wasn't the most comfortable place he'd stayed, and he was lonely on occasion, and still scared about what his future held—Lord knew he couldn't stay down there forever—he was, surprisingly, fine.

He had made the crypt his own. At the far end, behind the tomb in memory of the church's first reverend, he had his "bedroom." Ivy and Jim had brought blankets and pillows for him to use. To Bernie's relief, Ivy had been right and Jim wasn't as hostile as he'd worried he might be. Ivy had obviously had a word and explained Bernie's point of view and Jim, who was such a good young man, was now supporting Bernie in his hiding place, helping make it feel like home. He was, Bernie thought with a flush of shame, more comfortable there than he'd be in a trench.

To the side, was a long, low memorial to a former dignitary from Kew and his long-deceased wife. That had become Bernie's kitchen. He kept the food Ivy and Jim brought him there. It was mostly fruit and vegetables, but sometimes they brought bread or some cooked chicken or leftover meat from dinner, if they could get it. The good thing about it now being summer was the fruit and veg from Kew was in bountiful supply; he wasn't going hungry.

He was, however, rather bored. Ivy, bless her, had brought him a mismatched selection of books that she'd gathered from who knew where. But he found he missed the Gardens. He was longing to feel the sun on his face and the earth in his hands.

He'd been getting bolder each day, staying out in the churchyard for longer and longer instead of dashing out each morning and evening to relieve himself. And the other day, he'd noticed the graves at the back of the grounds were overgrown and unloved. That had given him an idea. He'd asked Ivy to bring him gloves, a trowel, and some secateurs and she'd agreed—after a fair amount of persuasion.

"It's risky, Bernie," she'd said. "What if someone sees you?"

"I really can't imagine anyone will. But if they do, I'll say I'm just helping out. They won't know I'm living here."

She'd pulled a face, but she'd brought the things he'd asked for. And now he was going to go outside and start tending the graves.

He had a routine now when he left the safety of the crypt. He'd open the door just a bit and listen careful, checking he couldn't hear voices or footsteps. Not many people came back this far, but occasionally someone came to visit an old grave or a child ran away from its parents. If all was quiet then he would carefully climb the few steps up to the path, keeping crouched down lower than the wall so if someone came around the corner he'd not be seen. And then he would nip out and casually saunter along, his hat dipped low over his face, as though he was just out for a walk.

Today he did the same, heading right to the very back of the church where the unkept graves sat in wonky rows. Bernie stood for a second, enjoying the sensation of the sun on his skin, and decided to start on the stone at the far end. He couldn't read the inscription, because the weeds had grown up so far that they hid the writing.

Nodding in satisfaction, he pulled out his secateurs and went to work.

It took a long time to cut back all the brambles, weeds and tangled tendrils that were looped over the gravestone, but he managed. Wiping his brow, he stood back to admire his handiwork and jumped in shock as a voice said: "Relative of yours?"

Bernie turned. Behind him stood a vicar, an elderly man with graying hair and a faded cassock.

"So sorry, I didn't mean to startle you," the man said. "I just wondered what you were doing. No one has been in this part of the churchyard for a long time."

Bernie swallowed, his mouth suddenly dry.

"I saw the graves a few days ago and felt bad that they were so overgrown," he said. "I like gardening so I thought I could help tidy them up."

"What a lovely gesture," the vicar said. "I'm grateful."

He made to walk along the path, but Bernic stopped him.

"Would it be all right with you if I carried on?" he said. "I'd like to clear this whole area, if I can. I can perhaps plant some flowers, too, to give it some color? And find something that will bloom in autumn so it's not too gloomy."

He realized he was talking too much and shut his mouth with a snap. But the vicar was smiling.

"I think that would be more than all right," he said. "Thank you . . . ?"

Bernie smiled back, before understanding he was asking for his name.

"Bernard," he said, and then caught himself. He shouldn't give out his real name, because what if word got back to Kew that there was a chap tending the church garden and someone put two and two together? He cast around for a solution and read a name on a nearby grave.

"Paul," he blurted. "Paul Bernard."

"Thank you, Mr. Bernard."

"Paul is fine," he said. His heart was beating faster and he thought he must look shifty, but the vicar showed no sign of suspicion.

"I'm Reverend Miller," he said simply. "I'll let you get on."

Bernie watched him go, then sank down on to the grass beside the graves, weak with relief. Ivy was right, it was risky him spending so much time outside. Perhaps he should go back in? Although he had a cover story now. And he was feeling so much better now that he was digging and pruning and weeding. With his hands busy he found he didn't have time to brood on the harsh words Mac had said or think about how Louisa, who he'd thought a friend, had betrayed him. Yes, he decided. For the sake of his sanity, he'd stay out just a little bit longer.

❦

Louisa was brooding, too. She felt so awful about Bernie that she couldn't get him out of her mind. She had been so certain, so sure, that she was doing the right thing when she left the feathers in his coat and in his bag that she never once stopped to question if it truly was the best way to act.

And now it was too late.

She was working alone today. She worked alone most days now. She wasn't sure if the other women knew what she'd done, or understood that she'd been responsible for Bernie being sacked and—she presumed— being called up. She didn't know if Ivy had said something to them, or if Mac had spread the word. But however it had happened, no one really spoke to Louisa now. No one was outright nasty, but no one shared small talk or chatted about their weekend. If Lou tried to ask questions about a fiancé, who was serving abroad, or an ill mother, or even trivialities like what they were having for lunch, she was shut down. So she'd stopped asking. She came to work each day, did what Mac asked her to do, and then she went home again.

122

It was a lonely existence. And with so much time on her hands she'd thought long and hard about Bernie and his insistence that war was wrong, that the German soldiers were just men and boys in different uniforms, and she'd come to see that he had a point. She still wasn't completely comfortable about some people fighting while others stayed safe at home, but she had changed her mind altogether about the white feather campaign.

"It's not right," she'd told some like-minded Suffragettes last week. "And I won't be a part of it."

The other women had nodded.

"I agree. It's not sitting right with me," said one, whose name was Effie and who was around Louisa's age. "My husband got one. My own bloody husband. He's a teacher, so he's not fighting, thank the Lord. And I heard Mrs. Parkinson's son got one when he was home because he'd had his hand shot off."

There was a murmur of discontent as the women all made it clear what they thought of that.

"We could still support the war effort," Louisa suggested tentatively. "Form our own group, and concentrate on helping in other ways?"

Effie frowned. "Like how?"

Louisa thought of Ivy, spending her spare time at the Federation in East London.

"A friend is working with Sylvia Pankhurst, giving milk and food to children whose fathers have been called up. Maybe we could do something like that. Something on the ground, as it were?"

"We could help soldiers, perhaps?" Effie said thoughtfully. "Support their families? Visit them in hospital?"

"I'd like to work on promoting peaceful solutions to conflict," said a young woman sitting across from Louisa. She was tiny, like a bird, but had a flinty, determined look in her eye. "I'm not sure war is ever the right thing to do. I've heard there's an organization called the League of Peace. I thought I'd go along and see if I can do anything to help them."

"Could I come?" Louisa said, surprising herself. "I'd like to know more about them."

The woman smiled. "Of course," she said.

Effie had nodded. "And let's not forget that we still do not have the vote," she said. "Women are keeping this country going while the men are away, and I am hopeful those in power remember that when the time is right."

The women had all cheered and Louisa had felt hopeful for the first time in months. It was a relief to have found some friends when work was so difficult. And it was difficult, she thought now, resting on her haunches as she weeded. Spending days alone with her thoughts wasn't much fun. But one good thing had come out of this whole horrible business— something unexpected: She'd gotten back in touch with her parents.

Louisa had realized over several sleepless nights that, just as she'd made a mistake with Bernie, perhaps there were bridges to be built with her mother, too. So the next time her mother wrote, she opened the letter and read the snippets of news from the village eagerly. Her mother hadn't mentioned Reg, and when Louisa replied, she didn't mention him, either. Instead she'd written her a chatty letter, asking about the farm and sharing stories of Kew. Her mother had replied swiftly, equally jovially, and enclosing a note from Louisa's brother, Matthew, who'd taken on most of the day-to-day running of the business. And since then there had been a few notes and letters. It was nice, Louisa thought, to feel part of a family again. Especially as her Kew family had fallen apart. And her misgivings about Reg coming to find her were clearly groundless. Perhaps he wasn't even in Kent anymore and he certainly wasn't worth worrying about.

She glanced up as Ivy walked by, carrying a basket full of carrots, lettuces and plums. The younger woman had hardly said more than a few words to Louisa since Bernie had gone. On more than one occasion, Louisa had wanted to ask her if she knew where he was, if he'd been called up, but she knew Ivy wouldn't tell her.

Recently, though, Louisa had been intrigued by some of Ivy and Jim's behavior. They were always together—that wasn't odd—but there seemed to be more whispering than normal. More tacit glances and tiny nods or shakes of the head. As though they were always making plans that others weren't allowed to be a part of.

And Louisa was pretty sure Ivy was taking produce from the Gardens. She knew things weren't always easy at home for the young woman, but she also knew Ivy's mother was a formidable housekeeper and a very proud woman and she'd never entertain the idea of her daughter stealing for her. So where was Ivy taking that food?

❧❧❧

Louisa bent down over her weeding, but from under the brim of her hat, she watched Ivy tip the contents of her basket into a soft fabric bag and hook it over her arm. She said something to the woman she was working with, who nodded and smiled, and then headed off, walking at a brisk pace toward the gate.

On a whim, Louisa put down her trowel and followed at a safe distance, hoping Mac wouldn't spot her abandoning her work.

Ivy trotted down the path and out onto Kew Green. Once she'd disappeared, Louisa upped her pace, almost running. She peeked out of the gate and saw Ivy dashing across the green to the church. Was she in need of spiritual guidance? It seemed unlikely.

Louisa loitered for a while, hoping Ivy would return straightaway, but when she didn't, she returned to her weeding. When Ivy eventually came back, Louisa couldn't help but notice that the bag she'd been carrying was now empty. Either Ivy had eaten a lot of fruit and veg, or she'd given it to someone.

With a rush of hope, Louisa realized it could be Bernie. He could be hiding out in the church, Louisa thought. They were places of sanctuary, after all. He could be hiding out, and Ivy and Jim could be slipping him food. The idea that Bernie wasn't huddled in a trench somewhere, facing death every day, because of her, made her weak with relief.

"I hope it's him," she said under her breath. "I do hope it's him."

She spent another sleepless night tossing and turning as she wondered what to do. Should she follow Ivy again and burst in? What if it wasn't Bernie? What if Ivy was helping the churchwardens or the vicar? Should she confront Ivy and ask her straight out? She'd surely just say no.

Eventually, as the birds began calling and dawn grew light round her drapes, Louisa made a decision. She got out of bed and went to her tiny kitchen, and she made some bread. She wasn't a great baker, but her mother had taught her the basics and her loaves were tasty. She kneaded and pounded the dough and by the time she was ready to leave for Kew, it was baked and smelling delicious. Louisa wrapped the loaf in paper and added a note that simply read: *Please forgive me.*

At work, she left the bread in her locker until they stopped for lunch and then took the loaf in its wrapper and she approached Ivy, who was sitting—as always—with Jim, under the shade of a large oak tree.

Steeling herself for rejection or rudeness—both of which would be rightly deserved—Louisa took a breath.

"Ivy," she said. "Can I have a quick word?"

Ivy looked up and exchanged a glance with Jim. "Needs to be quick because I've got somewhere to be," she said curtly.

Louisa nodded. "You don't have to tell me anything if you don't want to," she said. She'd been practicing what to say all the way to work this morning, until one of the other passengers on the bus had told her to be quiet. "But I wanted to give you this." She held out the loaf of bread and Ivy and Jim both stared at it. Neither of them took it. Louisa made a face. She wasn't doing very well.

"If you're going to see Bernie and you think he might need something to eat, I'd like you to give him this," she said in a hurry, her words falling over themselves as she spoke. "There's a note in there, but if you'd rather not give it to him, or if I've got this all wrong, then please don't worry."

Ivy and Jim were still looking bewildered, so Louisa bent down and put the bread on the grass beside them.

"Do what you want with it," she said. Then she turned and walked as fast as she could away from them.

She'd not got very far when Ivy caught up with her. She was ever so quick on her feet, that girl.

"Lou," she was saying. "Bloody hell, Lou, slow down."

Louisa stopped walking and turned to face her former friend. Ivy was red in the face and out of breath but her expression was kind.

"Was I right?" Louisa said hopefully.

Ivy glanced round to check there was no one in earshot and then she gave the smallest of nods. "You were right."

"Is he doing well?"

Ivy shrugged. "As you'd expect, really. I thought I'd come up with a plan to get him somewhere else, but so far Jim and me have drawn a blank."

"I feel awful," Louisa said. "I was so caught up with Mrs. Pankhurst's message, and I really believed I was doing the right thing. But I didn't think about the damage I would cause."

Ivy's expression softened even more. "Yeah, well you're not the first," she said. She rubbed her left arm and grinned at Louisa. The sight of that smile made Louisa's heart lift.

"Will you take him the bread?" she said. "And tell him I'm sorry."

Ivy nodded. "Course I will."

"And will you let me help?"

"Help?"

"I'm sure there must be a way for Bernie to avoid being called up," Louisa said. "What about teaching?"

"He won't do it. You should have seen the state of him when I suggested it."

"Then I'll find something else," Louisa said. "I'm going to put this right, Ivy. Just you wait."

Chapter 15

Louisa meant what she'd said to Ivy. She was determined to find a way to help Bernie. She just had to find out more about the legalities surrounding conscientious objectors—and she thought tagging along to the League of Peace might be the thing to do. But when she got in touch with the tiny woman from the Suffragette meeting—her name was Caro, which struck Louisa as being thrillingly bohemian—she was disappointed to discover that there wasn't to be a gathering for another week.

And she had another disappointment when Ivy came back from delivering the bread to Bernie.

"How was he?" Louisa said. She was worried about what Bernie thought of her and had decided if he wanted nothing to do with her that was his right. She wouldn't blame him in the slightest.

"He's hurt," Ivy said, choosing her words carefully. Louisa felt shame flood her again. Why had she acted so harshly?

"But he says to tell you of course he forgives you."

"Really?" Delighted, Louisa clapped her hands. "So I can go and visit him? In the church?"

"Shh." Ivy put her finger to Louisa's lips. "No, I don't think so. I think we need to keep this as quiet as we can. He's not in the church, so don't go thinking you can wander over there and find him."

That was so completely what Louisa had been thinking that she blinked in surprise.

"Well," she began, but Ivy shut her off again.

"The fewer people who know where he is, the better. That way it's more likely to stay secret, and it's only Jim and me who are taking the risk."

Louisa wanted to argue, but she knew Ivy was speaking sense. "But he's not angry with me?"

"Have you ever known Bernie to be angry with anyone?"

Louisa laughed. It felt like ages since she'd laughed and it was nice. "Never."

"Are you coming to Mac's thing this evening?" Ivy said.

"At the pub?" Louisa had been quite shocked when Mac suggested taking all of "his" gardeners out for a drink to celebrate their first year at Kew. Back home in Kent, the pub had been the place for the men to gather, and since she'd been in London she'd never set foot in any of the many inns around town.

"Come on, it'll be fun," Ivy said, tucking her hand into the crook of Louisa's arm, the way she always used to. "We deserve some of that."

"We really do," agreed Louisa. "Yes, I'll come along. It'll be a hoot."

And it really was. Mac was like a new man since the disappointment of discovering his hearing problem and not being allowed to enlist. He'd been asked to oversee the growing of food at Kew and was doing it so well, he kept being given pats on the back from men in high places. And though he was still upset about his hearing, with everyone in the know, life was much easier for him because all the gardeners simply made sure to face him when they were talking and he could read their lips.

He was less grumpy, much more jovial, and generally lots of fun to be around. And his initial reservations about the women gardeners had been replaced with a fierce, protective pride. He loved his "girls," as he called them, and spoke warmly of them to anyone who asked (and to many people who didn't ask, too).

At the pub, he bought beer and cider for everyone and toasted the success of their first year.

"I'm not afraid to admit, I was too stubborn to think this could work," he said.

"And pigheaded," heckled Ivy. Mac made a face at her and everyone laughed.

"And pigheaded," he conceded. "But I am very glad to have been proved wrong. You're all part of Kew Gardens now, girls. And that lasts forever."

He raised his glass. "To the Kew Gardens Girls," he said.

"The Kew Gardens Girls," everyone echoed. Louisa copied what the others did and drank a huge sip of her cider. It reminded her of home and made her eyes water a bit. She already felt slightly light-headed. It was warm in the pub and with all the gardeners gathered, she suddenly needed some air.

"Just going outside for a mo'," she told Ivy. She weaved through the groups of gardeners chatting and laughing and made it to the tiny front yard of the inn, where she took three large gulps of the cool summer evening air and looked up at the stars. Who'd have thought she'd end up here?

She stayed outside for five minutes or so, sitting on the low wall at the edge of the yard, just taking time to enjoy the quiet and the fresh breeze. But as she turned to go back into the pub, someone put their hand on her shoulder and made her jump.

She whirled round, expecting to see Mac or Dennis or one of the women and reeled in shock as she recognized the man standing in front of her.

"Hello, Lou," he said.

POSY LOVELL

He hadn't changed at all. His smile was still sarcastic and his eyes were still cold. And the hand on her arm was still squeezing that bit too tight.

"R-R-Reg," she stammered. "What are you doing here?"

"That's not the kind of welcome a man wants from his missus after so many months apart," he said. He pulled Louisa toward him and squashed his lips against hers. She could smell whisky on his breath and feel his beard prickling her skin.

"Stop it," she said, pushing him away. He let go, stumbling a little, and she realized he was very drunk. The thought scared her—he was always more aggressive, more prone to using his fists, more reckless, when he had a drink inside him.

"Reg," she said, trying to keep him calm. "It's nice to see you. I was just surprised, that's all. How did you know where I was?"

He gave her a nasty smile. "Your birdbrained brother."

"Matthew told you?"

"Nah, of course he didn't tell me. Your family are all as bloody tight-lipped as each other."

Louisa closed her eyes briefly, inwardly thanking her mother that no matter what she thought of Lou's decision to run away, she'd not revealed her whereabouts to Reg. Her new life would never have got started if he'd followed her straightaway.

"So what's Matthew got to do with you showing up?" She was trying very hard not to sound panicked.

"He was in the Three Crowns, wetting the head of another of his brats, and I heard him telling that idiot friend of his that he'd been in touch with you. So when he went to the lav, I checked the pocket of his jacket and found a letter."

He lurched toward her and Louisa backed away, putting the low wall between her and him. It wouldn't offer much protection, but it could slow him down if she needed to run.

"Why didn't you come to my house?" she said, cold fear dripping down her spine at the thought of his turning up on her doorstep. At least here she was in public, with Mac, Jim, Dennis, and the others just inside should she need them. Her eyes darted from side to side, planning an escape route if he went for her. It was astonishing how fast you could slip back into old habits.

"I went," Reg said. "But I wanted to watch you first, find out what you were up to."

Again, Louisa felt that shiver of fear. How long had he been spying on her without her knowing?

"I followed you to the park." He gestured with his head toward the gate of the Gardens. "You're a gardener?"

"Yes."

"But my farm wasn't good enough for you?"

"I tried my best with that farm," she said, annoyed at the implication. "I kept it going when you were out drinking the profits."

"It's gone now. I had to sell up."

Louisa nodded. She wasn't at all surprised, but she didn't say that. "I'm sorry."

Reg was suddenly morose, his eyes filling with tears. "That was my dad's farm," he said. "And his dad's before him."

"I know."

"And now I've got nothing."

He looked at Louisa. "It's your fault." His ruddy face contorted with anger. "It's your fault, you bitch."

He reached for her but Louisa stepped back quickly and he stumbled forward, steadying himself on the wall.

"What do you want me to do about it?" she said, feeling bolder as she heard the noise of her friends' laughter coming from the pub behind her.

"I need you to come home with me and sort it out. Come back, Louisa. I need you."

Just like that he was back to melancholy. He had always had violent mood swings when he was drunk and it seemed nothing had changed.

"I need you, Louisa," he repeated. His reddened eyes were brimming with tears again. "You owe me."

Louisa heard another burst of laughter from inside the pub. She thought about the good friends she had at Kew and how she'd started a whole new life in London, away from Reg and his fists, and she drew herself up as tall as she could.

"I owe you nothing, Reginald Taylor," she growled in his face. "It's you who owes me. You took my best years from me. You made me into a scared, cowering creature. And worst of all, you killed my baby."

She looked straight into his eyes, feeling her lip tremble as she thought of the child she'd longed for.

"I wanted to be a mother so much and you took that from me, too. But you know what? I'm glad now. Glad I didn't have a baby with you because no child deserves you as a father. You're a pathetic, drunken waste of space and you're not fit to breathe the same air as the men I know in London. Now, get going, before I call for help."

She folded her arms and stared at her ex-husband. She was shaking all over—she'd never once stood up to him like this. How would he react? If he came for her, she'd run into the pub and get help, she thought as he looked back at her, the shock of being spoken to like that obvious in his face.

"Bitch," Reg said again. He spat at her feet. Louisa didn't move. "Bitch."

Then, to Lou's enormous relief, he turned round and, without another word, wobbled off down the road toward the river and the bridge.

Breathing heavily, Louisa watched him go. She felt almost euphoric. She'd seen him off. Seen off the man who'd terrorized her for so many years. This was astonishing.

Giddy, she pushed open the pub door again and was immediately surrounded by her Kew friends.

"Where have you been?" Ivy said.

Louisa took her arm. "I've been laying some ghosts to rest."

Ivy raised an eyebrow.

"My husband turned up," Louisa explained. "He tracked me down. But I told him where to go and . . ." She blinked, still surprised by what had happened. "He went."

"Oh my goodness, are you all right?"

Louisa nodded. "I really think I am," she said. "I think I am."

"Well, come and celebrate."

Arm in arm the women rejoined the group of gardeners.

It was a lovely evening in the end. Louisa enjoyed every minute, chatting with her colleagues, laughing with Mac, teasing Jim and Dennis about working with so many women. She felt warm and happy and, she thought, as she searched for her bag under the table when it was time to go, she felt independent. She had no one to answer to, no man telling her what to do or when to do it. It was a good feeling.

"Do you want to stay the night at my flat?" she asked Ivy. It was a long trip back to Hackney at this time of the evening.

"Would you mind?" she said. "My mother will be angry if I waltz in at this hour."

"Not at all. Nice to have some company on the way home."

"I'll walk you to the bus stop," said Jim. He dropped into an extravagant bow. "After you."

Louisa led the way out of the pub, followed by her friends, and out into the quiet night street. She glanced over the green at St. Anne's, which was cloaked in darkness.

"I hope Bernie's all right," she said. "I want to help him."

"He's fine," Ivy assured her. "I think he quite likes it there."

She and Jim had their arms wound round each other, and as they paused to look at the church, Jim bent his head and kissed Ivy. Louisa watched them indulgently for a second—they were so sweet in their love for each other—and then wandered toward the bus stop. They'd catch up.

But as she walked along the side of the green, a figure came out from behind one of the trees and lurched toward her.

"Louisa," it slurred.

It was Reg, of course it was.

"Go away," she said, carrying on walking past him.

Surprisingly fast for someone as drunk as he was, he made a grab for her and pulled her by the arm. Caught off-balance, she stumbled and fell onto the ground.

Quick as a flash, Reg was on top of her, his sour breath in her face as he tried to kiss her.

"Get off," she squeaked, wriggling underneath him and twisting her head so he couldn't press his lips to hers. Looming above her, Reg held her chin in one hand and with an open palm, slapped her right across the face. She felt blood trickle from her nose and just like that, the memories of how he was when they were married flooded her mind and she was frozen in terror, all her earlier bravado abandoning her.

She stopped fighting. If she didn't move and didn't make a sound, he'd soon have had enough and she could go home.

Reg was panting now, still holding on to her chin, his meaty fingers digging into her jaw as he fumbled with his belt with the other hand.

"A man just wants what's legally his," he was muttering. "Bloody women think they can just do what they like."

His belt unfastened, he pushed down his trousers and, ignoring Louisa's gasping sobs, he started trying to pull her skirt up. But it had got caught beneath her when she fell and his weight on top made it tricky for him to loosen it.

"Bloody women," he said again. He pushed himself away slightly and suddenly he was off her. His sweaty body yanked upward by something Louisa couldn't see.

"What are you doing?" a voice growled in the darkness. "Get your filthy hands off her." It was Jim. Thank God, she thought. Thank God.

She sat up and watched Jim haul Reg by the collar, away from her. Ivy stood to the side, looking furious.

Are you all right? she mouthed to Louisa, and Louisa nodded, wiping the taste of Reg's mouth from her face and dabbing the blood from her nose.

"Get out of here," Jim was saying to Reg. "Go on, go."

He shoved the older man, and Reg windmilled round, wobbly on his feet.

"Get out," Jim said again.

"Sod you."

Once more, Louisa watched her husband walk away. But this time, he only went a few steps before changing his mind. He launched himself at Jim, getting one clear shot at the young man's face. Louisa winced as she heard Jim's nose crunch and Ivy shrieked.

Jim, though, was young and fit, and he was angry. He took Reg by the shoulders and pushed him off himself.

"Bugger off," he shouted. Reg went to hit Jim again but Jim swerved his fist and instead landed his own punch on the side of Reg's face.

Reg went down like a sack of coal. He thumped first onto the tree behind him and then slid, out cold, onto the grass at the edge of the green.

They all stood stock-still, staring at him as he lay, unmoving, on the ground.

"Is he . . ." Louisa gasped. "Is he dead?"

Jim, kind, gentle Jim was staring down at Reg in horror.

"I don't know." He was panicking, his breaths coming quicker and quicker. "I never meant to hurt him, I've never punched anyone in my life. I just wanted him to go away."

Ivy ran to her boyfriend. "It's not your fault," she said.

"I don't know if he's breathing," Louisa said. "What should we do?"

She bent down to Reg, but even being close to him when he was unconscious made her recoil. She stood up again. Along the street a little way, a group of men had left the pub and were coming in their direction. She didn't recognize them. Thinking quickly, she made her decision.

"You need to go," she said. "Jim. You have to leave."

"I'm not going anywhere," he said.

Louisa, feeling panic rising, gave him a push.

"Go," she said. "If you're here, they'll know it was you who hit him and you'll get into trouble. Ivy, take him away. Go into the Gardens. It's dark, no one will see."

Ivy's face shone white in the moonlight, but she nodded silently.

"Go on," Louisa urged. "I'll deal with this."

Quietly, Ivy tugged Jim's hand. Still looking shocked, he obediently followed as she led him to the gate and they melted into the darkness. Louisa waited, wondering how long they would take to find the key in Jim's pocket and let themselves in, until she heard the soft *clang* of the gate shutting again. Then, taking a breath, she let out a scream.

"Help!" she called. "Help! My husband's fallen and hit his head."

Chapter 16

Ivy clung to Jim in the dark Gardens. She could feel his heart thumping beneath his shirt and sweat trickling down his back.

"It's fine," she kept saying. "It's going to be fine. I'm sure he was breathing."

But she wasn't sure. Not really. He'd hit that tree with quite a thump and the way he'd been lying there, so still . . .

She shuddered.

"It's fine," she said again.

"What shall we do?" Jim looked young and scared and Ivy's heart twisted with love and worry for him.

"We'll stay here overnight," she said. "It's warm enough and we can find somewhere soft to cuddle up."

"And then what?"

"And then in the morning, we'll go to Louisa's and find out what's happening."

She paused as they heard footsteps running and shouts outside the gates. Someone must have found Reg. Or his body. She shivered again.

"Are you cold?" Jim pulled her closer to him. She wasn't but she liked being near him, feeling his body on hers.

"What if he's dead, Ivy? What if I've killed him?"

They started walking farther into the Gardens. Ivy wanted to be away from the gate, just in case someone caught a glimpse of them, unlikely as that sounded. She tried not to think about the last time she'd been in the Gardens at night, doing something wrong.

"You've not killed him," she told Jim. "He's a big bloke and he was drunk. He's just passed out. And if . . ." She stopped.

"If . . . ?"

"If something's happened, then we'll deal with it. Louisa's so quick-thinking, she'll have told a story to make it all seem all right. It's not your fault, Jim."

She pulled his arm to make him look at her.

"Reg was hurting Louisa. And if you hadn't come along when you did, he'd have hurt her a lot worse. He'd hit her—did you see her nose bleeding? And he was trying to . . ." She took a ragged breath. "He was trying to force himself on her. It's not right, Jim, and you stopped him. You're brave and wonderful and I'm so proud of you."

She was very close to tears, thinking about what could have happened, and what did happen, and what was going to happen now.

"No one will know it was you. Reg won't remember. And who would believe him, anyway? Drunken old git like that."

They'd reached a patch of lawn, under a huge spreading oak tree.

"Here," Ivy said. "Let's stay here. Look, there's a little nook between the roots that's just the right size for us. And it doesn't look like it'll rain, but if it does, we'll stay dry because of the leaves."

She sat down on the springy grass and gestured to Jim to follow, but he didn't.

"We could leave," he said, pacing up and down in front of Ivy. "We could go to Ireland. I've always fancied Ireland."

"We don't need to leave. It's going to be fine."

"What if I get sent to prison? I don't want to go to prison." Jim's voice was small in the darkness.

"You won't go to prison, my love. I won't let it happen."

"How can you stop it?"

"I'll hide you," she said. "I'll hide you away with Bernie."

Jim stopped walking. "That's it."

"What?" Ivy hadn't been serious when she'd said she would hide him.

"I'll enlist."

"No."

"It makes sense, Ivy. I'll sign up tomorrow morning. I could be training by Monday. No one will look for me if I'm in the army."

"No," she said again. She stood up and went to Jim. "You're too young."

He scoffed. "It's already July, I'll be eighteen in November, and I look twenty-one," he said. He was speaking the truth. His physical job meant his arms were thick and strong, and his body was taut with muscles. "There are kids much younger than me lying about their age and getting away with it. No one is going to question me. I'd be going at the end of the year anyway. This is just a bit early, that's all."

Ivy began to cry. It was like all her nightmares were coming true. With every bone in her body she longed for Jim to stay here in Kew with her, safe and sound, away from bombs and gas and guns. But she knew what he was saying made sense. The war showed no signs of being over any time soon and there was no doubt that come November, Jim would be enlisted anyway. At least if he went now, he wouldn't be in trouble for the business with Reg.

"I don't want you to go," she sobbed. "I want you here with me."

"I know, I know," he soothed. "But it's not forever."

"It's so dangerous."

"Look at me, Ivy. I'm a big lad. I'm strong. I'm healthy. I've got more chance than some of them against Jerry. I'll be home before you know it."

"I'll miss you so much."

He stroked her hair. "I know. I'll miss you, too. But I'll write to you."

In despair, Ivy sobbed harder.

"I can't read," she wailed. "I can't read your letters and I can't write them back."

Jim lifted her chin and looked at her. "We'll find a way," he said. "You can draw me pictures."

Ivy shook her head, lost for words. "I can't," she whispered. "I can't be without you."

Jim had looked scared and young before, but now he looked weary and older than his years.

"You'll have to, Ivy. We have to do this. We'll get through this, you'll see."

He pulled her close to him again.

"We should get some rest. The sun will be up about four and it'll wake us. And it's Saturday tomorrow; there will be visitors at the Gardens, no doubt. Especially if the weather's good."

He looked behind them at the little nook in the roots of the trees.

"I'll put my shirt down for you to sleep on," he said. He started unfastening his buttons. Only the slight shake in his hands betrayed how frightened he must have felt. Ivy watched, her mind whirling with emotions, and as Jim slipped off his shirt, she stepped forward and put her hand on his chest. It was firm and his skin was soft and warm.

"Jim," she breathed. He stayed still as she gently ran her fingers over his shoulders, and then he bent his head and kissed her deeply, almost taking her breath away.

"I love you," she said.

"I love you, too."

Amazed at her own boldness, she took the shirt from his hand and spread it out on the grass. He watched her, his gaze never moving from hers. Ivy unfastened her dress and shrugged it off and spread that down, too. She was only in her slip, but she didn't feel at all self-conscious. It just felt right.

Biting her lip, she sat herself down on the clothes and held her hand out to Jim.

"Are you sure?" he said.

"Surer than I've ever been about anything in my whole life."

He sat down next to her and they kissed again. Ivy's hands roamed across Jim's broad back and she gasped as he kissed her neck, sending shivers of pleasure through her body.

"This is the best way to say good-bye," she whispered. "It's the only way to say good-bye. I couldn't bear it, if something happened to you and we'd never been close like this."

"Shh," Jim said. "Nothing's going to happen."

She pulled away from him slightly and looked up at him.

"We don't know what's around each corner," she said. "We have to snatch every chance we get to be happy."

"You're right." Jim rested his forehead against hers. "You're right."

Then they stopped talking for a while as they lost themselves in each other.

⚜

They woke early with the sun nudging them into the morning as it rose above the trees. Ivy blinked and sat up. They'd slept intertwined, with Ivy's full skirt draped over them like a blanket. Now she pulled it up to hide her bare chest as she watched Jim sleep. The morning dew had dampened his hair and settled on his eyelashes and he looked peaceful.

She bent down and kissed his cheek and he opened his eyes.

"Morning," he murmured.

She nuzzled into him for a second, savoring his smell and the feel of his skin against hers.

"We need to go," she said.

"I'll be first in the queue at the recruitment office," Jim said, looking up at the sun. She could tell he was trying to guess what time it was and she loved him for his love of nature.

"Are you absolutely sure about this?" Ivy said.

He nodded. "It's the only way."

Ivy felt tears threatening again, so she swallowed. She had to be as brave as Jim was being.

"Do you want me to come with you?"

He shook his head. "I need to do this on my own."

"What will you tell your parents?"

"That it's the right thing to do. They won't be cross. My dad's talking about enlisting himself. He's only forty, so he's young enough."

"They'll worry."

He shrugged. "Not as much as they would if I was in prison."

Ivy shivered and felt around for her slip. She found it, slightly damp with the dew, and stood up to pull it on, feeling Jim's eyes on her as she did.

"Do you think he's all right? Reg, I mean."

"I hope so." Jim found his shirt and started getting dressed, too. "But even if he is, he's bound to be angry. If he reports me, there could be trouble. It's best if I'm out the way."

Ivy nodded. "Is this it, then? This is good-bye?"

She finished fastening her dress and looked at Jim. She thought her heart might burst with pride and fear and love and happiness and dread all at once.

Jim kissed her.

"It's not good-bye forever," he said. "It's just good-bye for now."

"Good-bye for now," she echoed quietly.

Jim sat down on the grass again to put his boots on. "I'm going to miss this place. The flowers and the trees. I'll not get to see how those new apple trees work out."

"Not this year," Ivy said. "But the apple trees will still be here when you get back."

"Draw them for me," he said. "When you do your diary, draw some extra pictures for me."

"I will."

They kissed again and, hand in hand, they started to walk toward the gates.

"Will you say good-bye to Mac for me?" Jim asked. "He's been so good."

Ivy's eyes prickled with tears again as she thought about how much Mac would miss Jim.

"What shall I tell him? He's bound to ask why you've gone so suddenly."

Jim shrugged.

"Tell him some of the lads from my street enlisted and it made sense for me to go at the same time?" he suggested. "He'll understand."

"And Louisa?"

"Tell Louisa the truth."

"She'll blame herself."

Jim sighed. "I know, but she mustn't. It was just bad luck, that's all. And it wasn't her fault Reg turned up, nor her fault that he attacked her. Any bloke walking by would have done the same."

Ivy wasn't sure that was true. Not all blokes were as brave and kind as her Jim. But she nodded anyway.

"What about Bernie?"

"Do what you can for him, won't you?"

"Course."

"Get Louisa to help you. She'll find a way to keep him from the Front, I'm sure of it."

They'd reached the gate. Ivy's tears were falling fast now, and she couldn't have stopped them even if she tried.

"Please don't go," she said. She clasped the front of his shirt and sobbed into the fabric. "I don't want to lose you. Please don't go."

They stayed like that for a while, arms round each other, both crying as they said their good-byes and kissed and laughed and cried some more. Until eventually, they couldn't put it off any longer.

"I love you, Ivy Adams," Jim said. "Stay safe."

"Come home to me, Jim," she said. "Come home soon."

They kissed once more and Jim gave her a jaunty salute.

"Look after the plants for me. Good-bye."

He walked off down the street, past the tree where Reg had fallen, toward the railway station.

"Good-bye," Ivy whispered. "Good-bye, my love."

Chapter 17

Louisa was expecting Ivy to arrive on her doorstep at some point, but she didn't expect her to turn up quite so early, nor in quite such a state.

She heard the quiet knock on her door as she was boiling her kettle to make tea. She'd spent a sleepless night going over and over everything that happened the night before in her head. Confronting Reg, Reg attacking her, and then Jim punching Reg all seemed like an awful nightmare. Every time she closed her eyes she saw Reg's sweaty red face looming over hers. Her nose was swollen and she had a large bruise on her cheekbone that stopped her getting comfortable, and in the end she gave up on sleep altogether.

When the knock on the door came, she opened it cautiously, worried that it could be Reg. But there was Ivy, sobbing her heart out, and still knocking quietly in case Louisa was asleep because she didn't want to wake her.

Louisa opened her arms to her friend and Ivy collapsed into her embrace, crying so heavily that she couldn't speak. Louisa led her inside, sat her down on the settee, and let her sob until, eventually, Ivy's weeping became less intense and her breathing less ragged.

"Ivy, my love, what's happened?" she said, handing her a mug of very sugary tea.

"Jim's enlisted," she said. She wrapped her fingers round the mug and held it close. "He's gone."

Louisa was shocked. That wasn't at all what she'd been expecting. "Enlisted? But he's only seventeen."

"He was worried he'd get into trouble for hitting Reg. He thought he'd killed him." She looked up at Louisa and her anxious expression made Louisa's heart contract with love for her young friend. "Did he kill him?"

"No, he didn't kill him. Reg is strong as an ox, the old bugger. He'd had too much to drink and he knocked himself out, that's all."

Ivy started to cry again, tears rolling down her puffy cheeks. "So Jim didn't need to go?"

Louisa made a face. "Reg remembered him. He was ranting about a young lad with muddy boots who'd hit him. It's possible someone would put two and two together. Though I told the constable who came that Reg had fallen over and he was talking nonsense."

Ivy put her head in her hands. "Jim said he'd be enlisted soon anyway and it made sense for him to go. And I know that it does, but it hurts so much, Louisa."

Louisa gathered her into her arms again. "I know," she said. "I know it hurts."

Ivy looked up at her, worry in her eyes. "What about you?"

"What about me?"

"Reg attacked you."

Louisa shrugged. "Not for the first time."

Ivy gently reached up and touched the bruise on Louisa's cheek. "He did this."

"He's done worse and he'd have done it again, if Jim hadn't been there."

Ivy looked proud. "What happened, Louisa? When we went into the Gardens we heard voices and footsteps. Did people come to help?"

Louisa nodded. "I shouted for help and a group of men who'd been in the pub came over. I told them my husband had fallen and they went to find a policeman. By the time they had found one, Mac had got there and he was wonderful. I managed to pull him aside and explain who Reg was and what had happened. He had a word with the constable when he arrived and said Reg was violent and shouldn't be allowed near me."

"Lovely Mac," said Ivy. "Did they listen to him?"

Louisa nodded. "The constable looked at my cheek, and he asked very kindly if I was telling the truth when I said Reg had fallen. I said—honestly—that he'd hit me. And they took him away. I asked if they could send him back to Kent and they said they would."

"So he's gone," Ivy said.

"He is, I hope."

"What if he comes back?"

"I've written to my brother, telling him what happened and asking him to keep an eye on Reg back home. He'll get the other men in the village involved, too. Seems Reg has been causing trouble all over."

"I'm glad he's gone."

"But Jim's gone, too."

Ivy lifted her chin, looking like she was trying to summon every ounce of courage she possessed.

"It was the right thing for him to do," she said.

"I'm so sorry, Ivy."

"It's not your fault. Not one scrap of this is your fault. If it's anyone's fault, it's Reg's and sounds like he's in trouble as it is."

Louisa looked at Ivy in awe. She was truly a wonderful person. Wise beyond her years.

"Thank you," she whispered. She took Ivy's hand.

"I am going to make amends for all the stupid things I've done. I'm going to help Bernie, and I'll help you, too."

"We've all done stupid things in our time. And I don't need no help."

"Will Jim write?"

Ivy nodded.

"I can help you read his letters. And help you write replies."

"Maybe," said Ivy. She looked a bit unsure. "I might have another idea, though."

"Really?"

"Tell you later." She gave Louisa a watery smile. "Bernie needs you, though. What can we do to help him?"

"I met a woman called Caro at a Suffragette meeting, who told me about an organization called the League of Peace," Louisa said. She filled Ivy in on how she hoped there might be a way for Bernie to stay.

"You could come to the meeting?" Louisa said, but Ivy shook her head.

"I can't," she said. "I've got Federation stuff to do. With so many men being called up, we're busier than ever before. Sylvia's rushed off her feet."

"You're a good woman, Ivy Adams," Louisa said. "Always thinking of others."

A shadow crossed Ivy's face. "Not always," she said.

⚜

Without Jim at Kew, there was more work to do, so the days passed swiftly, much to Louisa's relief. She was eager to get to the meeting of the League of Peace and get started on her quest to help Bernie. But there was no denying things were harder at the Gardens. Mac had even started talking about finding some more female gardeners to add to their team—

something Louisa would never have imagined him doing this time last year, when he was still grumpy and unwilling to trust them with any important jobs. They were no longer stuck on the herbaceous border or the rock garden—now they did everything the men had done. And they did it all well, too, Louisa thought proudly.

Mac, meanwhile, was fussing round his "girls" like a mother hen, checking they were all right every five minutes.

"Heard from Jim?" he kept asking Ivy.

"He's not been gone a week yet," she pointed out. "He'll write when he can."

Louisa watched Ivy for signs that she was worrying about keeping in touch with her beau while he was abroad, but she seemed calm. Maybe Bernie was going to help her? She itched to ask him, but Ivy said it was best she was the only one who knew where he was. Just in case.

Mac was worried about Louisa, too.

"He's definitely back in Kent, is he?"

"My brother wrote to say he's letting him sleep in the barn in return for some help around the farm. They're so short-staffed because all the farmhands have been called up, so even a drunken layabout like Reg is better than nothing. And Reg knows when he's on to a good thing. I can't see him coming back here." She lowered her voice. "I can't help thinking a spell in the trenches would do him the world of good. Sober him up. Make him realize there's others have it much worse than him. But legally we're still married, so for now, he's off the hook."

Mac nodded. "Seems unfair that Jim's off fighting when a waste of space like Reg stays behind. And as for Bernie . . . Well, I still feel bad about that."

Louisa felt a flush of guilt. "Don't feel bad," she said. "And don't ask any questions. But Bernie's all right for now. And I'm making it my business to sort something out for him. I'll tell you when it's all done."

Mac's astonished expression stayed with her all the way into town on the train and made her chuckle when she thought of it.

The League of Peace met in a large, drafty church hall in Mayfair. It was just like all the Suffragette meetings Louisa had been to over the years except with one striking difference—men were there. In fact, there were more men than women.

Feeling self-conscious and nervous, Louisa skulked into the hall and searched out Caro. She found her talking to a couple of men toward the back of the room. One was short and plump with a large mustache and a loud, hooting laugh, and the other was tall with reddish hair and bright blue eyes that had sadness in them.

"Caro," Louisa said, approaching the group.

"Louisa, I'm so pleased you could make it." Caro kissed Louisa on the cheek. Lou had to bend down because Caro was so small.

"We're going to get started in a minute or two. Today we're talking about how we can help the Red Cross."

"Lovely," said Louisa, though she knew all about the Red Cross and it didn't seem remotely useful for Bernie's predicament.

"Gents, this is my friend Louisa Taylor," Caro said. "We met at a WSPU meeting."

The men both murmured approvingly, much to Louisa's surprise. She'd not met a lot of men who supported women's suffrage.

"Louisa, this is Hector Burbage." She gestured to the man with the mustache and he grinned at Louisa.

"Pleased to meet you, Mrs. Taylor."

"Please call me Louisa."

"Hector."

"And Teddy Armitage."

The tall man shook Louisa's hand and smiled at her. She noticed that while his smile was genuine, it didn't quite melt away the sadness in his eyes. Then she realized she'd been holding his hand for a second or two too long and pulled her fingers away, flustered and flushing.

"Nice to meet you, Mr. Armitage."

His lips curled upward, ever so slightly. "Likewise."

"What brings you to the League of Peace?" Hector asked. He showed Louisa to a row of wooden chairs and she sat down. He sat next to her, with Mr. Armitage on his other side. Caro was one of the people hosting the meeting, so she'd gone up to the front of the room to get things started.

"I'm hoping to find out how I can help a friend," she said. "He's a conscientious objector, but I'm not sure what we need to do to make it all official."

"Teddy's your man for all that," said Hector. He nudged Mr. Armitage in the ribs. "You're the man for that, Ted."

Mr. Armitage—Teddy—looked alarmed. "The man for what?"

"Louisa here wants to know about conscientious objectors."

Teddy looked at Louisa across Hector's rotund belly.

"What do you want to know?"

"I have a friend. He's a Quaker and he doesn't want . . ."

At the front of the room a man stood up and clapped his hands for attention and the buzz of conversation in the audience stopped.

"Let's speak afterward," Teddy said to Louisa in an undertone. He looked straight at her and she felt that mix of flustered and flushed again. "I can help."

Louisa felt fidgety and impatient throughout the meeting, which was interesting but not as useful to Bernie as she'd hoped. When the speakers finished talking, and people started to move, she caught Teddy, who'd stood up and was putting on his hat.

"Excuse me, Mr. Armitage," she said. "Could I have a word about conscientious objectors?"

He turned to her and smiled that same funny sad smile. She felt a pull toward him—curiosity and concern mixed with something else.

"Of course," he said. "Are you in a hurry?"

"Not at all."

"Shall we take ourselves across to the park and enjoy the evening?"

"That sounds lovely, Mr. Armitage."

He looked at her with interest and smiled again. "Call me Teddy," he said.

Louisa nodded in agreement and together they left the hall. Teddy led the way through the side streets of Mayfair and out on to Park Lane, without speaking. They crossed over the road and went into Hyde Park. It was quiet at this time of the evening, but there was still warmth in the air and it was nice to be outside, away from the stuffy meeting hall.

"Shall we walk or sit?" Teddy asked.

"Walk."

Together they began strolling along the wide path that skirted the park.

"What do you want to know?"

Louisa took a breath. "My friend is a pacifist—a Quaker," she said. "He doesn't want to fight, but someone reported him and he's hiding away because he's scared he'll be enlisted."

Teddy nodded. "Good," he said. "Go on."

"He used to be a teacher, which would have meant he didn't have to enlist, but now he's a gardener."

"He won't go back to teaching?"

Louisa shook her head. "We've tried to convince him, but he had a bad experience and even talking about it makes him come across as peculiar."

Teddy thought for a while. "Would you let me make some inquiries for you? Ask around. There might be something I can do."

Louisa realized she'd been holding her breath. She let it out in a puff and beamed at Teddy. "Really?"

"I'm not promising anything, but there are ways round this."

They walked on for a few steps, even though he'd answered Louisa's questions and really she could go home now. She found she didn't want to leave, though. She wasn't sure why.

"How do you know so much about conscientious objectors?" she asked.

Teddy paused. "Shall we sit?"

He gestured to a bench and Louisa sat down, waiting patiently as Teddy gathered his thoughts.

"My wife died when our son, Philip, was born," he said. "So it was just him and me."

"I'm sorry," said Louisa.

"We had our ups and downs when he was young, but we rubbed along quite nicely. When the war started, he was nineteen."

Louisa could see where this was going. She looked at Teddy's sad face, and without thinking, she put her hand on his.

"Don't," she said. "Don't tell me if it's too difficult."

Teddy looked down at her fingers and then up at her face, but he didn't move his hand away.

"I'd like to," he said. "It's important.

"Philip said he wanted to enlist and I . . ." He took a breath. "I encouraged him. I said he should do his duty."

Louisa nodded. "I thought the same."

"He'd not been in France for six months when I got the telegram. They sent back his things. His uniform had a bullet hole in it. Can you imagine?"

Louisa couldn't. She squeezed his fingers but she didn't speak.

Teddy took a deep breath. "And all I could think was that I'd encouraged him to go. And for what end? What's it all for?"

"I'm beginning to wonder."

"Now I help young men who want to avoid being called up. I hate this ridiculous waste of lives. I don't want more men to die like Philip died."

He looked at her, like he'd forgotten she was there. Then he took his hand from under hers and put it gently in his lap.

"There are legal ways to register as a conscientious objector," he said. "Proper channels we can go through. If he's willing to do work elsewhere that could be considered contributing to the war effort?"

"What sort of work?" Louisa wasn't sure. "Nothing military?"

"No, no. They call it 'work of national importance.' Could be building roads or laboring on the railways. Some choose to work on the battlefields, driving ambulances."

Louisa tried to picture Bernie driving an ambulance or working on a road, and found she couldn't.

"You said he's a gardener?"

"Yes. That's how I know him. We worked together at Kew."

Teddy looked impressed. "You're a gardener, too?"

"They advertised for women to work there when their men signed up."

"Do you enjoy it?"

"I love it."

He looked at her, his blue eyes warm suddenly. She felt tingly under the weight of his gaze and, embarrassed, she looked away. What was this?

"Farmwork is considered work of national importance," Teddy said. "Growing food. Perhaps that would suit your friend better?"

Louisa stared at him. "Farmwork?"

"Yes?"

"Farmwork," she said, delighted. "Of course. Farmwork."

Teddy looked confused but pleased with her reaction. "Is that helpful?"

"It may well be," she said. "I might be able to find somewhere for him to work. If I can, could you sort out the official bits?"

"I could."

Louisa stood up, eager to get home and get started on the next part of her plan to help Bernie. "I'll be in touch."

Teddy's eyes met hers and again she felt that tingle as he looked at her. "I'll look forward to it."

Chapter 18

Ivy was watching the new gardener as she wandered round the rose garden. Humming. She had her hair neatly pinned up and she was wearing a long dress and a sunbonnet and holding a basket. Ivy glanced down at her own muddy overalls and boots. It looked to her as though this new gardener wasn't planning on getting dirty.

Annoyed, Ivy took a step toward her. She'd found that her temper, never far beneath the surface, was even quicker to flare up since Jim had been gone. She was missing him desperately and even receiving her first letter—of sorts—from him, which he'd sent to her at the Gardens, hadn't eased her pain.

She had tucked the envelope in her pocket so as to have it close and now she took it out and held it in her hands, gazing at his handwriting on the front. Louisa had read it to her, and she'd asked her to repeat it over and over, until Ivy knew it by heart. Jim had written:

My Ivy,

We have arrived in France and things aren't as bad as I feared. I have met some nice lads and would you believe, Ernie my old mate from school is here, too? It was good to see a familiar face. The men who have been here awhile say it's best in summer because the mud ain't so bad and the nights are warm. I miss you, Ivy. When we settle down to sleep, I look up at the stars and think about you doing the same. I am sending you something special—you'll know what it means.

Your Jim

She hugged herself, remembering his words—even if she wasn't sure she believed him when he said it wasn't as bad as he'd feared—and then she opened the flap of the envelope, ever so carefully, and peered inside, smiling. She had a plan about what to do with the tiny gift of love Jim had sent. She just needed to check with Mac first. But at the moment, he was fawning all over this new gardener. Ivy scowled. New gardeners were fine—great, in fact, because heaven knew they were all working as hard as they could now that Bernie and Jim were gone. But she really wasn't sure that this woman in her expensive dress was the right type for Kew.

"Ivy." Mac's voice behind her made her jump. "Come and meet our new recruit."

"I was just on my way to the palm house, Mac," she said. The female gardeners were allowed to work in every part of the Gardens now and Ivy adored the tropical greenhouse with its huge, foreign plants. Even if her hair did become even wilder as soon as she stepped through the doors.

"There's no hurry," Mac said. "Come and say hello."

Reluctantly, Ivy followed him across the rose garden to where the new woman was crouching down, smelling one of the blooms.

"Isn't this just wonderful?" the woman said. She had a clipped, cut-glass voice most unlike Ivy's London accent. "A beautiful, deep-red rose, meaning love."

"Actually, the dark crimson roses symbolize mourning," Ivy said.

The woman looked startled and stood up in a hurry. "Good heavens."

Mac sighed. "Ivy, this is Lady Winifred Ramsay, our newest recruit."

Ivy stuck out her hand, aware her fingernails were engrained with dirt. But if Lady Ramsay noticed, she didn't mind because she shook Ivy's hand with genuine enthusiasm.

"Hello, Ivy."

Ivy muttered her greetings.

"You two get acquainted," Mac said. "Can you show Lady Ramsay the borders, please? And I'll go and track Louisa down."

"She's in the veg garden with Dennis, I think," Ivy said. They'd expanded the vegetable garden yet again. That was good for Bernie, who was never in danger of going hungry across the green in his St. Anne's hideaway, but it was adding to their increased workload, too.

Mac nodded his thanks and headed off toward the vegetable patches. Ivy smiled awkwardly at Lady Ramsay, feeling grubby and unkempt.

"I'll show you the borders, Lady Ramsay," she said.

"Oh, call me Win."

Ivy blinked. "Really?"

"Absolutely. Lady Ramsay sounds like a stuffy old bag, wouldn't you agree?"

Despite herself, Ivy smiled, finding herself warming to the woman.

"Win," she said.

She led her down the broad path toward the herbaceous borders, telling Lady Ramsay—Win—some facts about the Gardens as they went.

"It's one of the longest borders in the world, so Mac says."

Win looked impressed. "All tended to by you girls?"

Ivy puffed up her chest. "Every bit."

"Wonderful," said Win. She looked round at the glorious display of flowers stretching in every direction. The Gardens really were at their best during summer and Ivy felt a flush of pride as she saw them through a stranger's eyes. The colors and scents, and the bees and butterflies darting among the plants all made Kew seem like a haven, a sanctuary, somewhere the poisonous tendrils of the war didn't reach.

As though she'd read her mind, Win glanced at Ivy.

"I saw you with a letter," she said. "Sweetheart off at the Front?"

Ivy pinched her lips together and nodded. "Just gone." She took a deep breath so as not to cry. "First letter."

Win squeezed her arm. "Then we shall keep each other's spirits up, because I know just how you're feeling."

"Really?" Ivy didn't want to be rude, but Lady Ramsay had to be well into her fifties and unless her husband was far younger than she, it seemed unlikely that he had enlisted.

"My husband, Archie, is serving in the Dover Patrol," Win said. "That's where we live, you see. I've just come up to our London house so I can help out here."

Two houses? Imagine. Ivy thought about her brothers and sisters spilling out of the terrace in Hackney and felt that rush of annoyance again. Fortunately, Louisa arrived before Ivy said anything she might regret.

"Mac said I had to come and meet our new gardener," Louisa said, striding over. Ivy saw, with amusement, that she reacted to Win in exactly the same way as Ivy had, running a disapproving eye over her hair, her dress, her basket.

"This is Lady Ramsay," Ivy said. Louisa looked surprised and unsure how to react. She paused and Win chuckled.

"Call me Win," she said. She held out her hand and Louisa shook it.

"Win's from Kent," Ivy told Louisa. She turned to Win. "So is Louisa."

"Marvelous, a local girl," Win said, delighted. "Whereabouts?"

"Tiny village called Cassingham, quite near Maidstone."

"I was just telling Ivy that I'm from Dover."

Louisa nodded politely, not overly interested.

"My husband's serving in the Dover Patrol. He's too old, really, but he's been in the Navy for donkeys' years so they snapped him up."

Win's smile wavered, just a bit. "But I miss him terribly."

Ivy and Louisa exchanged a glance. Ivy felt a sudden connection to this woman, realizing that however many houses she had, or how many pretty dresses she wore, the feeling of missing a loved one was the same.

"I find keeping busy in the Gardens really helps me," Ivy said. "You almost see time passing because the plants change every day. And I think every day that goes by brings me closer to seeing Jim again."

Win nodded.

"That's exactly what I hoped," she said. "I was rattling round in that big house down in Dover. And I kept looking out of the window, watching the sea, hoping I'd catch a glimpse of Archie's boat, and then worrying I'd see it attacked or sinking and not be able to do anything about it."

She swallowed a sob, and again Ivy felt sorry for her.

"And I thought to myself, 'Win, you're driving yourself mad here; get up to London and help with the war effort.' The only thing I'm really any good at is gardening so I popped in here and that charming Douglas said he'd find something for me to do. I was thrilled, darlings, because it's just what I need."

Ivy thought back to their first day at Kew, with Mac pacing along the line of recruits, quizzing them on their skills.

"He didn't interview you?"

Win shook her head. "Nothing as formal as that. I just said I'd help out where I could." She looked round at the flowers. "It's so delightful here, I thought it would keep my mind off whatever Archie is doing."

"Wait, you're just helping out?" Louisa said, frowning. "You're not working here officially?"

"Heavens, no. I've never had a job in my life."

Again, Ivy exchanged a look with Lou. "You're not being paid?"

Win let out a peal of laughter that send a couple of starlings whirling up from a nearby tree.

"Paid? No."

There was a pause.

"Let me take you to the borders and perhaps you can do some deadheading," Ivy said. She let Win go ahead and then pulled Louisa's hand to slow her down.

"She's not being paid," she hissed. "We need to talk about this."

"Veg patch at lunch," Louisa said.

And so, after a tiring morning spent discovering that when Win said she was good at gardening, what she really meant was she was good at telling gardeners what to do, Ivy found Louisa checking that the slugs hadn't eaten all the lettuces.

"She's not being paid," Louisa said, looking up as Ivy approached. "What's going on?"

Ivy crouched down next to her and examined a lettuce. "No idea. Sounds like she just decided it might be fun to wander round the Gardens every now and then, and Mac went for it."

Louisa snorted. "Mac's a sucker for a title and a nice accent."

"Apparently so." Ivy decided the lettuces were fine and moved over to have a look at the cauliflowers.

"Do you know what I'm worried about most of all?"

"That we'll have to start wearing dresses to work again?"

Louisa chuckled. They'd all worn dresses with aprons over them at first but, as time had gone on, most of the women had ditched their unwieldy skirts and opted for the same overalls the men wore.

"No," Louisa said, her expression suddenly serious. "No, I'm worried about what will happen if the chaps in the offices decide we shouldn't be paid, either. What will we do then?"

"That can't happen," Ivy said. "Can it?"

Louisa stood up and brushed down her overalls. "No idea. But why pay us if they can get posh women to do our jobs for nothing?"

"You can't compare us to Win, though. We've got knowledge and experience and expertise."

Louisa shrugged. "I know that, and you know that, and Mac knows that. But what about the people who are in charge? Times are tough, Ivy, and people are tightening their belts everywhere. All those men in the offices will see is numbers on a page in an accounts book—that's all we are to them."

Ivy let out a breath.

"Lord," she said. "What if you're right? What if they ask us to work for nothing?"

"I need a job," Louisa said. There was urgency in her voice—almost panic. "If I don't have a job, I can't pay my rent. And if I can't pay my rent, then I'll end up back on the farm with Reg. I can't have that, Ivy."

She looked like she might cry so Ivy stood up, too, and took her hands.

"I won't let that happen, Lou. Don't worry."

"What can we do about it, though?"

"I guess the first thing we need to do is speak to Mac."

Louisa nodded. "Yes, that's the best thing. Find out what's really happening and we can go from there."

"Do you know where he is? We could find him now."

"I saw him heading for the break room with Win."

"Let's go."

Together they wandered over toward the building, chatting quietly about which veg they could pick to take to Bernie.

"It's easy now, but Lord knows what we'll do in autumn," said Ivy. "We'll have to start pickling cabbage for him." She was only half joking. She'd been having sleepless nights wondering how much longer Bernie could stay hidden away in the crypt.

But Louisa smiled.

"Don't fret," she said. "I have something up my sleeve."

"Did you go to the Peace meeting?" Ivy had forgotten all about it, so absorbed was she in her grief and worry about Jim.

"I did." Louisa's cheeks flushed pink.

"And?"

"There was a chap there who knows everything there is to know about registering officially as a conscientious objector."

Ivy watched Louisa curiously as she explained about jobs of national importance. Her cheeks reddened every time she mentioned this Teddy who was helping her.

"He's nice, is he, Teddy?" she asked.

"Very nice."

"Hmm."

"What does 'hmm' mean?" Louisa looked flustered.

Ivy grinned. "Nothing," she said. "Carry on."

Still flushed, Louisa explained that she and Teddy were working on a plan.

"I don't want to say too much at the moment in case it doesn't work," she said.

"All right," said Ivy, more intrigued about Teddy than Louisa's plans for Bernie. "Just tell me if you need me to do anything."

They'd reached the building now. There was no sign of Mac, but Dennis was outside, leaning against the wall and smoking a cigarette.

"Mac about?" Ivy called.

He shook his head. "He's gone off with that posh woman. He's taken her to meet the bigwigs in the office."

"No," said Louisa, her eyes widening. "Well, that's that, then."

"Don't panic." Ivy's brain was whirring, as she tried to work out what they should do next.

"What?" said Dennis, who'd never panicked over anything in his life. Slowly, he pushed himself upright off the wall and ground out his cigarette. "Don't panic about what?"

"The new gardener, Lady Ramsay?"

"What about her?"

"She's not being paid."

"What do you mean?"

Louisa looked cross. "She means, Lady Ramsay is only here for fun. She's doing the work because she wants to. And we're worried that if she's working for free, they're going to end up expecting us to work for free, too. Or replace us with other ladies who'll do it instead."

Dennis looked uncharacteristically rattled. "Really?" he said. "Do you think that could happen?"

Ivy shrugged. "Dunno. But why would you pay for something you can get for free?"

"Sod." Dennis chewed his lip. "I can't afford to work for nothing. My dad's off driving ambulances and I'm the only one earning because my sister's too little and my mum's not well. There's little enough of my twenty-eight shillings left after we've paid the rent and bought food for the week."

Ivy looked at Louisa, her shocked face showing that Ivy hadn't misheard what Dennis just said. But she checked anyway.

"Little enough of your . . . ?"

"My twenty-eight shillings." Dennis looked at Ivy as if she were simple. "My wages, I mean."

"You get twenty-eight shillings?" Louisa said. "Every week?"

"Yeeeees."

Ivy and Louisa stared at him, and he stared back.

"What?" he said defensively. "Why are you looking at me?"

"Because we don't earn twenty-eight shillings every week," Ivy said. "We only earn twenty-one shillings."

"You do?"

Louisa looked stern. "Yes, we do. And that's not bloody good enough. We do the same work as you, we should get paid the same."

"Well," said Dennis, "you're women. You don't need to earn the same. It's not like you're supporting a family or nothing."

He let out a little shriek as Ivy grabbed his shoulder and pushed him against the wall.

"Say that again," she hissed.

"I just mean that men have responsibilities, that's all," he stammered.

"My dad goes off for weeks at a time," said Ivy. "My mum works, but her wage on its own doesn't go far with my brothers and sisters. They eat like horses, the lot of them. My wage covers the rent so they keep a roof over their head."

Dennis nodded. "I didn't know that," he muttered.

But Ivy wasn't finished.

"And Louisa here. She's totally independent. She owes nothing to no one. Earns her own money, puts food on her own table. Why shouldn't she be paid the same as a man?"

"You're right," Dennis said. "I'm sorry."

Ivy let go of his shoulder. "Course I'm right. Makes sense, doesn't it?"

"It does." Poor Dennis looked totally taken aback by Ivy's lecture. "Are you going to ask Mac to pay you more? He won't pay me less, will he?"

"Too right we're going to speak to Mac." Ivy's temper was flaring again. "We need to get this sorted out."

But Louisa put a calming hand on her arm.

"Hold on," she said. "We need to work out the best way to approach this. If we go in all guns blazing, he's bound to go on the defensive and before we know it, we'll be out on our ears. We need to present him—and the bigwigs—with reasons for us being paid the same as the men that they can't argue with. And we need to get the other gardeners involved, too. Let them know we're all being paid less just because we're women."

"What about Lady Whatsit?" said Dennis. "Should she be paid the same, too?"

Louisa made a face, but Ivy jumped in.

"Course." She thought for a minute. "It shouldn't be about whether we're men or women, should it? It should be about how long we've worked here and what jobs we do. So perhaps Win—Lady Ramsay—shouldn't get as much as us at the moment, because she's just learning. But once she's got the hang of it, then yes, she definitely should."

Louisa gave Ivy an admiring glance and she preened a bit, pleased to have impressed her friend.

"I reckon you've got a point there, Ivy Adams," Dennis said. "And I'm on board. I'll support you and the other women all the way. But I have to tell you—you've got a fight on your hands."

Chapter 19

It was like someone had lit a fire under Louisa, forcing her to act. Having Bernie to focus on was already helping her put the business with Reg behind her, and now she had the wages to think about, too.

With some help from Ivy, she'd spoken to all the female gardeners and found out they were all being paid the same as she and Ivy were. Dennis, bless him, had been as good as his word and had been very helpful, too. With Jim and Bernie gone, there were only a couple of younger male gardeners left, along with Mac. He'd had a word with them and found out that they, too, were being paid far more than the women. And when Ivy asked Bernie what he'd been paid before Mac sacked him, she was horrified to discover he had also been on the higher salary.

"He knew nothing when he started," she told Louisa as they left the Gardens one day after work. "We had to teach him everything we knew. How can it possibly be fair that he was being paid more money than we were?"

Louisa knew Ivy had been quick to anger since Jim had gone to the

Front, and generally she tried to keep her friend calm when she saw her temper start to flare. But this time she wanted her to be angry.

"It's not fair," she said. "And it's just the latest in a long line of things that aren't fair for women."

Dennis, who was walking behind the women, listening in to their conversation, chimed in.

"Well," he said, "you don't have to go and fight. You're safe in your beds at night, not in a trench."

"Yes," Louisa conceded. "But I bet there are women who would if they could, though."

Dennis shrugged. "Perhaps."

"Anyway, we're not talking about men, we're talking about women. Society is weighted against us and though we can fight for votes for women and other equal rights, I feel helpless when it comes to the big things."

Ivy nodded.

Encouraged, Louisa went on. "This is something we can change," she said. "This is somewhere we can really make a difference."

"So what shall we do?"

"I'm going to arrange a meeting of all the gardeners. We need to do this together."

Ivy nodded. "Good."

They'd reached the gates.

"Are you going home? I'll walk with you to the bus stop."

Louisa felt slightly embarrassed.

"I'm meeting Teddy," she said, feeling her cheeks redden as they did every time she spoke about her new friend. And whenever she thought about him, which was surprisingly frequently. "He's got some news about Bernie."

Ivy gave Louisa a mischievous grin, which she pretended not to see.

"Seeing a lot of Teddy, aren't you?"

"He's being very helpful."

Teddy was being helpful, that was true, but Louisa enjoyed spending time with him. He was gentle and sad, but kind and had moments of humor or levity that made Lou's heart sing.

"I know how short life can be," he had told her once. "And so I try to find the joy in everyday things. The sparkle of the sun on puddles after a shower of rain. The smell of bread in the morning."

He gave her a quick, sudden smile.

"I even try to find the positives in the sound of the children kicking their football against my wall."

Louisa had tried to take a leaf out of Teddy's book and every night before she went to sleep she would mentally list the good things that had happened that day. Praise from Mac, laughing with Ivy, eating for lunch tomatoes she'd grown herself, which tasted of the sun. It was a good way to end each day. She was sure that as she drifted off tonight, she'd add "spending time with Teddy" to her list.

He met her at the St. James's Park tube station and they wandered off toward the park together. They always headed for green spaces when they met. Partly, Louisa thought, because it made their conversation harder to overhear, and partly just because walking in the park had become something they did. She liked it.

"Tell me everything," she said as they walked. "What's new?"

Teddy looked pleased with himself. "It's all in place. As good as signed off."

Louisa felt light-headed with relief. "Really?"

"As long as you've got what we need?"

She went over to a nearby bench and sat down so she could riffle through her bag more easily.

"I do."

She found what she was looking for and brandished it triumphantly. "Here."

What she was gripping in her hand was a letter from her brother, Matthew. In it, he'd outlined how hard things were on the farm now that all their staff had enlisted. He wrote that their hops were ready and their apples would need picking very soon and how with so few farmhands to help, the fruit was in danger of rotting on the branches. He added that they had expanded their vegetable gardens and had recently bought three dairy cows, who were providing enough milk for all the children in Cassingham. But he was worried about how to keep things going. Matthew wrote:

> *My father does what he can, but he is not as fit as he was, and my children are too small to do much. Our farm is well-established and can easily provide food for our village, as well as providing a good harvest of apples for the wider community. But only if we have some help. I firmly feel that employment as a farmhand with us would be work of national importance and Bernard Yorke's particular skills will be extremely valuable.*

In a separate letter to Louisa, Matthew wrote:

> *Reg has gone to Folkestone to stay with his sister, who he says will look after him better than we do. He says he will be back, but frankly he is no use anyway and I'd rather he stayed away. Do not worry about him coming to London. Me and the lads from the pub had a word and he'll think twice before he bothers you again. Hope the enclosed letter does enough to ensure we can give your friend a job. We need his help desperately.*

Teddy read the official letter Matthew had written, nodding as he did.

"Perfect," he declared. "I'll take this tomorrow and register him. But it's stronger than the argument I made for another lad a few weeks ago and they approved that."

Louisa let out a gasp of air and leaned back against the bench.

"Oh my," she said. "I never thought we would do it. Can I come with you tomorrow?"

"What about work?"

"Mac will understand. He feels as bad about Bernie as I do."

Teddy smiled at her, and Louisa felt like the sun had come out on a rainy day. "I'd like you to come."

And so, the next day, she and Teddy made their way to the building that housed the tribunals for conscientious objectors. It was an imposing government office, close to the Houses of Parliament, but Louisa didn't let herself feel intimidated. She had to make this work. For Bernie's sake.

They had to wait rather a long time, in a long, quiet corridor lined with a horrible tiled floor. There were others waiting, too, and every time one of the dark wooden doors opened, everyone looked up hopefully, only to look down again when their name wasn't called. Eventually, a small mousy woman scurried through one of the doors, clutching a folder.

"Bernard Yorke," she said.

"That's us." Teddy stood up. "Are you coming in?"

Louisa nodded and stood up, too. "Of course."

In the end, it was quite straightforward. Frightening and rather too much like a courtroom for Louisa's liking but straightforward. There were two men at a table at the front of the room, and the mousy woman sitting to one side, taking notes.

"Ah, Mr. Armitage," said one of the men, not unkindly. "Here again, I see."

"I'm like a bad penny," Teddy said. "Sirs, I come to you today on behalf of Bernard Yorke, a former teacher who has found a hitherto undiscovered talent for growing plants. He wishes to register as a conscientious objector and instead work on a farm in Kent, growing food for the local area."

He stepped forward and handed Matthew's letter, along with some other paperwork, to the man who'd spoken. The man read it carefully and excruciatingly slowly and then handed it over to the other man, who did the same. Louisa felt a bead of sweat trickle down her spine and gather in the small of her back.

Finally, the first man looked up.

"This all seems to be in order," he said. "We will need confirmation of Yorke's wages."

"Of course. I'll arrange that," said Teddy. Louisa knew the conscientious objectors had to be paid the same as they would earn as a soldier—which wasn't much. But she also knew Matthew would give Bernie somewhere to stay and feed him and generally see him right.

The second man scribbled something on a form and handed it to the mousy woman, who took out a large stamp and thumped it onto the paper. Then she held it out to Teddy.

"All done," she said. "He should report to the farm before Friday or he will be arrested."

And that was it.

"I can't believe we've all been worrying for so long and that took less than quarter of an hour," Louisa said as they made their way back to Kew. Teddy hadn't wanted to come with her, but she'd talked him into it.

"I want you to tell Bernie what you've done for him," she said.

"You did all the organization with your family. I just helped with the paperwork."

Louisa patted his arm. "That's nonsense and you know it."

Ivy was waiting by the entrance to the tube station.

"You've been so long," she said, always one for a drama. "I've been waiting forever."

"It's only three o'clock," Louisa said mildly. "Ivy, this is Teddy Armitage."

Ivy gave Teddy an approving look and shook his hand with gusto.

"Pleasure to meet you," she said. "Let's go."

Together, they raced across the green to St. Anne's and, to their utter astonishment, found Bernie sitting on the grass at the back of the church, chatting with the vicar.

Ivy, who was leading the way, stopped abruptly, and Louisa charged into her, followed by Teddy, like they were clowns at a circus.

Bernie and the vicar looked round at the kerfuffle and Bernie stood up.

"Good heavens," he said. "Hello."

He came to Louisa and threw his arms round her, squeezing her tightly. "It's so nice to see you."

Louisa wasn't sure what to say.

"And you," she managed to stutter. "We weren't expecting to see you . . ." She lowered her voice. "Out here."

Bernie looked sheepish. "Ah, well, I've been keeping my hand in, as it were."

He stepped back and showed them a row of beautifully tended graves, each with its own little patch of garden blooming with flowers.

Ivy's and Louisa's jaws dropped. Teddy just looked confused. And the vicar didn't look surprised in the slightest. Louisa glanced from him to Bernie and back again.

"We've reached an understanding," Bernie said. "Reverend Miller and I."

Louisa blinked. "Goodness."

"Bernard has been most helpful around the churchyard, tending plots, planting flowers, cutting the grass," the vicar said. "Most helpful. Especially as I am getting rather forgetful in my old age."

He gave the women a very definite, rather cheeky wink.

"I sometimes forget things I've seen, or people's names, or whether I've left doors unlocked. I even leave books lying around where anyone could pick them up and sometimes I've even been known to forget where I've put a plate of food," he said.

Louisa looked at him. He seemed perfectly fine to her. He winked again and she let out a bubble of laughter. This nice man had been helping Bernie, too.

Unable to hide her glee any longer, she turned to Teddy.

"Bernie, this is a friend of mine, Teddy Armitage. He helps men who want to register officially as conscientious objectors. And he's done it for you."

Bernie looked like he might fall over.

"What?" he said. "What do you mean?"

"I mean, I've arranged for you to work with my brother, Matthew, on our family's farm. It's all sorted out. Matt will give you somewhere to live. And as long as you get there by Friday, you're off the hook. You'll be doing work of national importance, and you won't be called up."

Bernie's face went red, then white, then red again. Teddy held out the official form and he took it, gazing at it in wonder.

"I don't need to fight?" he breathed.

"No."

"Why would you do this for me?"

"Because it was my fault you lost your job," Louisa said. "It was my fault Mac reported you, and it was my fault your landlady kicked you out. And I was wrong, Bernie."

Bernie shrugged as though the awful things Louisa had done were of no consequence to him. "You were just doing what you thought was right."

Louisa nodded. "Yes, but I was wrong. And I'm sorry."

Bernie waved the form at her. "You've more than made up for it."

"Teddy did all the official bits," Louisa said, not wanting to take all the credit.

Bernie turned his gaze on to Teddy. "I'm a stranger to you. Why would you work so hard for someone you've never met?"

Teddy shifted from one foot to the other.

"I lost my son, early in the war," he said awkwardly. "Don't like to think about those who don't want to go being forced to fight."

"You're a good man."

Bernie and Teddy nodded at each other in a manly way. Louisa thought they both really wanted to hug but it simply wouldn't have crossed their minds to do so.

"You can go today if you like," she said. "Matt's expecting you. And there are trains from Charing Cross until evening."

Bernie looked amazed. "And it's all official? I don't need to worry about being spotted or arrested?"

"All official," Teddy said.

Ivy threw her arms round Bernie and hugged him.

"I'm going to miss you so much," she said. "I'll come to Charing Cross with you, shall I? See you off."

"I'd like that. I'd like you both to come."

"I can't," Louisa said, genuinely sorry. "I've got a meeting with the gardeners later."

"What about?"

"Wages," Ivy said, a flash of anger in her eyes. "Remember, Bernie? I was quizzing you the other day about what you'd been paid."

Bernie chuckled. "I do remember and I reckon Mac needs to watch his back, with you two on the warpath," he said.

Ivy looked up at the clock on the church tower.

"In fact, you need to get going, Lou," she said, nudging her.

Louisa nodded. "Then I'll say good-bye, Bernie. But when you're settled, I shall come and visit. It's time I went to see my parents and met my new baby niece."

"I'd like that."

They hugged, and Louisa turned to Teddy. "Shall I walk with you across the green?"

He nodded.

"I can never repay your kindness," Bernie said, clasping Teddy's hand. "And I am so sorry about your son."

Teddy smiled. "Live life," he said. "That's the best way to repay me."

"I shall."

Feeling emotional, Louisa led the way out of the churchyard and across the green. As they reached the gates of the Gardens, they paused.

"Do you know the way back to the station?"

Teddy nodded. "I do."

To Louisa's surprise, he reached out and took her hand. "I can't imagine not seeing you so frequently," he said. "I've very much enjoyed getting to know you."

Louisa felt her cheeks flame again, but she was thrilled with his words.

"I feel the same."

"Would it be all right if, perhaps, we went walking again? Perhaps at the weekend?"

Louisa's smile was so broad it felt like she might split her cheeks wide open.

"I'd like that very much."

Tentatively, Teddy leaned forward and kissed Louisa lingeringly on the cheek. She breathed in the smell of him for a second before he let go.

How extraordinary to feel so connected to a man, after everything that had happened with Reg. How extraordinary and how wonderful.

"Then, Louisa Taylor, I will see you very soon."

He tipped his hat at her, and warm with happiness, Louisa watched him walk away.

Chapter 20

Floating on air, Louisa headed to the break room, where she'd arranged to meet with all the female gardeners. She hoped enough of them would get on board with her efforts to secure them pay equal with the men's because she knew this sort of fight was always easier as a team.

To her surprise—and delight—every single female gardener showed up. Except Ivy, of course, who was off at Charing Cross saying good-bye to Bernie but had promised to be back as soon as she could. There were so many women there that Louisa decided it would be better to go outside, so they all gathered under one of the large trees and sat on the grass while Louisa talked. Dennis was there, too, which helped Louisa argue her case.

"We do exactly the same work as the men," she said. "In some cases, we've been here longer and have more experience working with plants than they do. They're only being paid more because they are men."

"It's because they're breadwinners, though, isn't it?" said one gardener, called Harriet. She looked worried as she spoke. "They need to support their families."

Louisa nodded. "Yes, many of the men who work here are the bread-winners in their homes," she agreed. She looked round at the women sit-ting on the grass in front of her. "Can I just ask for a show of hands? How many of you are the only one earning in your household?"

About half the gardeners put their hands up.

"And how many of you would be in real trouble if you weren't bring-ing in a wage?"

Now everyone raised their hands—including Harriet. Louisa smiled.

"We all need money. Some of us are single, some of our husbands are off at the Front—or back with injuries and unable to earn. Some of us live with our parents and need to contribute. Someone's personal circum-stances aren't relevant here. What matters is the work they're doing and how much they deserve to be paid for that work."

There was a murmur of agreement.

"But what can we do about it?" another woman called from the back of the group. She was a similar age to Louisa, bringing up three children alone, and was lean and wiry and strong as an ox. "What if they think we're just causing trouble and they sack us all?"

"That's the thing about working together," Louisa said. "They simply can't sack us all. If we're all in agreement, we can present a united front to Mac and the bigwigs. If they say no, then we'll move on to something else, come up with a different plan, but for now we all need to be speaking with one voice."

"Hmm," the woman said, obviously not completely on board.

Louisa looked at her.

"I don't know you, not really." She searched her memory for the wom-an's name. Frannie, that was it. "But we've worked together a few times, haven't we, Frannie?"

"We have, yes."

"I know how hard you work. I know how fast you dug out the new vegetable patches, and how strong you are."

Frannie looked pleased. "It needed doing and I always think it's best just to get on and do something."

"Do you think Dennis here could have done it faster?"

"Not a chance."

Dennis looked offended, and then shrugged.

"She's got a point," he conceded, grinning. "Fran's faster than I am."

"And could he have done it better?"

"Nope. It is what it is. Either it's dug or it's not. There's no better about it."

Louisa wasn't sure that was true, but it didn't matter. "Right. So you dug it faster, and just as well as Dennis could have?"

"Yes." Frannie raised an eyebrow at the woman sitting next to her, obviously not sure where she was going.

Louisa was doing some sums in her head.

"And yet for that morning's work you got paid one shilling and six-pence, while Dennis got two shillings."

Fran's eyes widened. "Well, when you put it like that."

"It's not fair."

"No, it's not."

The women all started talking again and Louisa shushed them.

"We're doing men's work while they're away. If the gardeners all came back from the Front tomorrow, they'd pay them properly so we know they've got the money."

"We can't all go and demand extra pay, though, can we?" Fran was still being bullish.

"No, that would just get them defensive, I think."

"So what, then?"

"I'd like to write a letter, spelling out our requirements, and have all of you sign it. Even you, Dennis, if you're willing? And the other men if we can get them on board."

"What are our requirements?"

"To be paid the same as the male gardeners for doing the same job."

"What about the new recruits?" someone called.

"I think there should be a probationary period, perhaps, when they're paid less, but then after a few months they should earn the same as the rest of us."

Louisa was enjoying this. She'd missed the focus of being a Suffragette while the war was on, and Reg's reappearance had reminded her how unfair things were for women. She couldn't divorce him, much as she wanted to. She couldn't vote while he—drunken layabout that he was—could. Good as she was at her job, she knew she was just taking care of it while the men were away, and that after the war she'd be out on her ear. It all made her want to scream with frustration and anger. But she wouldn't scream. No, she'd fight for her rights instead.

She looked at the women gathered in front of her.

"Who is with me?" she said.

Slowly, all the women raised their hands—even Dennis stuck his mud-encrusted fingers up in the air. Louisa clapped with excitement.

"Excellent," she said. "I'll get the letter written up this evening, and I'll circulate it round for you all to sign. We should get cracking on this as soon as we can. I don't know about you, but I'm finding it hard to give my all at work, now that I know we're not valued as highly as our male colleagues."

The women all chuckled and muttered in agreement. Dennis looked slightly shamefaced and Louisa felt proud of him for coming to the meeting and being on their side. He was a good lad. Just as Jim was. She wondered, as she always did when she thought of Jim, what he was doing now and if he was safe. She hoped that he was—and not just for Ivy's sake.

Speaking of the devil, Ivy appeared. She was slightly red faced and had a smear of train dust on her cheek, but she looked happy.

"Sorry I'm late. Had to see a friend off on a train," she said to the group, but really to Louisa. Relieved that Bernie had gotten off all right,

Louisa waited for Ivy to sit down on the grass with the others and opened her mouth to carry on . . .

"Hello, girls. What's all this?" a voice said. Louisa looked round and her heart sank as she saw Lady Ramsay trotting across the lawn toward the group.

"Just a staff meeting," she said, hoping Win wouldn't stay. But Win looked round at the other women in delight and waved hello to several of them. How did she know so many of the other gardeners already?

"Wonderful," she sang. "Charming." She sat herself down on the grass next to Harriet. "What are we discussing?"

"Wages," said Harriet.

Louisa rolled her eyes. She didn't want Win involved, because it was finding out she was just a volunteer that had led to this whole thing. And somehow she didn't think someone with a title and two houses would be interested in their struggle to make ends meet. She tried to meet Ivy's gaze to see if she felt the same, but Ivy was watching Win with a mixture of amusement and affection.

"What about them?" Win looked curious.

"We've just discovered that we all get paid less than the men, for doing the same job," Fran explained.

Win blinked and looked up at Louisa, realization dawning in her eyes. Louisa braced herself for Win to announce that she didn't get paid at all for her *charming* job, *darling*. But instead Win gave her a small nod as if to say, "That stays between us."

"You get paid less than the men?" Win said to Fran. "Well, that's simply ridiculous, my darling. You're keeping this place running and, let's face it, it's hardly an easy job, is it? I've only been here five minutes and I'm exhausted."

Despite herself, Louisa laughed. She'd sorely misjudged Win. She'd assumed that because of her nice dress, neat hair and cut-glass accent that she wouldn't be one of them. But she really was. Ivy had been right about that, too.

Louisa grinned at Win. "I thought I'd write a letter, spelling out our demands, and have everyone sign it," she told her.

Win made a face. "Really?"

"Well, I think it makes sense to be clear about what we want."

"Absolutely. I just think we should take some action, too." Win got up and went over to where Louisa was standing in front of the group. "You know who I've always admired? The Suffragettes."

A disapproving whisper spread among the gardeners.

"They burned down the tea pavilion," Louisa said in an undertone to Win. "Not many of the gardeners here approve."

Win smiled and addressed the group again.

"Oh heavens, I know they've made some mistakes. Haven't we all, darlings? But we all know about them, don't we? We all know what they want and we're still talking about it, even though they've been quiet recently."

She was right. Louisa and Ivy smiled at each other. Who'd have thought someone like Win would talk this way?

"What I propose is some direct action," Win was saying.

"I ain't burning anything," said Fran, looking mutinous.

"Absolutely not. No, I propose something a little more . . . mathematical."

"Mathematical?" Louisa was confused but Win looked gleeful.

"At the moment, you're being paid three-quarters of what the men get, right?"

"Right."

"So, why not do three-quarters of the work?"

"What do you mean?" Harriet said. "Just down our tools?"

"That's precisely what I mean. You work twelve hours a day, don't you? So I propose you stop after nine. Why should you work for the extra quarter of a day that, to all intents and purposes, you're not being paid for?"

Louisa stared at her. This was brilliant. Simple, but brilliant. A hub-bub of voices started up as the women all discussed it. Louisa could tell from the tone that they were on board.

"Send your letter," Win said. "Explain what we're going to do. And then we'll take action." She turned to the group once more and they all quietened down to hear what she had to say.

"We'll win this fight," she said.

As the women cheered and surrounded Win, asking questions, Ivy found her way over to Louisa.

"Bloody hell," she said, looking at the women gathering round the new recruit.

"Bloody hell is right." Louisa was amused and unexpectedly pleased that Win had got involved. "I never for one minute expected that."

They both laughed.

"Bernie got on the train all right, did he?"

"He was quite excited I think. Looking forward to getting his hands in the dirt again."

Louisa thought of the well-cared-for churchyard and grinned. "He's been doing enough of that at St. Anne's. I'm glad it's all worked out, though. I felt so awful about everything."

"It's worked out better in a way because of your involvement," Ivy pointed out. "If you'd not given him the feathers, he'd still be worried about being found out every day. And perhaps someone else would have exposed him anyway."

Louisa made a face.

"I suppose," she said. "It's not going to be plain sailing down in Kent. Matthew said not everyone was thrilled at the idea of him employing a conchie, official or not."

"Bernie's tougher than you think."

"I hope so."

They looked round as Win approached.

"Darlings," she sang. "What an exciting meeting. I'm so glad I came."

Louisa grinned at her. "We're glad you came, too. It's a great idea to work three-quarters of a day to make our point."

"Well, I just thought to myself, 'What would Mrs. Pankhurst do?' and it came to me in a flash. I think the Suffragettes are simply wonderful women."

Louisa and Ivy exchanged a look again, but this time Win caught it. She was sharp as a tack, that one.

"What?" she said. "What aren't you telling me?" She looked from Ivy to Louisa and back again, and she gasped. "Are you Suffragettes? How thrilling."

Quickly, Louisa steered Win away from the other gardeners who were still milling about.

"Shhh. We keep it quiet here because Mac's not keen after the pavilion fire. We don't want to lose our jobs."

"But you are Suffragettes?"

The women both nodded.

"We were," said Louisa. "Things have got rather quiet now, with the war going on. I've got a meeting I go to regularly, though there's not much action happening."

"Could I come? To a meeting?"

"I don't see why not." Louisa suspected her Suffragette friends would adore Win immediately. "Ivy's got more involved with the Federation over in East London."

"With Sylvia?" Win talked as though she was a close personal friend of Mrs. Pankhurst's daughter. "How marvelous. I hear she's doing some rather exciting things over there."

Ivy nodded, her eyes wide with wonder at everything Win was saying. "You should come and see."

"I'd like that."

Louisa watched the two women forming a bond and found she was pleased for them both. Ivy's family life was chaotic to say the least and having older women she could rely on could only be a good thing. She smiled. Perhaps having an older woman around could be good for her, too. She was pleased to be back in contact with her own mother but the memory of her siding with Reg would always hurt, and she missed having someone to talk to who could share experiences and offer guidance.

She smiled at Win.

"I think you're going to be a very good addition to the Kew Gardens Girls," she said.

Chapter 21

Ivy was smitten with Lady Ramsay. She'd never met anyone quite like her before. It wasn't just that she was posh and well-educated—Ivy had met lots of women like that through the Suffragettes. And it wasn't that she cared about what Ivy considered to be "normal people." After all, Sylvia Pankhurst ticked all those boxes. It was more that Win was all those things and, on top of it, she was an absolute hoot. She was just such fun to be around: willing to learn everything there was to know about gardening, not afraid to get her hands dirty, and curious ("I'm horribly nosy, darling," she would say) about everyone's lives outside of Kew.

Louisa wrote the letter outlining the women's plan to work three-quarters of a day, and together, she, Ivy and Win gave it to Mac.

"I know you're not the one who'd make a final decision," Louisa said as she handed it over. "But if you come round to our way of thinking I know the managers will listen to what you have to say."

Mac had looked dubious. "I didn't expect this from you."

"Really?" Ivy said, raising one eyebrow.

Mac, despite himself, laughed. "Yes, maybe I expected it from you, Ivy Adams. But not you, Louisa."

It was Louisa's turn to look surprised. "I've been known to make a bit of trouble in my time, Mac," she pointed out, and Mac laughed again.

"Christ, you're right." He looked at Win. "But not you, Lady Ramsay."

Win lifted her chin, showing off her long, elegant neck and peered at him down her nose.

"I'm the worst of the lot," she said.

Mac knew when he was beaten.

"Fine," he said. "I'll read the letter and I'll think about it."

"Don't think for too long because we're only doing three-quarters of our usual work. I imagine things will fall apart rather quickly," Louisa warned.

Then they'd walked out, leaving Mac staring after them in shock.

⎯⎯ ❧❦❧ ⎯⎯

On their first shorter day, when the time to down tools drew near, Ivy went round the Gardens, spreading the word and asking each gardener she passed to tell another. Eventually, just after the chimes of the hour rang out across the green from St. Anne's clock tower, the women all gathered by the break room, looking nervous and thrilled about what they were doing.

"I was thinning out the border," Fran complained.

"It'll keep until tomorrow."

"I was pleased to stop weeding," said another gardener, flexing her fingers. "It's so boring."

"Same again tomorrow," Win reminded them. "Let's keep it up as long as we can. I don't reckon it'll take them too long to notice how much you all do."

"We all do," Ivy corrected her. Far from being the liability she and Louisa had expected, Win had already proved herself to be a big help around the Gardens.

"Can I take you charming girls for tea to celebrate our first day of direct action?" Win asked. Ivy accepted eagerly, but Louisa frowned.

"I can't, sorry," she said. She didn't look very sorry, much to Ivy's amusement. "I'm going for a walk with Teddy."

Ivy squeezed Louisa's arm to show she was pleased for her, but didn't say anything because Louisa was liable to clam up every time she was asked anything about Teddy.

"Just you and me, then," Win said. "Shall we?"

Win offered Ivy her arm and together they wandered across the Gardens to the gate nearest the bridge. Summer was in its final flourishes now, and everything felt hot and sleepy. Even the bees looked drowsy as they buzzed slowly round the heavy-headed flowers. Ivy didn't like late summer as a rule, but this year she was trying to embrace it because it was another sign that time was passing.

She led the way over the bridge and then to a tea shop that Win pronounced, predictably, "charming" because it had a view of the river.

"So, Ivy," Win said, when they were both seated and had ordered tea "and two slices of your most delicious cake, thank you, darling" from the cheerful waitress, "I want to know everything about your sweetheart."

Ivy felt a lurch of sorrow and fear, as she always did when she thought of Jim, and then of happiness as she thought of their letters.

"His name is Jim and he's the sweetest, kindest, gentlest man you could ever meet. And he's a wonderful gardener."

"Good with his hands?" Win winked at her and Ivy blushed.

"Win!" she said, shocked.

Win laughed a throaty chuckle and gestured for Ivy to carry on.

"He's funny and brave and really clever."

"Is he handsome?"

"So handsome."

Win beamed at her. "And is he writing you wonderful love letters? My Archie's been sending me the most gorgeous notes. He's been writing sweet nothings that he's not said out loud since we were courting. It's quite the eye-opener."

Ivy looked down at the table. Should she fess up to her difficulties with reading and writing? What would Win think?

"Well," she said, "we've been doing something a bit different."

"Different?"

"I can tell you, but it's better if I show you. I'll take you after tea, if you don't mind going back to the Gardens?"

"Not at all," Win said, clearly intrigued.

"In the meantime you can tell me all about your Archie. Bet he's handsome in his naval uniform."

Win's eyes gleamed. "Isn't he just," she said.

They ate their cake and drank their tea and talked about Archie's job in the Dover Patrol, preventing the Germans from entering the English Channel.

"Sounds dangerous," Ivy said, then kicked herself for saying so as she watched Win's smile falter.

"It is dangerous. It is. Archie downplays it, but I have nights when I can't sleep for worrying."

"Is it just you and him? No kids?"

Again Win's smile faltered and again Ivy felt rotten for saying the wrong thing.

"We were never blessed with children, but we have lots of nieces and nephews. I'm very proud to be an auntie."

"I bet they love you," Ivy said honestly. "They're lucky to have you."

Win waved away her compliments, but she looked pleased. "Would you like to have children one day? You and your Jim?"

"I'm only sixteen, Win," Ivy said. But she had to admit she'd thought about it. Or perhaps more honestly, she'd worried about it. She took a swig of tea and forced herself to grin at her new friend.

"Jim says we'll get married one day." But then it was there again, the terror of never seeing him again. Of never being his wife. She felt sick suddenly and pushed away her plate without finishing every crumb of cake like she did usually.

"Had enough?"

Ivy nodded.

Win fixed her with her sharp eyes. "Then why don't you show me how you and your Jim are keeping in touch?"

Together, they walked back across the bridge and into the Gardens. Dennis was just finishing work, looking exhausted.

"Nice afternoon, eh?" he called to them as they passed.

"Lovely, thank you," Ivy shouted back, feeling ever so slightly guilty but still proud of what they were doing.

She led Win round the back of the break room and across to what had once been a neglected corner of the Gardens.

Then, taking a breath and avoiding Win's curious stare, she explained what was going on.

"I never learned to read and write properly when I was little," she said in a hurry. "I was always trailing after my dad at the market or running round the Gardens. I was never that interested in letters and stuff. When I started work here, our friend Bernie said he'd teach me and he did—a bit—but not enough for writing letters or reading them."

"I see," Win said.

"So when Jim enlisted, I was so scared because I thought we'd not be able to keep in touch and I knew I'd miss him so bad. But, like I said, he's clever, and he came up with a plan."

"Which was?"

Ivy stepped back and, with a flourish, showed Win the patch of garden she was standing next to.

"Ta-da," she said softly. "This is my letter garden."

Behind her was a riot of color. There were some tiny seedlings, some bigger plants, lots of flowers, and a few herbs. It wasn't very organized, but it was well looked after and Ivy was very pleased with it.

"What's this?" Win said. "What have you done here?"

"Jim doesn't write me letters. He knows there's no point because I can't read them. Instead, he sends me things from France. To grow."

"Ohhhh," Win breathed. "How wonderful."

Having not told anyone what she was growing in her little patch of garden until now, Ivy found she was suddenly eager to share everything with Win.

"The plants all mean things," she explained. "Jim and me, we've always talked about the language of flowers. It used to be a thing people did, years ago—they'd send little posies to each other with hidden meanings."

"That's what you meant when you said the red roses meant mourning," Win said, understanding dawning on her face.

"Well, yes, that's true. But I was nasty to say it," Ivy admitted.

"These flowers all mean something?'

Ivy clapped her hands. "Yes, but I never know what they mean until they grow. Jim sends me seeds, you see. Or bulbs. And I plant them here and they grow and I understand what he was telling me."

Win looked around her in wonder. "Every plant here, they all have a hidden meaning?"

"They do."

"Like what?"

Ivy bounced over to a patch of pink carnations. "He sent me these first. These were the first seeds he sent. I wasn't sure what to make of it, but I asked Mac if I could plant them somewhere and he said I could use this patch here. I planted them, and these carnations grew."

"And they mean?"

"I'll never forget you."

"Oh." Win's eyes filled with tears. "How sweet. What else?"

"He sent me hyacinth bulbs," Ivy went on. "I'll plant them in a few weeks and they'll flower at Christmas. I don't know for sure, but I reckon they'll be blue, because they mean constancy of love. And this is heliotrope."

She showed Win a small green shrub.

"I don't think it'll flower until next year, but there's enough there for me to recognize it."

"What does that symbolize?"

"Eternal love."

Win was speechless with delight.

"This is the most romantic thing I've ever seen," she said. "I can't believe it."

Ivy was thrilled that her letter garden had such a good reception. "I know. I'm so lucky."

"Do you send him seeds?"

She shook her head. "No point, is there? He's got nowhere to grow them."

"So what do you send him?"

"I'll show you."

Ivy sat down on a nearby bench and pulled her sketchbook out of her bag. Since Bernie had given it to her, she'd filled it with drawings of flowers and pressed cuttings and it was bulging.

Very carefully, she opened it to a page she had marked, and showed Win what was inside. It was a frond of fern, pressed flat and stuck to a page of writing paper.

"I'm going to send this one tomorrow."

"Does it have a secret meaning?"

Ivy nodded. "Bonds of love," she said. "Never to be broken."

Win pulled out a handkerchief with WLR embroidered on the corner and dabbed her eyes.

"This is simply precious," she said. "Precious."

"I press the flowers and leaves in a book Bernie gave me and when they're done I send them. Sometimes I draw them instead. I draw the flowers that I've grown from the seeds, and I draw the garden, too. I want him to see what he's given me."

She showed Win her sketch pad with the many pictures inside. Rapt, Win leafed through the pages, sighing at almost every drawing.

"My goodness," Win said. "This is really something." She nodded. "I think your Jim is a keeper, Ivy. Don't you ever let him go."

Ivy shuddered as she spoke, feeling doom hanging heavy overhead.

"I won't," she said. "But it's not up to me, is it?"

There was a moment's silence as the two women thought about how helpless they were, and then Win forced a smile.

"Perhaps you could help me send something to my Archie?"

"Course I could. What do you want to say?"

"Be strong?" Win suggested. "Is there anything that says that?"

Ivy nodded. "Bit of a weird one, strength. It's thyme, the herb. So your letter will smell good, too."

"Charming," Win muttered. "What about patriotism? Is there anything along those lines? I could be telling him to stay strong for England."

Ivy had never thought of combining two plants to make a longer message. She liked the idea and told Win so.

"England's a rose, obviously, you could send one of those. Or, if you want to encourage him to be patriotic, you need nasturtiums."

"Could you draw some for me?"

"No need," Ivy said. "They're all out right now. Shall we go and pick some?"

"Mac won't mind?"

"Not if he doesn't know."

With a cheeky grin over her shoulder, Ivy led Win first to the kitchen garden, where she cut a sprig of thyme.

"Smell that," she said, thrusting it at Win.

Win took a deep breath in and smiled. "Wonderful."

From there they went to the glorious rose garden, where Ivy had first seen Win, and picked a red rosebud. Not the deep, blood-colored crimson but the brighter scarlet that meant "I love you" and symbolized England.

"Roses are hard to press when they're blooming because the petals drop," Ivy explained. "But a bud presses lovely and the color lasts longer."

Win nodded. "This is simply thrilling," she said. "What next?"

"Nasturtiums, in the borders."

They weaved their way through the plants to the herbaceous border and Ivy crouched down by the nasturtiums.

"Yellow will look nicest, I think. With the red of the rose and the green thyme."

"I agree."

Ivy snipped a couple of flowers.

"You can eat these," she told Win. "But I wouldn't want to. They're much too pretty to end up in my belly."

Win laughed and Ivy was pleased. She liked entertaining this clever, caring woman.

"Now what?"

"Now we tie the plants together with a piece of ribbon into a little posy. Do you have a heavy book? Like a Bible or an atlas?"

"Yes."

"When you get home, tuck the posy inside and pile some other books on top. Or anything heavy." She frowned as she thought about pressing the flowers at her house. "I put mine under my mattress. My sister and I share a bed, so there's plenty of weight on it."

As soon as she'd said it, Ivy regretted her joke. It was true, she did share a bed with her sister, but Win didn't need to know that. A nice lady like her would be bound to be shocked at the idea of lanky young women—almost grown—sharing a bed because there was neither room nor money for them to each have one of their own.

But Win simply nodded.

"That'll do it," she said. She looped her arm through Ivy's.

"Thank you, darling," she said. "You've shared something really special with me today and I love it."

Chapter 22

The women worked three-quarters of their usual day for a whole week. Things were already starting to fall apart. The herbaceous border was looking a bit weed-choked, there were lettuces in the vegetable garden that should have been picked days ago and the raspberries were hanging heavy on the plants because no one had been to check them. Dennis was doing his best, bless him, and Mac was working all hours, but still the lawns were untidy, the wisteria needed pruning and there were lots of flowers that needed to be deadheaded. The women were forcing themselves to ignore the jobs that were crying out to be done—it wasn't easy, but they all told themselves and one another that it would be worth it in the end. And didn't all the unpicked veg, rotting fruit and out-of-control lawns prove that the women were far more valuable to Kew than the men had realized? Louisa was confident that a few more days of untidy borders and Mac would crack.

The other thing that was different was how much time the women had. It was an odd feeling, and Louisa found herself at a loose end.

"What are you doing after work?" she asked Ivy as they got changed out of their overalls. Ivy had been disappearing each day, muttering about "making the most of the time" and Louisa was interested to know what she'd been doing.

Ivy smiled at Louisa.

"I've got something to show you," she said.

Intrigued, Louisa followed her round past the kitchen garden to a patch of rough earth. At least, it had been a patch of neglected dry soil the last time Louisa had been near it. Now it was a garden.

"Oh my," she breathed. "What's this?"

"It's my letter garden."

Louisa was confused. "Letters?"

"Jim sends me seeds from France, and I plant them here. All the plants have messages—you know, like we were learning?"

"Ivy, it's wonderful," Louisa said. "Really beautiful."

She felt a bit teary. Since that first letter, she'd not been asked to read anything for Ivy, so all this time she'd been wondering how Ivy and Jim were keeping in touch. Now she knew.

"Has anyone else seen this?"

"Just Mac; he gave me the patch of garden to use. And Win."

Louisa was slightly hurt that Win—the newcomer to their group—had seen it before she did. But Ivy obviously read the expression on her face and squeezed her arm.

"I showed Win because she's in the same boat as me, isn't she? With her Archie off in his patrol. I helped her pick some flowers to press for him with a message."

"You send Jim pressed flowers?"

"I do." Ivy looked proud and Louisa gave her a hug.

"This is wonderful. Can I look round?"

"Help yourself."

It wasn't big, and the flowers were higgledy-piggledy, presumably because Ivy wouldn't always know what they were before she planted them, but the garden was beautiful.

"Did Win like it?" Louisa called, admiring some carnations.

"She did. I think she's lonely, Lou. She told me she'd wanted to have children, but it never happened. I felt sorry for her."

Louisa felt the rush of sadness and helplessness she always experienced when something reminded her of her own failure to have a baby. She felt an ache inside for her lost baby and for Win's struggle.

"There's a WSPU meeting later, in Wandsworth," she said suddenly. "Shall we see if Win wants to come along?"

Ivy grinned. "Great idea."

And so, later on the three women got on the bus heading east.

"What a thrill," Win said, looking round at all the other passengers. "I've never been on an omnibus before. Don't we have to tell the driver where you want to go like when I get a cab to work?"

Ivy and Louisa both laughed.

"It just stops at certain places and you get off at the one nearest to where you're going," Louisa explained.

"How do you not know this?" teased Ivy, the affection she felt for the older woman plain to see. "I know you're all lah-di-dah, but even ladies need to get places."

"Archie normally drives me where I want to go."

"He has a car?" Louisa was impressed.

"Oh yes, he loves all that sort of thing—motorcars, trains, ships. Never ask him a question about a boat, Louisa, for your own sanity. He'll talk your ears off."

"I'm looking forward to meeting him," Louisa said.

"Oh, he'll love you. I've told him all about you in my letters. We're hoping he'll get leave in the autumn, so perhaps you'll meet him then."

"I hope so," said Ivy, squinting out of the dirty bus window. "We're almost there, Win."

They gathered their bags and Louisa rang the bell, which Win thought was "wonderfully clever, darling," and they jumped off the back of the bus at the next stop.

The meeting was in the town hall on the crossroads by the shops. Louisa led the way, as it was her local group, and showed them into a medium-sized room on the first floor.

Inside were about fifteen or twenty women of various ages. Louisa waved to Caro, from the League of Peace meetings and she came over to say hello.

"These are my friends, Ivy Adams and Lady Ramsay."

"Call me Win, darling," Win said, shaking Caro's hand.

Caro hugged Louisa. "I hear you've made quite an impression on Teddy."

Louisa's face flamed, as always.

"Oh, I don't know about that," she said airily. "Who said so?"

Caro grinned. "Teddy."

Louisa tried not to smile, but she couldn't help it. "He's a lovely man. I'm enjoying spending time with him."

"Well, he definitely thinks the same about you," Caro said. "He was quite giddy when I saw him last."

Giddy? Louisa couldn't imagine Teddy being giddy, but she was pleased to hear it. She did enjoy spending time with him and though she was nervous about the prospect of a new romance after everything that had happened with Reg over the years, she found when she was with Teddy all those fears simply vanished. She'd even told him what happened with Reg, and the baby, and her mother—things she'd not spoken about with many people—and he'd been so understanding and kind that she liked him even more for it.

"Louisa, are you daydreaming? The meeting's about to start," Ivy said, prodding her and shaking her out of her reverie. "Let's sit down."

They all sat and Louisa was amused to see how excited Win was, simply about being at a meeting.

"Don't expect too much," she whispered. "Things are so quiet. We're not taking any action, not campaigning, not doing anything, really. Just keeping it all ticking while the war's on."

Win shrugged. "It's just heavenly to be among all these clever women," she whispered back. "All these bright minds, working together for a greater good. Isn't it charming?"

Louisa laughed. "It most certainly is."

The meeting was about how to keep the Suffragettes' cause in the minds of people on the street, while things were so hard and everyone was focused on the war.

"It's a balancing act," the woman who was leading the meeting said. "We want people to remember us and what we stand for, but we don't want to be accused of taking focus off the soldiers and the people doing war work."

She looked round at the women. "Any ideas?"

Next to Louisa, Win raised her hand. "I have an idea."

Lou and Ivy looked at each other. Ivy widened her eyes and Louisa shrugged. It was, she thought, possible for Win's idea to be absolute perfect—or completely wrong.

"Could you stand up so everyone can see you? And would you mind sharing your name? I don't think we've seen you here before, have we?"

Win stood up and did a funny little bow to the women looking at her. Louisa stifled a laugh.

"Hello," she said gaily. "I'm Lady Winifred Ramsay, though I'd much rather you all called me Win."

A murmur spread round the room. The Suffragettes prided themselves on welcoming anyone from shopgirls to princesses, but they were still impressed by a title. And who could blame them? Louisa thought. It was a sad fact that the upper classes still had more clout than working-class people. If they chose to use that clout to further the cause of votes for women, then so much the better.

Win cleared her throat.

"I'm here today with my friends Ivy and Louisa. We all work at Kew Gardens. Most of the male gardeners have gone to the Front now, and we're doing their jobs. It's important work, anyway, because the Gardens really are a jewel in the nation's crown, but it's also vital with regards to the war, as we are growing more and more food. But recently, my friend Louisa here discovered the female gardeners are being paid far less than the men for doing the same work."

Again, a murmur spread across the hall. This time tinged with disapproval. Win nodded.

"It's awful, darlings. These women are working all hours, keeping things going at the Gardens while the men are away and they are not being valued."

She smiled.

"So we're campaigning for equal pay. And we're doing it by only working the hours the women are paid for. We get three-quarters of their salary so we're only doing three-quarters of the work."

The room was silent; everyone looked at Win and she wobbled, slightly.

"That's right, isn't it, darlings?" She looked down at Louisa and Ivy, who were both gazing up at her in awe. "That's what we're doing."

"It is," Louisa said. "That's exactly it."

Onstage, the chairwoman clapped her hands. "That's absolutely wonderful," she said.

Wobble over, Win smiled again.

"So, I thought, we should make sure women doing men's jobs are all paid the correct amount," she said. "Bus drivers, conductors, factory workers, railway guards, firefighters—all of them. If we fight for equal rights here, then surely votes will follow?"

The room erupted into cheers as everyone gave Win's idea their approval. Win sat down in her seat and Ivy and Louisa both gave her well-done pats.

"So clever," Louisa whispered. "You're amazing."

When the noise died down the chairwoman looked directly at the three Kew Gardens Girls. "What can we do to help?" she said.

Win grinned. "I was hoping you'd say that."

⁕

What Win wanted was the support—the loudest, most visible support—of the Suffragettes.

"Things are being affected already," she explained. "But the men in charge are digging their heels in. They're not budging. I thought a bit of protesting from you, and they might be shamed into giving the women equal pay."

When the Suffragettes agreed to get involved, Louisa and Ivy had organized things, arranging for the women to protest outside the main building at Kew, where the bosses worked. They sorted out placards and banners and worked hard all weekend, getting everything ready.

When Monday dawned, they arrived at work—slightly bleary-eyed after their late nights—and were heartened to see women already gathering outside.

"I've arranged to go and speak to the bosses," Louisa told the women, who were clutching their placards and looking eager to get started. "It will really help our cause if you can be causing a bit of a commotion while I'm there."

"Righto," said Caro. "Let's go, troops."

The women began marching up and down next to the entrance to the Gardens, shouting, "Equal pay for equal work!" and waving their placards. As the gardeners arrived for work, they were all thrilled to bits to see such support, thanking the Suffragettes as they passed.

"Isn't this marvelous," commented Harriet as she entered. "How lovely to know we're not alone."

"We can return the favor if women in other jobs need us to," Louisa pointed out. "We can fight for equal pay for everyone."

"We most certainly will."

Louisa watched the Suffragettes for a little while, then she headed into the main building and up the sweeping wooden staircase to the offices. Mac was waiting at the top, looking frazzled.

"Morning," he said.

She smiled. "Morning."

"Before we go in, I just want to say you're right," Mac said gruffly, not looking at her. "You girls should absolutely be paid the same as the men and it's wrong that you're not. You've got my support."

"Really?"

"Really."

Louisa threw her arms round him and hugged him. He peeled her off, looking embarrassed.

"That's enough of that. Shall we go in?"

Together, they knocked on the office door and went inside. The director of Kew was a man called Sir David Prain. He wasn't there that day, nor had Louisa been expecting him to be. But she found she was facing two rather high-up men, which made her stomach lurch with nerves.

"Ah, Mrs. Taylor?" one of the men said. He had gray hair and fluffy sideburns. "What's all this kerfuffle outside?"

"It's the women from the WSPU, sir," Louisa said. "They're supporting us in our campaign for equal pay."

The men looked at each other and frowned. "Word has spread?"

"Indeed. I believe women in other jobs are considering campaigning in a similar fashion."

Mac cleared his throat. "If I may speak?"

"Go ahead, Mr. MacMillan."

"I was unsure about employing female gardeners initially," Mac said. He sounded as though he'd practiced and Louisa loved him for it. "But my girls have more than proved themselves to be up to the job. They're fast, strong, creative, talented. They're just as good as the men—better in some instances. For the last week, the women have been working three-quarters of their usual day to make the point that they're only paid three-quarters of the men's salary, and let me tell you, we are missing their efforts enormously. It makes no sense to me that they're paid less. No sense at all."

There was a pause and the bigwigs looked at each other again.

"But men are breadwinners. They have families to support."

Mac shrugged.

"There's a war on," he reminded them. "Most of our women are the breadwinners now, while their husbands are away."

"Could you excuse us for a moment?" the other man said. He was younger, with swept-back hair.

"Of course."

The two men huddled together, angling their chairs away and speaking in an undertone, as Louisa strained to hear. She looked at Mac and he held his hands out as if to say "No idea" and she smiled. This was excruciating.

Eventually, the men turned back to Louisa and Mac.

"We have agreed," Sideburns said. "Your female gardeners will be paid the same as the men."

Louisa wanted to throw her hands in the air and whoop with joy, but instead she nodded politely.

"That's good to hear, sir," she said. "Thank you."

The younger man bent his head to the ledger in front of him, picked up his pen and started to write. The older one pushed his chair back and rose to go. The meeting was obviously finished. But not as far as Louisa was concerned.

"There's one more thing," she said.

The younger man sighed and put down his pen. "Yes?"

"One of our gardeners isn't being paid at all. I trust that she will be included in this equal-pay decision?"

The man tutted. "Sounds as though she is a volunteer. Paying her could be awkward . . ."

"Her name is Lady Winifred Ramsay," Louisa said.

He and the older man looked at each other. The older man gave a small nod.

"Fine," he said. "Lady Ramsay will be added to the payroll."

Louisa gave him her best, broadest smile. "Thank you."

Outside the office she and Mac hugged and jumped up and down like excited schoolchildren.

"We did it, Mac," she squealed, thrilled to bits at the result.

"You did it," he pointed out. "You, Ivy, Win and that bunch of reprobates out there." He gestured through the large window at the top of the stairs, through which the tops of the Suffragettes placards could be seen, bobbing up and down as they marched.

Louisa nodded.

"It's amazing what you can achieve when you put your heads together," she said.

Mac raised an eyebrow. "Does that include sorting out those lawns and deadheading the petunias?"

Chuckling, Louisa started down the stairs.

"I'll get right to it," she said. "Once I've told the girls what they're really worth."

Chapter 23

Win was a heroine for a few weeks, her popularity among the gardeners well and truly cemented. As a mild September became a rainy October, the Kew Gardens Girls worked harder and with more dedication than ever before, preparing the land for winter; picking fruit and vegetables and taking it to the Kew Women's Institute for bottling, pickling, and preserving; digging up potatoes; and starting to plant the bulbs that would bring color in spring.

Things were good, as far as Ivy was concerned, except for the hollow in her heart where she missed Jim. He'd sent her more seeds, tiny little black specks that she'd scattered across every spare bit of earth in her letter garden. She hoped they'd survive the winter. She concentrated on tending the garden, trying to ignore the niggle in her brain that told her she had something else to worry about, too. Maybe if she didn't think about it, it wouldn't be true. Because if it was true and she was . . . Well, she wasn't going to think about that now. Not yet.

She was pleased that Win was so settled, too. She and the older woman spent a lot of time together, bringing each other comfort while

Jim and Archie were away. And Louisa spent a lot of time with Teddy, who had brought a light to her eyes that Ivy was thrilled to bits to see.

But then everything changed.

On a blustery day in early October, the three women were wandering toward the break room in search of a cup of tea after spending the morning in the soggy herbaceous border. Louisa was telling them about her plans to visit Bernie.

"I know they've been rushed off their feet with the apple harvest and the cider making," she was explaining. "But now things have calmed down, I thought I might go down and visit for a weekend." She took a breath. "And I thought I might take Teddy."

"You're introducing him to your parents," Ivy teased. "That's a big step."

Louisa giggled like a schoolgirl. "I just want to show him the farm. Nothing more."

"I think it's wonderful. He's a charming man," Win said.

"He really is."

"Reg won't be there, will he?" Ivy didn't want to think about what could happen if Louisa's fist-happy husband came face-to-face with her new beau. But her friend shook her head.

"He's still in Folkestone, according to my brother. I think his sister's keeping him on a short rein for now."

"No more than he deserves," muttered Win, who'd never even met Reg but was firmly on Louisa's side.

"Bernie sounds really happy," Ivy said. "That last letter he sent, the one you read out loud the other day, was lovely."

"It really was. He's working hard, but he and Matthew seem to get along quite nicely. And he said he's not had any trouble. People either don't know he's a conscientious objector, or they know but they don't care."

They carried on chatting for a moment, but as they passed the entrance to the admin building, Mac appeared.

"Win," he said. He had an odd expression on his face that Ivy couldn't quite read. "Percy in the office needs a word."

"With me?" Win was squinting through the drizzle at him. "Are you sure?"

Mac swallowed. "I'm sure."

Win shrugged.

"I'll catch you up, darlings," she said to Ivy and Louisa, as she headed into the building. But Mac caught Ivy's arm as they went to continue on to the break room.

"Stay here," he said. "She's going to need you."

Ivy's stomach plummeted into her boots and she felt an icy chill that wasn't just the rain.

"Mac?" she said, scared.

But he shook his head. "Not my place to say."

Louisa and Ivy stood at the bottom of the sweeping wooden staircase, where just a few weeks earlier, Louisa had bounced with joy after winning their fight for equal pay. Now the stairs seemed too big and too imposing for joy.

They didn't speak, but Louisa reached for Ivy's hand, and Ivy took it gratefully, squeezing her friend's fingers. Mac stood by them in silence, twisting his hat in his hands.

Eventually, there was the sound of a door shutting up above. Then footsteps echoed through the quiet building. Ivy looked at Louisa, whose eyes were already filled with tears.

Slowly, Win came down the stairs. Her head was held high, but her face was white and drawn. As she reached the bottom, she nodded at her waiting friends.

"My neighbor, Edith, saw the post boy delivering a telegram to my flat this morning," she said. Her voice was small and shaky. "She very kindly intercepted it and brought it here in case it was important.

"The telegram says Archie's boat was attacked by a U-boat two days ago. It says the men fought bravely, but despite their efforts, their boat sank. It says there are no signs of any survivors."

Lifting her head higher, she took a deep, shuddery breath.

"It says Admiral Lord Archibald Ramsay is lost at sea."

She stumbled, and Louisa and Ivy both reached out to her at once. She clung on to them, but she didn't cry.

"Take her home," Mac said to them in an undertone. He wiped his eyes, then fumbled in his pocket and handed Louisa a shilling. "Get a cab. Look after her."

Louisa stayed with Win, who was wide-eyed with shock, while Ivy raced back to the break room to pick up their bags and coats. Then they took a cab down to Win's mansion block, on Wimbledon Hill.

It was a newly built, large yellow-brick building with black window frames. The main glass front door was open and fortunately Win's flat was on the ground floor. Ivy didn't think her friend had the strength to climb stairs.

Win fumbled with her key before Louisa gently took it from her and opened the front door. Inside was by far the nicest home Ivy had ever been in. The lounge had pretty pink patterned wallpaper and a huge, soft sofa. There was a big fireplace with a clock on the mantelpiece, and a photograph in a frame of a much younger Win with a handsome man in a naval uniform. Archie, Ivy presumed, feeling sick with sorrow for her friend.

"Sit down," Ivy urged Win. "Sit."

Louisa touched Ivy's arm gently and nodded at Win—she was still wearing her damp, mud-spattered overalls. She'd ditched her dresses and hats as soon as she started working properly as a gardener, which Ivy had loved. It meant Win was really one of them. But Louisa realized that spreading dirt all over Win's lovely home wasn't the best idea.

"Ivy, could you find Win's dressing gown and slippers, perhaps?" she said. "Are they in your bedroom, Win?"

Win nodded. She'd not spoken since they'd left Kew.

Ivy squeezed Win's hand and then headed off down the hall to find the bedroom, opening doors to the bathroom—how fancy—and a broom cupboard, before she got lucky and discovered the large, airy bedroom. It had a big bed with a brightly colored counterpane and a big, dark wood headboard, a matching wardrobe, and—hanging on the back of the door—Win's dressing gown. Ivy took it, noticing with a pang of sadness that Archie's was hanging there, too. She found slippers under the bed and took them back to Louisa.

"Let's get you changed," Louisa said to Win. Like a mother with a child, she helped the older woman take off her mucky clothes, bundling them up so they didn't shake mud onto the rug. Win didn't object, obediently holding out her arms so Louisa could take off her overalls, and stepping out of her trousers.

Ivy helped her into her dressing gown while Louisa found some water and a sponge and gently cleaned Win's hands; then she curled up on the settee and to their surprise, she went to sleep.

"My mum always says sleep is a healer," Ivy said quietly. They were standing by the big square window at the far end of the lounge. It overlooked a park and they watched the leaves being whipped from the trees in the wind.

"I think it'll take more than sleep to heal this."

Win woke just as the afternoon was darkening into evening. Ivy and Louisa were sitting quietly in the lounge. Ivy was putting together a letter for Jim, enclosing a sketch of the garden as it had been in full glory just a few weeks ago before autumn descended, and Louisa had found an old Robert Louis Stevenson book on Win's brimming shelves and was engrossed in tales of pirates.

"Darlings," she said, as she opened her eyes and saw them there. "You're here."

She sat up, blinking. Her hair was all tangled on one side, where it had been against the cushion and the kohl round her eyes was smudged. Ivy found that seeing Win looking less than perfect made her heart hurt.

"We didn't want you to be alone," Ivy said, tucking the letter into her sketchbook. "We didn't want you to wake up and have no one here."

Win gave them both a weak smile. "You're so thoughtful."

"Are you hungry?" Louisa said, putting down *Treasure Island*. "I can make you a sandwich?"

Win shook her head. "A cup of tea, perhaps?"

"I'll boil the kettle." Louisa got up and headed for the kitchen, stopping on the way to put a comforting hand on Win's shoulder. Win reached up and patted her hand, showing her she was glad she was there.

"Is there anything we can do?" Ivy asked. "Anyone else you need to tell? Does Archie have brothers and sisters?"

"A brother. I should write to him."

"Louisa could do it." For the hundredth time, Ivy wished she could write.

"That would be good. I don't think I could find the words." Win's eyes filled with tears and Ivy was glad. Win hadn't cried yet and Ivy was worried she was bottling it all up.

"I'll tell Lou. Anyone else?"

Win took a breath, blinking away the tears. "Hundreds of people, darling."

"Are there a few people we could contact, and get them to spread the word, perhaps? A couple of friends who could let others know? It will be too difficult for you to tell people over and over."

Win looked weary but she nodded.

"I'll give you my address book and mark a few names," she said. "Thank you, darling."

There was a knock on the door of the flat and Win looked startled. "Who's that?"

"I'll go and see."

Ivy found a small woman with jet-black hair standing at the door.

"I'm Edith," she said. "I took Win's telegram to Kew."

"Thank you," Ivy said. "It was kind of you to realize what it was."

The woman bit her lip. "Is she all right?"

Win appeared in the door of the lounge. She'd straightened her hair and rubbed the makeup from under her eyes.

"Edith, darling," she said. She took her neighbor's two hands in her own. "Thank you for caring."

"I'm so sorry about Archie," Edith said.

"I will miss him dreadfully."

"Will you let me know if there's anything I can do?"

"I will, my darling. But for now I have my Kew Gardens Girls with me and I need to be getting on."

She kissed Edith on the cheek, bustled her out of the flat and shut the door firmly. Then she leaned against the back of the door and closed her eyes briefly. Ivy watched, concerned.

"Win?" she said.

Win opened her eyes and stood up again. "I'm fine."

"You don't have to be fine," Ivy said, thinking of how she'd fallen apart when Jim went. "You don't have to put a brave face on for us."

"Where's Louisa with that tea?" Win said.

Louisa and Ivy stayed with Win for the rest of the day, not wanting her to be alone. And as the evening became night, they had a huddled conversation in the kitchen.

"We can't leave her by herself," Ivy said.

"I agree. She's being very stiff upper lip, but I'm waiting for her to fall apart."

"I'll stay." Ivy made the decision without thinking twice.

"Sure?"

She nodded. "It's only one night."

Louisa made sure Win was settled into bed before she left and then she kissed Ivy good-bye.

"I'll see you in the morning," Louisa said. "Try to get her to eat something."

"I'll take care of her."

Win, who'd seemed relieved that someone was staying, lent Ivy a nightgown, which was far nicer than any of Ivy's best dresses, and told her to make herself comfortable in the spare room. Then she'd gone into her own bedroom and closed the door quietly.

Now, with Louisa gone, Ivy hovered outside Win's door, wondering if she should knock.

"Win?" she whispered. There was no reply. "Win? I'm going to bed now, but just shout if you need me. I'm right next door."

Again there was no reply. Hoping that meant Win was asleep, Ivy went into the guest room, took off her clothes and pulled on the soft nightgown, enjoying the feeling of the fabric on her skin. She couldn't resist swishing around the room for a second before she climbed into bed.

"It's like a wedding dress," she murmured to herself, then felt bad because Win had a wedding dress once and a wedding and a husband, and now he was gone.

She got into bed and wriggled down under the covers, feeling bone tired suddenly and desperately sad for her friend. And as she drifted off to sleep she heard sobbing from the room next door.

Chapter 24

Ivy woke early the next morning, after a restful night's sleep—how luxurious to have a bed all to herself—which she felt guilty about. She couldn't hear any sounds in the flat so, hoping that meant Win had finally cried herself to sleep at some point during the night, she went in search of tea and toast. She found tea in the cupboard and a loaf of bread in the bread bin and was cutting thick, uneven slices just as Win walked in. Once again, Ivy's heart ached to see her friend look so different from her usual self. Her hair was loose and messy, falling over her shoulders in a tangle. Her face was bare and blotchy, and her eyes were swollen—from crying, Ivy assumed. She looked old and tired and so, so sad.

"I thought you might be hungry?" Ivy said. "Do you think you could manage some toast?"

Win made a face. "Maybe one slice?"

"Go and sit down and I'll bring it to you. Would you like a cup of tea? I'm making a pot."

"That would be lovely, darling."

Win sat down at the little table by the window in the kitchen and gazed out at the park. Ivy didn't like to think about how many breakfasts she'd shared with Archie, sitting there.

Obviously thinking along similar lines, Win said: "In Dover, Archie always has breakfast in the orangerie. Even when it's raining cats and dogs. You can imagine how noisy that is."

"I can," she said, though she'd only ever worked in an orangerie, not sat down to enjoy breakfast.

On the stove, the kettle whistled and she picked it up with a tea towel and poured some boiling water into the teapot, swirled it round and poured it away again before she added the tea and filled it up.

"Warming the pot," Win said approvingly.

Ivy smiled. "My mum would have my guts for garters if I made tea in a cold pot."

"There's a toast rack in the cupboard," Win said. Ivy found it and stacked the hot toast from the grill in it.

"And the marmalade and butter are in the pantry. I should help you, really, but I don't have the energy."

"Don't you worry, it's nice to be able to help."

Ivy put the teapot on the table and as she did, Win grabbed her hand.

"Will you stay?" she said.

"Course. Mac won't mind one day."

Win shook her head. "I don't mean today. I mean, will you move in? I can't bear the thought of being here by myself. And you understand, Ivy. You know what it's like because of Jim being away. I thought perhaps we could keep each other company?"

Ivy stared at her. "You want me to live here?"

"Do you think your mother would mind?"

"I think she'd dance with joy. And my sister would be so happy, she'd probably pack my bags for me."

"Then it's settled." Win looked up at Ivy hopefully. "Isn't it?"

Spontaneously, Ivy leaned down and hugged her friend. "It's settled."

She sat down at the table and spread marmalade on toast for Win.

"Try to eat that," she said. "Might give you some more energy."

Obediently, Win nibbled at the crust of her toast.

"What do you want to do today?" Ivy asked. "Is there anything you need to do?"

"I want to go to work."

"Oh, Win. I'm not sure that's a good idea."

"It's better that way. I'll keep busy. I'm not the only woman to have lost her husband and there's a lot to do at the Gardens before the frosts come."

"If you're sure?"

"I'm sure." She swallowed a piece of toast and stood up. "I'll go and get ready."

Ivy cleared up the plates, not sure what to think. She was definitely pleased to move in with Win—even for a short time—and help out where she could. Especially now, with Archie gone and . . . She shook her head. This was no time to be thinking of her own troubles. She had to focus on Win for now.

"Ready?" Win appeared in the doorway, looking like her old self. Her hair was brushed and neatly tied up, she was wearing one of her dresses, and she had rouge on her cheeks and a slick of lipstick on her mouth.

"You look lovely," Ivy said, surprised.

"'Chin up, back straight, smile on,' Archie says."

Ivy smiled. "And you're sure you're going to be all right?"

For a second, Win's determined look vanished and Ivy saw a glimpse of the broken woman beneath.

"Oh, darling, I'm not sure I'll ever be all right again," she said. Then it was back. "But I'm Lady Winifred Ramsay and I'm not going to let my Archie down."

Ivy offered her an arm and Win took it. "Then let's go to work."

Their days fell into an easy pattern. Each morning, Ivy would make toast and tea and cajole Win into eating. They'd travel to Kew together—on the bus now that Ivy was there. She couldn't bear to think of the indulgence of taking a cab when there was a perfectly good bus route. They would work hard all day—at least, Ivy would. Win had rather gone back to her old habits of drifting round the rose garden or wandering in the palm house but Mac didn't mind. He liked having her around—they all did—and he was happy to give her easy jobs for now. Ivy, thinking of what helped her when Jim was away, gave Win some seeds he'd sent in his last letter. Which had been days and days ago now, though she tried not to count up how long it had been precisely because she'd only panic.

It was the tiny black specks Jim had sent that had given her the idea. Ivy had discovered they were poppy seeds, though the meaning of poppies—consolation or imagination or even wealth, if they were yellow—didn't seem relevant. But then one day, a few weeks before, Mac had come to visit her letter garden with something to tell her.

"I got chatting to a lad in the pub last night," he'd said. "He was on leave, from France."

Ivy had stiffened, scared it was bad news, and Mac put his hand on her arm comfortingly.

"He told me the battlefields are covered in poppies. Apparently, they grow in the churned-up earth. He said the soldiers think of them as a sign of hope—that something so pretty can grow in such a hellish place."

"Hope," Ivy said. "That's what he meant."

"I reckon so."

"Is it too late to plant them?" she'd asked, looking at the leaden sky that threatened yet more rain.

To her delight, Mac had shrugged.

"No, not if you get them in before the end of the month. Plant them now and you'll have a great display come spring."

Ivy had planted most of them, but there were so many of the tiny seeds, she'd saved some and now she was glad. She gave them in a twist of paper to Win.

"Take a patch of my letter garden and scatter the poppy seeds there in memory of Archie," she said. "In hope of happier times to come."

Win had nodded gratefully, and now she was often found pottering round the letter garden, keeping an eye on things. Ivy had worried she would find Win intrusive, but she didn't—their shared feelings of loss united them.

After work, they would go home. Often Louisa would visit, on evenings when she wasn't busy with her League of Peace work or seeing Teddy. And Win had found a whole new group of friends in the Suffragettes. She'd thrown herself into the organization, desperate for some way to fill her days.

"Janet thinks we'll start direct action as soon as the war's over," she told Ivy after one meeting. "Wouldn't that be thrilling, darling?"

Ivy had shifted uncomfortably on the sofa. "Depends what it is," she muttered.

"And we're protesting at the bus depot on Friday, campaigning for equal pay for their female drivers and conductors," Win went on. "Our fight at Kew has inspired others to take up arms. Metaphorically speaking."

But while Win kept her chin up, Ivy heard her crying alone in her bedroom every night. And every morning her eyes were red and her face blotchy with tears.

"She's dealing with it in her own way," Louisa said, when Ivy told her about her worries for Win. "It's the way some women are—strong as an ox on the face of it. She won't want us to think she's not coping."

"She is coping," Ivy pointed out. "I'm just worried she's so sad."

"It's not been long. It will get easier for her," Louisa said. "Teddy says there are days now when he doesn't think of Philip as much. But there are also times when something reminds him of his son so sharply it's as painful as it was when he was first killed. It's unpredictable. That's why we just need to be there for her."

Ivy had shuddered at the thought of people getting used to living without their loved ones.

November had arrived, bringing with it frosty mornings and dark evenings. With things much calmer down on the farm, Louisa was planning to visit Bernie the following weekend, so she'd come round to visit Ivy and Win to see if there was anything they wanted her to take. With a drawing of Kew in autumn by Ivy in her bag, she was staying for tea.

"Can you read to us this evening?" Ivy asked as the two went back into the lounge, where Win was sitting by the fire. Louisa, enjoying the Ramsays' bookshelves, had taken to reading to her friends when she visited. They were halfway through *Jane Eyre* and Ivy was enjoying it enormously.

"You could learn to read it yourself," Louisa said. Ivy had given up trying to learn once Bernie had gone. She just didn't have the heart.

"I don't want to."

Win looked up. "I could teach you."

"Really?"

"I'm not a teacher like your Bernie was, but we might be able to muddle through together. What do you think?"

"I'd like that."

Win put her glasses on.

"How much can you read?" she said. "What words do you know?"

She picked up the newspaper, which was on the side table next to her, and held it up to Ivy.

"Can you read this headline?"

Ivy glanced at it. There were a few words she recognized.

"It's about the Front," she said.

"What about it?"

Ivy tried to read the words, but her eyes had filled with tears.

"It's something about gas," she said. "Are they using more gas on our soldiers, Win?"

Win turned the newspaper round to look at the story and then quickly folded it up and put it away.

"No, no," she said. "Nothing like what happened at Ypres, you mustn't worry."

But Ivy saw Win exchange a worried look with Louisa and her heart pounded with fear.

"What?" she said. "What's happening? Is Jim in danger? He's in France."

Louisa put her arm round Ivy and held her tightly.

"Jim's fine," she said calmly. "You know he's fine because you hear from him all the time, don't you? He sent you those poppy seeds. He's fine."

But panic was rising in Ivy's chest.

"I don't know," she said. "I don't know he's fine."

Win looked alarmed.

"Darling, I know how you feel. I used to feel awful whenever I read news from the war, worrying about Archie . . ."

"And the worst happened," Ivy cried. "Archie was lost."

"But there's no reason to think something's happened to Jim, no reason at all," Win said.

Ivy took a breath. "There is a reason," she said.

Win's face went white and Louisa squeezed Ivy tighter.

"What's happened?" she said. "What haven't you told us?"

"He's not written for weeks. Not since he sent those poppy seeds."

Louisa frowned as she tried to remember. "But that was, what? The start of October?"

"End of September," Ivy whispered. "It was five weeks and three days ago." Who had she been fooling, pretending she wasn't counting?

"Why didn't you say anything?" Win said, then she nodded. "Because of Archie? You didn't want to upset me, while I've been grieving for Archie."

Ivy gave her a small smile. "I felt awful, worrying about what might have happened to Jim while you've been dealing with what really has happened to Archie."

"Oh, darling, you silly girl," Win said. "You should never dampen your own feelings to protect mine. Never."

Louisa had been thinking. "It's autumn in France, too. Maybe there aren't any flowers for him to send?"

Ivy jumped on this tiny bit of hope. "Maybe." But then the despair came back. "But there are trees, surely? Or he could write to me, knowing Louisa would read it for me, if he had nothing to send."

There was silence as all three women racked their brains for a good reason why Ivy had not heard from her sweetheart.

"You've been sending drawings and cuttings to him as usual?"

"I have. I send something every few days. I can't bear for him to think I'm not worried about him."

Louisa bit her lip and again, Ivy watched as she and Win glanced at each other. What were they thinking? Did they think the worst?

Despite her best efforts at holding back the tears, she started to cry.

"I'm so worried that something's happened to him. Has he been gassed? Could he be lying dead in the mud somewhere? I can't get it out of my head, the idea that he's dead."

"Hush," soothed Louisa, gathering Ivy into her embrace like a child. Win came over and sat on her other side, one hand on her arm, letting her know she was there.

After a little while, Win spoke. "You may not want to hear this," she said, "but they'd tell you if something had happened. Reading that telegram was the worst moment of my life, but at least I know for sure."

But Ivy shook her head. "They wouldn't tell me, though, would they? They'd tell Jim's mum."

"She'd tell you, Ivy. She wouldn't leave you in the dark." Louisa's face was serious. "Would she?"

Ivy shrugged. "Dunno. She's always been really nice to me, but she might not even live in London anymore. I don't know."

"Perhaps we should pay her a visit?" Louisa suggested. "Just to be sure."

Ivy nodded. "There's something else," she whispered.

"What?"

Ivy got up and went to the sideboard, where she'd left her sketchbook, then she sat down on the settee again, leafing through it until she found the right page.

"This is the letter I'm getting ready to send Jim. I'm planning to post it tomorrow, but I thought I should show you first." She breathed in deeply. "Because you need to know this, too."

She opened the page she'd marked with her finger and showed them a small bunch of dried white flowers. Tiny blooms with delicate edges.

"I pressed these ages ago, before Jim went away," she said. "I never dreamed I would need them one day."

Win leaned over to get a better look.

"Gypsophila?" she said. "What does that symbolize?"

But Louisa was one step ahead, looking for all the world as though Ivy's flowers had confirmed something she already knew. "It's baby's breath. That's what some people call it, isn't it?"

Ivy couldn't look at her. Instead, she stared at the sketchbook on her lap and simply nodded.

"Ivy, are you expecting? Are you expecting Jim's baby?"

A fat tear rolled down Ivy's cheek. She didn't brush it away; instead she let her hands drift down to her stomach, cradling the baby she now knew was growing inside.

"I am."

She forced her gaze up to meet Louisa's and then Win's, frightened she was going to see judgment in their eyes. Instead, she just saw love and sympathy and kindness—and that made her cry even more.

"I don't know what to do," she sobbed. "I don't know what to do."

Louisa took one of Ivy's hands and Win took the other.

"We are going to work it all out together," Louisa said. "It's all going to be fine, you'll see."

Ivy let her head drop onto Louisa's shoulder, feeling so grateful for her support that she could burst. Yet she couldn't quite believe what her friend was saying. She was unmarried, expecting a baby, and she hadn't heard from the baby's father in weeks. Lord only knew what Mac would say when he found out—or her mother. She shuddered at the thought of anyone finding out her shameful secret and wanted to scream in misery at even the idea of Jim dying on a battlefield in France, never knowing he was going to be a father.

"It's all going to be fine," Louisa said again. But Ivy just shook her head. She didn't think anything was going to be fine, ever again.

Chapter 25

I'm at a loss as to what to do for the best," Louisa told Teddy as they traveled down to Kent the next day on the train. "Ivy's so sad—she's just fallen apart. She and Win are giving each other a lot of comfort, and we've promised her we're going to stand by her. But it's not going to be easy."

Teddy took her hand, sending warm waves of pleasure up her arm.

"I don't think anything is easy right now," he said. "But I think Ivy is lucky to have you and Win."

Louisa let her head rest on his shoulder. She felt like the lucky one, to have met Teddy at a time when she thought she would never find love. Their courtship was slow but steady, because they had both been so wary at first. They'd both suffered losses and terrible heartaches, but they found strength in each other and Louisa thought the world of this sad, gentle, kind man. She wasn't sure what would happen or where things would go; after all, she was still legally married to Reg. But she found that didn't matter to her, not really. Instead, she was living for each day as it came, enjoying Teddy's company and making the most of the time they had together. That was why he'd come with her to Kent; she didn't want to spend a weekend away from him, and by the haste in which he'd agreed to accompany her, it seemed he felt the same.

Of course, she felt slightly nervous that Reg could show up, but Bernie and Matthew had both assured her that he was still down in Folkestone with his stern sister.

Matthew met them at the station, in the horse and cart that after all her time in London seemed old-fashioned to Louisa. Old-fashioned, but familiar and comforting. She introduced Teddy, and Matthew eyed him cautiously, until Teddy commented that he'd spent a few summers on a hops farm as a child and suddenly they were the best of friends.

Louisa chuckled to herself as they trip-trapped through the lanes toward the farm. Men really were the simplest of creatures.

"Bernie sounds to have settled in," she said as they approached her old home, and Matthew nodded eagerly.

"I can't lie, I was a bit alarmed when I first saw him," he said with a laugh. "With his hair all over the place, and that funny bandy-legged walk he's got. I thought, 'Blimey, what's Lou landed me with?'"

Louisa grinned. "But?"

"But he's such a fast learner and he's really interested, you know? He's been doing loads of reading about yields and how to maximize the use of the land, and coming up with ways to make more money from the crops. He's a proper asset."

He paused to swing the cart round a corner, then continued: "Jenny thinks he's wonderful, and the children adore him. He's been teaching Lettie her alphabet."

"And he's sleeping in the barn?"

"He was, but Jenny's cleaned out the old boot room for him. He's got a bed in there now, and it's next to the kitchen, so it's warmer. Looks like being a nasty winter."

Louisa nodded. She and the Kew Gardens Girls had already discussed the awful weather they'd been having—though today was a rare dry day—and agreed the same.

"I'm pleased it's working out," she said. "And Mum and Dad? Are they all right?"

"Same as ever," he said. "They like the cottage, though Mum spends most of her time helping Jenny anyway."

Their parents had moved out of the large farmhouse, to let Matthew, Jenny and the children make it their home now that Matthew did most of the work on the farm. They lived in a cottage nearby and Louisa would be seeing them today for the first time since she'd left. Her letters to her mother had gone a long way toward easing the tension between them but she was still nervous about seeing her parents in the flesh.

Matthew turned the cart into the entrance to the farm, and there by the farmhouse was Jenny—looking a little older but still with the same broad smile that Louisa remembered and with a plump toddler on her hip. Two older children chased each other in circles round her feet, and Louisa's parents were sitting on a bench at the front of the house. Suddenly, all her nerves disappeared. Matthew slowed the cart, but before it had come to a complete halt, Louisa was jumping out and rushing over to her mother and father. There were hugs and some tears and lots of apologies on both sides as they all tried to say everything that they could to make right the distance between them.

Eventually, Louisa became aware of Jenny and Teddy and the children all standing awkwardly to one side, and she stood back, wiping her eyes.

"Everyone, this is my friend, Edward Armitage. He's the man who helped Bernie get approval to come and work here. These are my parents, Bill and Nora Hamilton, and Matthew's wife, Jenny."

"Call me Teddy," said Teddy, shaking everyone's hands. "Delighted to meet you all."

Jenny introduced the children—Lettie and Roddy—who shyly greeted Louisa but who obviously didn't remember her—and the baby, whose name was Ellen.

"Gosh it's funny to be back," Louisa said as Jenny led them all inside for tea. "Everything's so familiar and yet so different."

"I'm glad you've managed to build bridges with your parents," Teddy said, speaking only to Louisa. "Family is so important."

She nodded. "I needed time, to heal and to come to terms with my mother's reaction. But my time with the Suffragettes opened my eyes, really. I understand now she was worried for me—she thought I wouldn't be all right on my own, that I needed a man and that even a man like Reg was better than no man at all."

"She should have helped you, though, when you asked."

Louisa nodded again. "She should have. But I know she feels awful that she didn't and we can both put it behind us and move on."

Teddy squeezed her hand. "Wise words."

"Auntie Louisa, Mummy made a cake," Roddy said, bounding up to them and taking Louisa's hand. "Come and see. It's got cherries on top." Touched by how quickly he'd accepted her as part of the family, she let him lead her into the big kitchen, which like everything was the same but different. The big fireplace and the range hadn't changed, but there was a new table and a pretty tabby cat curled up on one of the chairs—at least until Roddy prodded it. It hissed in annoyance, jumped onto the stone floor and tiptoed snootily out the back door.

"Tea?" Jenny said with a smile.

"That would be great."

While they waited for the kettle to boil, they chatted about Kew and the farm. Matthew and Louisa's dad, Bill, asked all sorts of questions about the vegetable patches at the Gardens, and Lou glowed with pride as she shared tips about how to get the potatoes growing better and what crops to grow over winter. She felt even more like a proper gardener when her dad got up from his chair and found some paper and a pencil and started making notes about what she was saying.

"We've expanded so much and we could do a lot more," Bill said, tucking the stub of pencil behind his ear. "Lord knows, the villagers can do with all the food they can get."

Louisa thought the war seemed very far away down here, unlike in London, where there were signs of the conflict everywhere, with soldiers home on leave around the place and all the posters and the like. But it seemed she'd been wrong and the war had sent its poisonous tendrils into every part of England, even this tiny corner of Kent.

"Is it tough?" she asked.

Her mum, Nora, shuddered.

"All the men have gone, more or less," she said. "Obviously the farmers are still here, but there are no farmhands, no casual labor. Neville from the pub? With the red hair? He went."

"Isn't he too young?" Louisa was trying to remember him, but the only image she could conjure up was of a small mop-headed boy with freckles.

"Sixteen," her mum said. "He was killed after a fortnight."

Teddy winced and Louisa glanced at him, checking he was all right. He gave her a small nod in reply.

"Teddy lost his son, Philip," she told her mum, feeling Teddy's hand discreetly finding hers under the table and giving his fingers a reassuring squeeze. "He was killed early in the conflict."

"I'm so sorry," Nora said. Teddy bowed his head briefly, acknowledging the sympathy.

"And a friend at work, her husband was in the Dover Patrol and he's lost at sea. His boat was sunk by a U-boat."

"Bloody Jerries," muttered her father. "Bloody war."

"That's partly why I'm so pleased you could help Bernie," Louisa went on. "No one should be forced to go to that hell, not if they don't think it's the right thing to do."

"Is that why you helped Bernie? Because of your son?" Nora asked, watching Teddy with interest. Louisa wondered if she could see they were holding hands under the table, so she let go of Teddy's fingers.

"It is," Teddy said carefully. He always spoke more slowly and more cautiously when he was discussing Philip. It was as though he'd rehearsed what to say when he was asked, so he didn't have to think about the horror behind his words. "I have always wondered if Philip wanted to enlist to impress me. And of course I encouraged him to fight for king and country. When he died, I felt awful. I still feel awful."

Nora patted his arm. "You shouldn't blame yourself," she said. "We all make mistakes as parents." Her eyes met Louisa's, and Lou smiled at her, realizing that was another apology of sorts.

The back door opened and Lettie and Roddy both shouted: "Bernie! Bernie!"

Louisa looked round and there, looking sturdier, healthier and ruddier than she'd ever seen him before, was Bernie.

She rushed over to him and gave him a hug. "Bernie, you look wonderful."

He beamed at her. "So do you," he said, holding her at arm's length and examining her face. "Something's agreeing with you."

He glanced at Teddy and gave Louisa a knowing smile. She made a face at him, urging him not to say anything because she was, after all, still a married woman. He understood.

"And, Teddy," he said. "Good to see you."

The men shook hands and Jenny fussed round Bernie, pouring him tea and serving him an enormous slice of cherry cake.

"All good in the top field," he told Matthew. "That's ready for planting. And I've swept up all the leaves in the orchard."

"Great."

Louisa smiled at the conversation. "You sound like you've settled in."

"I love it," Bernie said. He sounded a bit surprised about it. "It's all the things I loved about Kew—feeling the connection to the earth, seeing time passing—but added to that is the feeling that I'm doing my bit, you know? Not just hiding out."

"You're definitely doing your bit," Matthew said. "We couldn't have expanded the vegetable patches as we have without Bernie."

"Would you like me to show you round?"

"I'd love it."

So Louisa, Teddy and Bernie all pulled on their coats and boots and headed outside.

"Shall we start at the top and work our way down?" Bernie said. The farm was on a slope, so they'd always called the different areas the top and the bottom.

"Let's go."

They wandered up along the footpath to the top field, while Bernie explained what they were planning to plant.

"Cabbages, obviously," he said. "More potatoes, and maybe some cauliflowers for now. But there's scope for more."

They admired the fields, the hops poles, and the orchards—bare now, but Bernie assured them the harvest had been a good one—and listened to Bernie's idea to experiment with growing mushrooms.

"Listen to me, banging on," he said eventually, as they skirted the duck pond and the new henhouses.

"How's Ivy? She sends me drawings, bless her."

Louisa paused. "Can we sit down?"

Bernie gestured to a hay bale on its side by the henhouses and they all sat on it.

"What's happened?"

Louisa grimaced. "Ivy's in a bad way. Jim's stopped writing."

"No," Bernie said, his face paling.

"I'm afraid so. So obviously poor Ivy is convinced he's dead, but poor Win lost her Archie recently and she's adamant Ivy would have heard, officially, if Jim had been killed."

"Gosh, what an awful thing," Bernie said. He looked stricken. "What an awfully horrible thing to happen."

"That's not even all of it."

"It's not?" Bernie looked alarmed.

Louisa glanced round to check there were no small children lurking nearby who could overhear, and then said: "She's expecting. Ivy's expecting a baby."

"Oh heavens."

Louisa nodded grimly. "I know."

"What's she going to do?"

"She's going to have a baby," Louisa said with a small smile. "And then Win and I are going to help her."

"What about Jim?"

She shrugged. "I suppose we'll just hear when we hear. Ivy and I are planning to visit his mum and see if she's heard anything."

"He could still be alive," Teddy put in. "Men often end up in hospital without anyone knowing who they are, so their families don't know for months."

"Exactly," Louisa agreed. "He could be injured. Or there could be another reason for his letters stopping. It doesn't necessarily mean he's dead." She swallowed a sob.

"He could still be alive," she echoed.

Bernie nodded.

"I might know a way to find out for sure," he said. "Don't say anything to Ivy yet, but I might have something up my sleeve."

"Really and truly?" said Louisa, grateful for any help they could get. "Thank you."

Chapter 26

Bernie had been bursting with pride as he showed Louisa and Teddy round the farm. He'd felt a bit awkward at first, given it was Louisa's childhood home, but she asked so many questions and was so interested that he was soon enjoying showing off his hard work.

But the news about Ivy and Jim had stopped him in his tracks. He knew Jim had been sending Ivy seeds to plant, and had thought it a wonderful idea. And he knew that something had to have happened for Jim to stop writing. Fortunately, as he'd said to Louisa, he had an idea about finding out what that was.

The rest of the afternoon passed in a happy blur. Bernie was very pleased to see Louisa and Teddy were close. He wondered if there was any way they could become a proper couple. Could Louisa divorce Reg? He'd heard about couples divorcing but never met anyone who'd been through it. It seemed unfair, though, that Louisa couldn't move on with her life while Reg was doing whatever he wanted down in Folkestone.

"How are the locals being with you?" Louisa asked as they waited for

Matthew to bring round the horse and cart for their journey home. She and Teddy could have stayed but Louisa had said she wasn't sure how things would be with her parents so she'd decided to just come for one day—for now. She was sure she'd be back soon.

Bernie considered her question. There was Mrs. Lannister in the post office, who was always terribly nice, and the men in the pub had been standoffish at first but were now pleasingly accepting.

He smiled. "They're very nice."

But Louisa fixed him with her sternest glare.

"Are they, Bernie?"

He caved at once. "They are nice, that's the truth. But . . ."

"But?"

"They don't know I'm a conchie."

Teddy winced at the term, which had become an insult. Bernie had even heard some of the village children using it as a way to annoy one another.

"Don't say that."

Bernie shrugged. "It's the truth."

"Will you tell them?"

"Matthew says no one need know, and I'm inclined to agree."

Louisa and Teddy looked at each other. Bernie knew they would be worried about his keeping more secrets.

"I'm not lying. If anyone asks outright, then I'll tell them," he assured them. "I'm just not going to announce it to anyone and everyone."

"If you're sure?"

"I'm sure."

Matthew pulled the cart round to the front of the house and Louisa picked up her bag.

"Just be careful, Bernie," she said, kissing him on the cheek.

Bernie had a few more jobs to do in the evening. Then, as soon as he'd eaten, he hurried into his room to start putting his plan into action.

He was very happy at the farm, and having a proper bedroom had simply made him feel more at home. It wasn't fancy—just distempered brick walls and an iron-framed bed. But he and Matthew had made bookshelves from more bricks and planks of wood and a desk from an old door he'd found in the barn, sanded down and varnished, and those things had made the room his own.

Now, he sat down at his desk and pulled a notepad toward him. Teaching at the same minor public school he'd attended as a boy may not have turned out to be the best decision he'd made, but it had certainly come with some positives and he intended to use the old boys' network to his advantage.

Thinking, he tapped his lip with his pencil. Who might be able to help? He'd start with his old school friend Wally. He was at the War Office now, Bernie believed. And Wally owed him a favor because Bernie had pulled some strings to get his son into St. Richard's when Wally had forgotten to put him on the waiting list.

He wrote down "Wally" on his pad.

Then there was Tobias Jackson's father. Tobias was at Oxford now, and doing rather well by all accounts, thanks in no small part to the reference Bernie had given him. Wasn't his father a field marshal? Or possibly he'd been promoted since Bernie last heard news of him. Yes, he'd most certainly be useful. Now, what was his name? He paused, drumming the end of his pencil on the desk. Jackson. Jackson . . .

"David," he said out loud. He scribbled it down. Who else? What about that irritating lad who'd been grumpy as anything in class, surly and silent, and then sang like an angel in choir? Sylvester, someone? Wasn't his father an MP? In fact, wasn't he now a minister? Bernie had seen his name somewhere recently.

With a flash of memory he dashed into the kitchen and found yesterday's newspaper under the sleeping cat. He picked her up to retrieve it and she mewed in irritation.

"Hush," he said, scratching her under her chin as he put her back down on the chair. She curled up and went back to sleep, and Bernie went back to his room.

He turned the pages of the paper quickly, scanning for the photograph he remembered seeing.

Yes, there it was. Marcus Francis-Evans. Goodness, he was in the wartime cabinet. He wondered if he would be able to help. Bernie hadn't had a lot to do with Sylvester at St. Richard's—the boy wasn't much interested in the classics, preferring to spend his time playing piano and singing. Could he ask for his father's help now? Why would he help him? He probably wouldn't even remember Bernie Yorke, a former teacher at his son's school.

He'd remember Vivienne, though. Beautiful, talented music teacher Vivienne.

Thinking about Vivi made his stomach lurch. He couldn't possibly contact her now and ask for a favor. Could he?

He thought about Ivy, pregnant and alone, worrying about what had happened to Jim. And he thought about how she and Jim had looked out for him, hidden him at St. Anne's, brought him food when he was hungry. And he thought that however difficult it would be to get in touch with Vivienne, he would do it. For Ivy.

❦

The next day, Bernie had a stack of letters on his desk, each addressed to an old friend or a former pupil's father. In each one he'd explained briefly that a good friend of his had lost contact with her fiancé—he thought that sounded stronger than "sweetheart"—and was desperate to hear word of him.

This young woman has an astonishing character, he wrote. *She is kind and always puts everyone else's feelings above her own. She looked out for me when I was at my lowest and I believe she saved my life. I hope you can help me now, when she is in her hour of need.*

Then he'd carefully reminded the recipient of the favors he'd done for them over the years.

I hear Tobias is making a mark for himself at Oxford, and is tipped to be a future prime minister, he wrote. Or, *I trust Lawrence is enjoying his time at St. Richard's and making good friends, as we did.*

When it came to the letter for Marcus Francis-Evans, he simply wrote about Ivy and how much she meant to him and what she'd done for him. Then he sealed the envelope and put it inside another with a note for Vivienne. It had taken four attempts before he managed to get the right balance between the airy tone of catching up with an old friend and reminding her that her cruelty and disregard for his feelings had cost him his job and almost his sanity.

I wondered if I may ask you a favor, as a former colleague and friend, he wrote. *I know you were close to the Francis-Evans family, and nurtured young Sylvester's considerable talent. May I ask you to pass on the enclosed letter to his father, and perhaps let him know it's of vital importance? I trust you are well and happy. I'm sure you would want to know that I have put the miserable business at St. Richard's behind me and hold no ill will toward anyone from that time.*

He tucked the stack of letters into his pocket and went to check with Matthew that it was all right for him to pop to the post office.

Matthew agreed, and Jenny asked him to pick up a few things from the shops. So Bernie wrapped up in his coat and hat—it was another blustery day—and headed off down the lane to the village.

Mrs. Lannister greeted him like an old friend, chattering away as he stuck the stamps on his letters.

"And you'll never guess who my husband thought he saw this morning," she said. Bernie made a noncommittal noise that could have meant anything from "Oh my gosh, who was it?" to "Honestly, I could not care less." Mrs. Lannister was always telling him stories about people he didn't know; he took it as a compliment that she forgot he was a newcomer to Cassingham.

"Reg Taylor," she said in triumph. Bernie winced. He paused in the licking of his stamps and looked at her.

"Reg Taylor?"

"Like a bloody bad penny. He always turns up sooner or later. My Stevie, he said he was down at the coast, Dover, I think."

"Folkestone," Bernie said.

"Folkestone, that's it. Staying with that sour-faced sister of his. No wonder he's slunk back up here with his tail between his legs—can't be much fun down there with her."

"What's he like?" Bernie was curious about Louisa's husband, and he didn't feel like he could quiz Matthew about him.

Mrs. Lannister looked at him, brow furrowed. "Don't you know him?"

"He'd gone before I arrived."

"Of course." She let out a peal of laughter. "I always forget you're not a Hamilton by birth. You're part of that farm now."

Bernie was pleased but still eager to hear about Reg.

"What's he like?" he asked again.

Mrs. Lannister leaned over the counter and cupped her chin in her hand, thinking.

"He's one of those that goes round thinking the world owes him a living."

Bernie nodded. He'd met plenty of those men in his time.

"And he's a drinker. And when he drinks, there's no telling what he'll do. He's handy with his fists, he's rude. But when he's sober, he's a nice chap. Good company. Popular among the lads in the village."

"Poor Louisa," Bernie muttered under his breath, but Mrs. Lannister had ears like a bat and heard him.

"She's well rid, if you ask me. I always admired her, going off like that. Very bold."

"She is."

Mrs. Lannister stood upright, signaling their conversation was over.

"I imagine you'll meet Reg soon enough if he's back," she said. "He'll show up somewhere before too long. Wanting something, no doubt."

⁓

Matthew said the same when Bernie told him the news.

"He'll turn up here, I imagine," he said. He was under the cart, flat on his back, mending one of the wheels so Bernie couldn't see his face. But he could hear the tone of his voice, which sounded less than impressed. "He always comes here when he wants something. He was so put out when Louisa left him that he thinks we owe him. He can't see that she left because of the baby."

Bernie liked how Matthew was solidly, quietly supportive of Louisa. "Will you help him?"

Matthew was quiet for a moment.

"I'll let him sleep in the barn over winter, I suppose. I wouldn't want any man outside with the weather so wild. But no. I don't think we'll help him. I think it's time he found his own way."

"That's a nice thing to do." Bernie admired Matthew's sense of right and wrong, which to him seemed in keeping with his own Quaker belief in tolerance. "He might enlist. Married men are being called up now. And he's not working."

"I don't imagine they can find him," Matthew said. "But he's too old anyway, which is lucky for him; but luckier for the army, in my opinion. I'd not want to be in a trench with him."

Matthew slid out from underneath the cart and looked up at Bernie.

"If he's going to show up anywhere, it'll be in the pub. I'm going for a drink later if you fancy it?"

Bernie didn't drink, not really. He occasionally had a brandy if he'd had a shock—he'd had quite a lot of brandy when the whole Vivienne thing happened—but he rarely joined the men in the village pub. He was tempted, though. Intrigued by the prospect of meeting the man Louisa had run from.

"I might do that," he said to Matthew. "Thanks."

Chapter 27

And so, later that evening, Bernie and Matthew headed down to the pub. Because the village had a lot of farms, there were still a few men around, so the pub was normally busy enough. Bernie hadn't been in it before, but he knew Matthew's friends, and he knew the farmhands and most of the villagers. They all greeted him like an old pal and offered to buy him a drink—he asked for a small beer—and after a while, Bernie relaxed, enjoying the company and the laughter. It was nice to be out with other people, rather than reading alone in his room—which he also enjoyed, but perhaps not every night.

After about an hour, Matthew nudged him.

"Told you," he said, nodding his head toward the door. "Reg."

The man who'd entered had a ruddy complexion and thinning hair. Bernie knew he was only in his early forties, but he looked older. He was slightly unsteady on his feet as he came through the door like a returning hero.

"Look who's back, lads," he said.

The men all looked up and Bernie was sure he saw more than one of them wince. But some of the older farmhands smiled and patted Reg on the back, and someone bought him a drink.

He stayed at the bar for a while, getting through his first beer in the blink of an eye and telling tales—to everyone and no one—of what he'd been getting up to in Folkestone. Bernie began to see what Mrs. Lannister had meant when she said he thought the world owed him a living.

". . . so I told him where he could stick his bloody job," Reg was saying, hooting with laughter. He pushed his empty beer glass across the bar. "Stick another one in there, Jeanie."

The barmaid, Jeanie, pushed it back. "Not unless you show me your money."

Bernie hid his smile. He liked Jeanie, who took no nonsense. She had a little boy, a sad-eyed lad called Peter who was missing his dad dreadfully while he was away at the Front. Bernie sometimes sat with Peter and read to him, or just chatted to the boy about what he was up to. He was a sweet child.

Reg sighed.

"Things are a bit tight now, Jeanie love," he said. "I'll see you right, though. Don't I always?"

Jeanie glared at him. "Never."

Reg turned to the bar. "Hear that, lads? She says I never pay up. Anyone stand this old friend a drink?"

There was a pause and for a moment, Bernie thought no one would offer. But eventually one of the farmhands from down in the valley raised a finger to Jeanie.

"Put it on my tab," he said in a resigned voice. Jeanie nodded and filled Reg's tankard. Bernie could see Reg trying to look down the front of Jeanie's dress as she pulled his pint, and he felt repulsion. Matthew obviously recognized the expression on his face because he grinned at Bernie.

"He's a waste of bloody space, that man," he said. Bernie chuckled, enjoying feeling part of something with the farmer.

But then everything changed. Reg took his tankard full of beer and turned, raising it to the pub, and as he did so, he spotted Matthew and Bernie in the corner.

"Matt," he said. "My brother's in the bar, lads, and he's not even said hello."

"I'm not your brother," Matthew said quietly through gritted teeth. Then: "Hello, Reg."

Reg came over to their table. Matthew didn't ask him to sit down.

"How are things on the farm?" Reg said. "Bet it's hard work, with the lads away. I heard Alex went."

Matthew nodded, looking into his pint. "He did. Things were tough for a while."

"Need any help?"

Matthew drew in a breath and met Reg's red-rimmed stare.

"You can stay in the barn over winter, but you need to go in the spring," he said. "And I don't need your help because it's winter now anyway, so there's not as much to do. And frankly, Reg, you're a liability on the farm. You always end up costing me money. We've got Bernie now, anyway."

Reg's eyes narrowed. "Who's Bernie?"

Bernie gave a small wave.

"Hello," he said nervously. "I'm Bernie."

Reg turned his bloodshot stare on to Bernie, who felt himself recoil from the beery breath. Reg had sunk a few beers since he arrived and he'd not been sober then. He looked to Bernie's inexperienced eyes like he was spoiling for a fight. Matthew clearly thought so, too. He stood up and put his hand on Reg's arm.

"Let me buy you a drink," he said.

Reg shook him off. "In a minute," he said. "First, I want to take a look at the runt who's taken my job."

Bernie's heart was pounding. He hated confrontation and aggression of any sort.

"What can he do that I can't?" Reg asked Matthew, his glare still fixed on Bernie. "He's only small. Skinny fella like that can't lift baskets of apples like I can."

"You'd be surprised," Matthew said. "And he certainly doesn't drop apples like you do. Bernie's stronger than he looks, he's fitter than you, younger than you, he doesn't drink away the profits like you do, and he's sober."

Reg snorted. "Sober."

Then he looked round at Bernie again.

"And younger."

Bernie froze as Reg thumped on the table with his two fists.

"Younger," he repeated. "Young enough to enlist, eh?"

Bernie wasn't sure what to say. At a loss he looked to Matthew for help, but he just shrugged.

Sensing weakness, Reg pounced. "So why haven't you, then?"

"Why haven't I?"

"Enlisted."

Bernie wasn't ashamed of being a conscientious objector; he was certain in his beliefs and he knew he was doing his own bit by working at the farm. But he found he couldn't quite get the words out now, faced with Reg's red, angry face and the knowledge of what this man had done to Louisa.

"You're a conchie," Reg said in triumph. A bit of spittle flew from the side of his mouth and landed on the table in front of Bernie. "You're a bloody conchie."

He grabbed hold of the front of Bernie's jumper and pulled him upright.

"I ought to take you outside right now and give you a good hiding," Reg growled. "I should beat the living daylights out of you."

Finally, Bernie found his voice.

"Why don't you, then?" he said. "Why not punch me? Go on. Or do you only hit women?"

Reg's face got a bit redder. "I'm a real man. Not like you, you bloody coward."

Bernie, filled with courage he'd never thought he had, laughed in his face.

"I may be a conchie," he said, "but at least I've never hit a woman. I've never beaten my wife black and blue, or punched her so hard she lost her baby."

Reg's face was purple now. He twisted his hand so his grip on Bernie's jumper increased, and it tightened round his neck. Bernie raised his head to free himself slightly, but he didn't move.

"Louisa's told me all about you, and what you did," he said. "You drank away your inheritance—the farm your father worked hard to build up—and you drank away your marriage and you killed your baby. I'd rather be a conchie than a baby killer."

Reg let go of his jumper and Bernie stumbled backward, putting a hand on the table to balance himself.

"Listen to the lies he's spouting about me," Reg declared to the pub. Everyone was standing still and silent, watching the altercation. All Bernie could hear, apart from Reg's drunken ranting, was his own breathing and his own heart thumping. "He thinks he can say rotten things about me—him a newcomer to Cassingham and me having lived here since I was a lad, and my father and grandfather before me. What kind of a man must he be to make up such shit?"

Matthew took a step forward so he was standing next to Bernie.

"A good man," he said. "A truthful man. A better man than you, Reg Taylor."

Reg spluttered with anger. "A coward and a conchie, more like."

"Bernie works hard on the land, just as you should have. His efforts feed the families in this village. What have you done, Reg?"

Bernie felt a warm glow of friendship, hearing Matthew speak up for him. Reg was still spluttering, mumbling about knowing your own and family.

Behind the bar, Jeanie raised her voice. "Bernie's been so good to my Peter, looking out for him while my Kenneth's away. He's a treasure."

"Peter's a good lad," Bernie said, not wanting to take credit.

Mrs. Lannister, who'd been standing by the door, having arrived to track down Stevie just as Reg started his rants, came over and gave the drunk man a prod in the ribs.

"You could do better than take a leaf out of Bernie's book," she said. "He helped Stevie with the thatching last week. Wouldn't take nothing for it, neither."

"I was interested to learn," Bernie told her, but she waved his comments aside.

The landlord of the pub, a thickset man called Ernie, with heavy eyebrows, who Bernie was more than a little scared of, appeared at Reg's side.

"Right," he said. "I think that's quite enough of that."

Bernie's shoulders slumped. "I'm sorry. I'll go."

But Ernie put his huge hand on Bernie's shoulder.

"You're going nowhere," he growled in his ear, and Bernie stayed exactly where he was, barely moving a muscle. His heart pounded harder.

Ernie reached out an arm and took Reg by the collar. "Bernie's part of Cassingham now," he said. "He's one of us, and he's doing as much as he can to help. Whereas you are a despicable, no-good baby-killer and a wifebeater and if I ever see you in here again, I'll kick you into next week. Understand?"

Reg seemed to shrink under Ernie's glare. He nodded, and without another word, he turned and slunk out of the pub.

"I'm not sorry he's gone, even though his drinking is always good news for my takings," Ernie said. He slapped Bernie on the back, so hard Bernie almost fell over. "What will you have, lad?"

⁂

The next morning, Bernie found he couldn't stop thinking about the previous night's events.

"Do you know where Reg might have gone?" he asked Matthew. "Could he be in your barn?"

"Probably." Matthew shrugged. "I should move him on, really."

But Bernie shook his head. "Don't, not yet."

"Bernie, he's a nuisance and a drunk. He needs to go."

"He deserves a second chance."

"He's already had a second, third, fourth chance and he's blown every one."

Bernie was determined, though. "Can I have a chat with him? See if I can get through somehow."

"If you really want to." Matthew looked dubious. "But this is absolutely the last time. If he can sober up and start helping, he can stay. Otherwise, he needs to go. However bad the weather is."

"Thanks," Bernie said.

Matthew rolled his eyes but in a good-natured way. "It's the old barn behind the hops poles."

So Bernie trudged through the poles in the wind and rain to the barn and found Reg sitting on an old cider barrel, smoking a cigarette.

"Look who it is," he said as Bernie approached. "Bloody Bernie, the conchie."

Undeterred by the hostility, Bernie upended another barrel and sat down next to him.

"Matthew wants to throw you out," he said. "Thinks you should move on."

"Come to help me pack?"

Bernie smiled. "No," he said. "I talked him into letting you stay."

"Why would you do that?"

"Because everyone deserves a second chance and because everyone's got something to offer."

Reg snorted. "And he agreed, just like that, did he?"

"No. There are some conditions."

"Course there are."

"If you can stay off the drink and help around the farm, you can stay."

Bernie expected aggression from Reg, but what he actually got was resignation.

"I can't, can I?" he said. "I've tried to stay away from booze so many times, but each time it gets harder."

"I can help you, if you'll let me."

Reg looked up at Bernie and the younger man felt a wave of sympathy as he saw the hope in those red-rimmed eyes.

"Will you?"

"It won't be easy."

"I know."

"Then come with me. Bring your things—you'll be away for a little while."

"Where are we going?"

Bernie thought about whether to tell Reg or just take him, and he decided it was better he knew.

"Salvation Army in Maidstone," he said. "They're good people, Reg. Caring, considerate. And they understand men like you and your issues. They can help—if you're ready to try."

Reg nodded. "I'm ready," he said.

"Let's go."

With his head bowed, Reg gathered up his belongings, which were scattered across the barn, and gave Bernie a half-drunk bottle of whisky he produced from somewhere.

"Will you throw this away for me, Bernie?"

"Course."

Together they walked across the front of the barn toward the hops, but then Reg stopped. "Will you do something else for me?" he said.

Bernie looked at him suspiciously. "What?"

Reg took a breath and for a moment, a fleeting moment, Bernie thought his eyes were filled with tears. But surely he was mistaken?

"Can you tell Louisa I'm sorry. About the baby. About everything?"

Bernie shook his head. "That's something you can do yourself, Reg. When you're better."

"When I'm better," Reg said in wonder. "When I'm better."

"Come on," Bernie said. "Sooner we're there, sooner you'll start recovering."

He strode off down in between the hops poles, and after a moment's pause, Reg followed.

Chapter 28

January 1917

Louisa stared at the wonky handwriting on the envelope. Reg had never been one for penmanship and the mix of upper- and lowercase letters meant she recognized his scrawl immediately. But why was he writing to her? What could he possibly have to say?

She was alone in the break room at Kew, having come in to find a pair of dry gloves; hers were wet from clearing snow from the path and her fingers were icy cold. She'd found the letter sitting on the side, along with some others. Many of the gardeners had their post delivered to Kew—they were there so often it just made sense. But what didn't make sense was Reg writing her a letter.

She pulled out a chair and sat down at the table, turning the envelope over in her hands. She hated the way any remembrance of Reg brought back all the old feelings—the fear, the impotent rage, the helplessness. When she was feeling charitable, as she found she was more often these days, she could see that though his actions sent her life off down a different path, it wasn't a bad one. She had her friends at Kew, and the Suffragettes, and now she had Teddy. She smiled, thinking of her beau. But she didn't have her baby. And she still had nightmares occasionally where she was back on Reg's family farm, listening for his footsteps coming up the stairs and trying to work out if he was drunk just from the sound of his tread. She frowned again as she looked at the letter.

"Just open it, Louisa," she told herself. "How bad can it be?"

She knew Reg had briefly returned to Cassingham and then had gone again. From Matthew's letters, it sounded as though Bernie had something to do with it—though what he'd done, Louisa couldn't imagine and she'd not asked. Sometimes, with Reg, it was better just to let sleeping dogs lie.

Taking a breath, she slid her finger under the envelope flap and pulled out the letter inside. There was just one sheet of paper, covered in Reg's unruly writing with a few words crossed out and one small ink spot. She blinked at the address on the top—the Salvation Army mission in Maidstone.

"What on earth . . . ?" she mumbled as she read.

Dear Louisa,

I am writing to say sorry for all the wrongs I have done you over the years. I am living in Maidstone now and working at the mission. They are good blokes and they have helped me stop drinking and see that I had to change my life. Your friend Bernie brought me here after we had a bust-up in the pub and though I was angry at first, I see it was the right thing to do. He is nice though a bit of an odd one and I owe him a lot.

Louisa, it is not easy looking at what I've done with sober eyes. I was a bad bloke back then and a bad husband. And when I think about the way I treated you, I feel so guilty. I am sorry for hitting you. And Louisa I am so sorry that you lost the baby. Our baby. I know nothing I say now will ever put that right, but you should know that I think about it every day and wish things could have been different.

I don't blame you for going away, not one bit. And I won't blame you if you rip up this letter and put me out of your head forever. But I just wanted to say sorry.

Your husband,
Reg

Louisa sat for a little while, reading and rereading Reg's words. She thought about the terrible day when he'd lost his temper so badly and hit her, over and over again, even though she cried out to him, reminding him she was carrying his child. And when her stomach started cramping and the bleeding started, she'd wept for so long that her eyes swelled and she could barely see. The day she'd delivered their baby was the worst day of her life. She had only been just over halfway through her pregnancy, with a tiny bulge to her stomach. But the labor pains had been searing and the pain in her heart worse. She didn't see the baby; the midwife bundled it up and took it away before Louisa had really known what was happening. There had been no funeral; there was no grave to visit. But it had felt like a death to Louisa.

She breathed in deeply. Could she forgive Reg now? She tested her feelings gently and decided that no, she couldn't. She suspected she would never forgive him for what he'd done. But knowing he was sorry, that he, too, thought about their child, who had never taken a breath, that helped a little. She smiled, a small, sad smile. She was glad he'd had help to stop drinking and she was glad Bernie had been the one to do it. He was remarkable, that man.

"What's that?"

Louisa looked up to see Ivy, longing in her eyes. "Is it a letter? Is it from Jim?"

There had been no word from Jim all winter, just endless reports from the Front of awful conditions, gas attacks, and daily casualty lists. They'd visited Jim's mum and been half relieved and half devastated to discover she'd not heard anything, either. Things felt very bleak as far as Ivy was concerned, and though Louisa and Win tried to keep her spirits up, it wasn't easy.

"I'm afraid not, my love," she said, hating to dash her friend's hopes. "It's from Reg."

Ivy forced a smile. "Silly, to keep thinking he'll write," she said. "I just can't help it."

Louisa reached out and took Ivy's hand. "I know," she said.

There was a pause as Ivy took in what Louisa had said. "Reg?"

"Would you believe it?"

"What does he say?"

"He says sorry."

Ivy snorted and Louisa chuckled.

"That's what I thought at first, but I've read it over and over and I think he's sincere. It's all down to Bernie."

Ivy made a face. "What? Read it to me."

She sat down at the table with a grunt, loosening her waistband as she did. She was so tiny that her pregnancy had been easy to hide so far, but she was getting further along now and Louisa knew she must be uncomfortable, though she never complained.

"Ready?"

Ivy nodded, and Louisa read out the letter.

"Goodness," Ivy said when she'd finished. "That's a turnup for the books."

"Isn't it just?"

"What do you think?"

Louisa shrugged. "I can't forgive him."

Ivy ran her hand over her swelling stomach. "Don't blame you."

Louisa watched her friend gently caressing her baby and nodded. "But maybe it's time to put it all behind me."

"You should plant something," Ivy said. "As a memorial to your baby."

Louisa blinked away tears. "That's a lovely idea."

Ivy was thinking. "Lilies," she said. "They're a symbol of a mother's love."

Touched, Louisa could only nod.

"I'll give you a corner of my letter garden," Ivy said. "There's a patch in the corner that catches the sun just at the right time. We'll do it in the spring."

"Thank you," Louisa said, and Ivy smiled at her.

"We're family now, Lou. Need to look out for each other."

Louisa fixed her with a stern look. "Speaking of which . . ."

Ivy threw her head back, clearly recognizing from Louisa's tone what was coming.

"I don't want to," she said.

"Ivy, look at the size of you. Someone will realize soon. You need to tell your mum, and probably Jim's mum, too."

"I know," Ivy said. "I'm just scared about what they'll say. Mum will be worried about money . . ."

"There's no need," Louisa jumped in. "You know that. Win's said you and the baby can live with her for as long as you want. And I'll help whenever I can. This baby is going to have one mother and two very devoted godmothers."

Ivy smiled. "I know. But it's not right, is it? Expecting when I'm not married, and I've no idea where Jim is or even if he's ever coming home. I'm worried about what everyone will think."

"I understand. I'll come with you when you tell your mum, if you like?"

"Yes, please. She won't get so angry if you're there."

"You don't need to tell Jim's mum yet, I don't think. Wait until the baby arrives," Louisa said thoughtfully. "If you think that's best. But you will have to tell her one day."

Ivy shrugged. "I know."

"Do you know what?" Louisa leaned over the table conspiratorially.

"What?"

"I bet you're not the only girl in this position."

Ivy looked surprised. "Really?"

"Course not. All the men off at the Front? Sad good-byes and no time for weddings? There are bound to be lots of war babies being born."

Ivy smiled. "I suppose."

"And it's not ideal, but listen, if the worst happens and Jim doesn't come home . . ."

Ivy winced at her words and Louisa felt a stab of guilt. She took Ivy's hand.

"If he doesn't come home, then we can buy a wedding ring and you can call yourself missus."

"But . . ." Ivy began, and Louisa shushed her.

"We'll make this work," she said. "The three of us together."

"Four," said Ivy, patting her stomach with a smile.

"Four."

Louisa paused again, because there was something else she wanted to say and she wanted to make sure she said it right.

"You need to tell Mac."

"No."

"Ivy."

"No, absolutely not. He's such a moral bloke, Mac. He's so black and white about things. He'll be disappointed." Ivy's eyes filled with tears. "I can't bear for him to be disappointed in me."

Louisa shook her head. "He adores you, Ivy. And he adores Jim, too. He might be shocked but I don't think he'll be disappointed."

Ivy made a face. "I don't want to."

"Ivy, you're tired and uncomfortable, and it's only going to get worse. You can't bend down properly anymore. You're breathless. I saw you pushing the wheelbarrow up that ramp the other day and I was terrified. It's so slippery on the paths at the moment because of the snow, and there's you pushing a wheelbarrow. What if you'd slipped and fallen onto your belly?"

Louisa felt her voice catch and she took a breath, trying to calm down.

"I'm just frightened that something's going to happen to you. Or to the baby. I lost my baby because of Reg's violence and your baby is only here because of it. The little one feels like a miracle and I couldn't bear to lose another child, even if it's not my own."

Ivy hugged her tummy. "I'm fine," she said, but her voice was uncertain. "You don't have to worry about me."

"But I do worry."

"I need to work, Louisa," Ivy said. "If I'm doing this on my own, being a mum to this baby without Jim next to me, then I need money. Babies need clothes and somewhere to sleep, and then they grow up into children who need shoes and books and unbelievable amounts of food, if my brothers are anything to go by. It's a lifetime commitment, isn't it? And I know you and Win are standing by me, and believe me, I'd be lost without you, but I don't want to rely on you forever."

"I hear what you're saying," Louisa said truthfully. She did understand the point Ivy was making—who knew what could happen in the future? Lives could be snuffed out in a second, babies born, relationships built. Ivy was young, but she was sensible, and preparing for life as a mother was the right thing to do.

Louisa thought for a minute.

"You could still work," she said slowly. "As long as Mac's on board, we can arrange the jobs so you do less physical things. You can order plants, and sweep the paths, and trim the hedges, perhaps. There's not so much to do right now anyway, because it's so cold. We can easily make allowances for your condition."

Ivy considered it. "There's lots I can still do. For now, anyway."

"See? It's all fine. You just need to tell Mac."

"I'll think about it, is that good enough?"

Louisa rolled her eyes. "For now," she said. "But I'm going to keep nagging."

"S'all right. I quite like it," Ivy said with a little smile. "Shows you care. Right, best get back out there before Mac wonders where we've got to."

She stood up with a grunt, rubbing her back. "Oof."

"Keep doing that and everyone will realize you're expecting," Louisa joked.

Ivy stuck her tongue out and Louisa smiled to see her friend in good spirits. Things were tough for her, there was no doubt, but she was confident they could do this together. At least, she hoped they could.

She shoved Reg's letter into her locker, picked up a pair of dry gloves and looped her arm through Ivy's.

"Come on, then, fatty," she said. "Let's get going."

Chapter 29

Later that day, Ivy lay on the settee in Win's flat, exhausted by a hard day's work and wondering if Louisa might have a point. She probably should tell Mac the truth about her pregnancy but she just couldn't imagine saying the words. She'd not said them out loud to anyone. Perhaps she could give him some baby's breath, she thought wryly. Then he could work it out like Win and Louisa had done.

She sighed, arranging one of the cushions behind her head so she was more comfortable. Win didn't like her lying on the sofa; she said it was unseemly. But Ivy was tired and she needed to lie down, and she liked being able to see the park out of the lounge window; her bedroom was on the other side and didn't have the same view.

Win was out for the evening. Ivy didn't know where, but she assumed she had gone to another Suffragette meeting. Since Archie's death, Win had thrown herself into the fight for women's suffrage with vigor, regularly meeting up with her new friends and planning all sorts of action for when the war was over. If the war was ever over. It seemed never-ending, with worse news almost every day.

She felt the baby wriggling and put her hands on her belly.

"Hello," she whispered. "Hello, baby."

As she was dropping off to sleep, a knock on the door roused her. She sat up. Who could that be? She knew Louisa was spending the evening with Teddy and no one else ever visited. Perhaps Win had forgotten her key. She heaved herself up off the couch and waddled to the door. And there, standing in the hall was a group of Suffragettes all carrying bundles, bags and boxes. Win was right at the back, looking very pleased with herself.

"Hello!" Win called. "Can you let everyone in?"

Bewildered, Ivy stood aside and watched as the women trooped into the lounge, carrying their loads.

"What's all this? What's going on?" Ivy had no idea what was happening.

Henrietta, one of Louisa's Suffragette friends who Win had adopted, walked by with laundry basket full of fabric. She smiled at Ivy. "Come and see," she said.

Ivy followed her into the lounge.

"It's all for you," said Henrietta. "For your baby."

Ivy's jaw dropped. "How did you . . . ?"

Win gave her a sheepish smile. "I told them."

Ivy was bewildered. "What is all of this?"

Henrietta put her basket down on the floor with a *thump*. "This is baby clothes," she said. "None of it new, of course, but it's all clean and mended. Things our littl'uns have worn and grown out of. You'll be amazed how messy they get."

Ivy had no words.

"And this is nappies," said another woman, whose name, Ivy

thought, was Elizabeth. She held up a bundle. "Some are a bit thin, but they'll do."

"Clothes for you," another one—Sophie—said, holding up a bulging bag. "A few bigger dresses and skirts. We thought you might want to be discreet, and a few larger bits will help."

Ivy blinked fast, trying to stop the tears that were welling up in her eyes from falling. "It's all for me?"

"That's not all," said Henrietta. She stepped to one side, showing a pretty wooden crib, painted with purple and green flowers.

"Lucy's husband's a carpenter," Henrietta said. "He made this for you with leftover wood from work. And Mary Clark painted the flowers."

Lucy and Mary both raised their hands. Ivy was crying properly now.

"Suffragette colors," she sobbed. "You painted the flowers in Suffragette colors."

Mary chuckled. "Well, of course."

Win came over to Ivy and put her arms round her. Feeling totally overwhelmed, Ivy wept on her shoulder.

"I'm not sad," she told the watching women. "I'm not sad, I'm happy."

When she'd gathered herself, she sat down and blew her nose loudly. Win sat on one side, Henrietta on the other, while Mary, Lucy, Sophie and Elizabeth all sat on the floor.

"Why would you do this for me?" Ivy asked.

"Because you need help," Henrietta said simply. "You need help and we're in a position to give it."

"When I told them about what had happened with Jim, everyone was so concerned," Win explained. "And then one day I let slip about the baby. I'm sorry, Ivy, I know you wanted to keep it quiet. But I said something and Henrietta here put two and two together."

Ivy took her friend's hand. "Don't worry."

"Win explained you were finding it all a bit tricky, with not knowing about Jim, and working and that, so we thought we'd do what we could. When I mentioned it to the others, everyone wanted to pitch in."

Ivy gave them all a watery smile.

"Thank you," she whispered. She blew her nose again. "Thank you so much."

Henrietta patted her knee. "We know what you've done for the cause over the years. The sacrifices you've made. Olive told me . . ."

With horror, Ivy realized what Henrietta was about to say.

"Nothing," she said quickly. "It was nothing." She'd never told anyone what she'd done on that dark evening when she was a young girl, and she certainly didn't want Win to find out now. If Win knew, then it would only be a matter of time before Louisa found out and she wasn't sure how her friend would take the news, given how much she loved Kew. Mind you, she loved the Suffragettes, too. Perhaps she'd understand?

Henrietta was looking at Ivy with concern. "Are you feeling ill?"

She forced a smile. "Just overwhelmed. I can't believe you've all been planning this."

"It's not much, just a few hand-me-downs. But you deserve this, Ivy. Your baby deserves it."

Ivy reached into the bag of baby clothes and pulled out a tiny knitted cardigan.

"Ohhh, look at the size of it," she breathed. "It's lovely."

"My Albie wore that," Mary said. "Now he's taller than me. It doesn't seem possible."

Ivy chuckled. "I don't reckon my baby will ever be as tall as your Albie, not with me and Jim as its parents."

"We know it's tough, not knowing where Jim is or what's happened to him," said Elizabeth, worry etched in her face. "We've all had a taste of what that's like. Win's lost Archie, and Sophie's nephew was killed, and I've lost my brother. We want to help you, be here for you when the baby's born. We're not blood-related, but we're family."

Ivy felt a rush of love so powerful she almost felt dizzy. They were family. These were her sisters, sitting here with her, promising to look after her. She was so lucky to have them. It was as though the worry that had weighed her down for months and months was suddenly lifted. This would be all right, she thought. Even if—God forbid—Jim didn't come back, she would be all right. Because she had her baby, a tiny creature created from the love she and Jim shared, and she had her Suffragette sisters, who would stand by her, no matter what.

"I think we should have tea," Win said. "I'll go and make some. And I think there might be some shortbread in the cupboard, if Ivy's not polished it all off."

"I did," Ivy admitted. "But Edith brought round some more."

Win bustled off to start making tea, and Elizabeth and Sophie went to help. Ivy began opening the bags and admiring all the clothes the women had brought.

"This is wonderful," she said, holding up a loose-cut skirt. "This could be useful for work."

Henrietta frowned. "Win said you've not told anyone at work."

"No."

"Do you think it's time?"

Ivy hugged a little pair of knitted bootees to her chest. "No."

"Ivy?"

"You sound like Louisa."

Henrietta smiled. "Louisa is very sensible."

"She's worried I could hurt the baby by doing such physical work."

Henrietta nodded. "It's possible. You've not got long to go now. You don't want to take any risks."

"I'm scared to tell Mac, though. What if he turfs me out of Kew?"

"What if who turfs you out of Kew?" Win came into the room carrying a tea tray and caught the end of what Ivy was saying.

"Mac," Ivy explained. "I was just saying to Henrietta that I'm frightened to tell him about the baby. Because I'm scared I'll lose my job."

"Piffle, darling," Win said. "Mac adores you. As he should, because you are adorable."

"He adores me now," said Ivy glumly. "He might change his mind when he realizes I'm expecting and I'm not married."

"I'm sure he won't."

Henrietta and Mary had been whispering and now Henrietta looked up with a cheeky grin.

"If the worst comes to the worst, and he does sack you," she said, her smile growing wider, "we'll start another campaign to get you your job back. We'll march up and down outside like we did with the wages."

Ivy laughed. "I believe you'd do it."

"Oh, we'd do it."

"So don't you worry one bit," Mary said. Ivy smiled at her. She was a woman in her late fifties or possibly early sixties, with a dimpled smile and the energy of a far younger woman. "We're here to support you in any way you need us to. And that baby will have a whole bunch of aunties on hand to cuddle it and rock it to sleep and tell it off when it's cheeky."

"Then my baby will be the luckiest baby in London," said Ivy. "Just as I'm the luckiest girl."

"Will you tell him?" Henrietta said. "Tell Mac, and get him to look after you, too. You know you should."

Ivy took a breath. "I will tell him. I'll tell him tomorrow."

Chapter 30

When tomorrow came, she was so nervous she thought she might vomit. She practiced different ways of saying it.

"I'm having a baby," she said, looking at her face in the mirror as she tried to tame her hair. "I'm expecting."

Louisa was thrilled when Ivy told her she was going to tell Mac that day.

"You know it's the right thing to do," she said. "You'll feel better once it's done."

"I don't know what to say. I've been practicing."

"Just tell him you're having a baby—Jim's baby—and I promise you he'll be happy," Louisa said.

"You can't promise that," Ivy said darkly.

"Do you want me to come with you when you tell him?"

Ivy did want Louisa there, more than anything, but she knew she had to pull her socks up and do this herself, so she shook her head. "I'll be fine on my own."

They had been walking to work from the bus stop—Win was starting later, as she had the morning off to meet with a group that was organizing a memorial to the Dover Patrol—and were approaching the gates.

"Will you do it now?"

Ivy gritted her teeth. "I s'pose."

"Best to get it over with."

She nodded and drew a sharp breath as she saw Mac up ahead, going into the break room.

"Now?" she said.

"Now."

She couldn't walk very fast now because the baby pressed on her lungs and made her breathless, but Ivy speeded up as much as she could and, steeling herself, she pushed open the door to the break room. Mac looked up as she entered and smiled to see her.

"Morning, Ivy."

"Mac, could I have a quick word in private?"

"What's happened? Is it Jim? Have you heard something?"

"No," reassured Ivy. "No, I've not heard anything. But it is about Jim. Sort of."

Mac pulled out a chair. "Tell me."

Ivy wanted to cry because he was being so nice. But, not looking at Mac, she forced herself to speak.

"Before Jim went away, he and I . . ." She trailed off. Mac didn't need to know all the details. She tried again.

"I'm expecting," she said in a hurry, looking down at her lap. "I'm having a baby. Jim's baby."

Mac didn't speak. Bracing herself for judgment, Ivy slowly looked up, and to her confusion, she saw tears in his eyes.

"Are you angry?" she said, her voice wobbly. "Are you disappointed in me? I've let everyone down."

A tear fell onto her clasped hands and she wiped it away. "I'm so sorry."

There was a pause, and then Mac reached out a hand and took Ivy's fingers in his.

"Ivy, of course I'm not disappointed." He sniffed. "I'm happy."

"Happy?"

"I love Jim like he's my own," Mac said. "That lad's been with me since he was a young scrap of a thing, and I've taught him everything he knows—and now he knows more than me. And I miss him, Ivy. I'm so frightened that he's not coming home."

Ivy nodded, not trusting herself to speak in case all her pent-up emotions came flooding out.

"Now you tell me you're carrying his child. A little bit of him. And you think I'm disappointed?"

He nudged her.

"You could never disappoint me. None of you Kew Gardens Girls could ever make me less than proud."

Ivy wasn't sure about that, but she was so delighted by his reaction that she pushed those misgivings aside. "Louisa told me you'd be fine."

"She's a good woman."

Ivy grinned. "She is."

"Were you really worried about what I'd say?"

"I thought you might think I was bringing shame on Kew Gardens, being pregnant out of wedlock."

Mac patted her hand.

"No one needs know you're not married," he said. "We'll tell everyone you and Jim tied the knot before he went."

Ivy blinked at him. "Really?"

"We'll see you right," he said. "Don't you worry."

Ivy couldn't believe how nice everyone was being. "But what will people think?"

Mac snorted. "I don't care. And, let's be honest, you're not the first girl to be pregnant with a fella elsewhere."

"That's what Louisa said."

"See? Good woman."

Ivy smiled again. "You don't think people will talk?"

"Well, people in glass houses shouldn't throw stones." He grinned suddenly. "What would you have done, if I'd thrown you out?"

"The Suffragettes said they would campaign to get me my job back, like we campaigned for equal wages."

Mac's face was a picture. "Did they indeed? Those bloody women." But his eyes were smiling.

"You've changed your tune."

He nodded, grimacing slightly. "Can't say I agree with their methods, but let's just say I'm coming round to the argument." He paused. "Don't tell them that, though."

Ivy laughed properly, so thrilled that Mac was on her side and things were looking up—if only Jim was there to see how pleased Mac was about the baby. Did he even know about the baby? Had he ever got the letter with the baby's breath? She might never know.

"When are you due?"

"Spring."

"Not long. I can't believe you've kept it from me this whole time."

She shrugged. "I didn't know how to tell you."

"Next time, you come to me earlier."

Ivy hooted at the idea of there being a next time, and Mac smiled, too. Then he looked serious again for a moment.

"We need to make sure you're not working too hard. What were you thinking, keeping going like that?"

"I need the money."

"You still at Win's?"

She nodded. "The Suffragettes are helping, too. They brought me clothes and a crib. You should see it, Mac."

"Bloody women," he said with a smile.

With another weight lifted off her shoulders, Ivy spent the morning happily tidying up in the temperate house, not working too hard, taking rest breaks when she needed, and enjoying the warmth inside instead of the bitterly cold winter's day outside. She felt so much better now that the Suffragettes were helping and Mac was on her side. Just two things continued to bother her: She was still desperately hoping that Jim would get in touch, obviously, and she had a confession to make to Win and Louisa.

So, that evening, she gathered them together in Win's lounge.

"I want to tell you how grateful I am, how lucky I feel, and how I don't know what I'd do without you," she said.

Win took her hand. "Darling, I would have been lost without you when I got the news about Archie. This isn't all one-way."

Louisa nodded. "And you stuck by me when I made that awful mistake about Bernie. And you didn't blame me when Reg turned up and Jim enlisted. You're a wonderful friend, Ivy. Like Win says, this goes both ways."

Ivy made a face. "You might not agree when I tell you this."

Louisa and Win looked at each other and Ivy almost changed her mind. Almost.

She took a breath.

"A few years ago, things were really bad at home. Dad was off on one of his disappearing acts, Mum had not long had Elsie and was up to her elbows in washing and nappies, and the boys were under her feet . . . You know how it is? I wasn't going to school but no one cared. I was wild, really. And I met this woman called Olive one day. She was speaking in the street about how women were just as clever as men, but no one gave them a chance to prove it. And I thought about Mum working her fingers to the bone, and Dad swanning off when he felt like it. We got chatting and she was so kind to me, girls. So kind."

Louisa looked like this was a familiar tale. "Suffragette?" she asked.

"Suffragette."

"But . . . ?" Win was frowning. "It sounds like there's more to this story."

Ivy nodded. "This was back in 1913. Things were really hotting up with the WSPU. All sorts of things happening—women being arrested left, right and center, windows broken, stones being thrown. You remember."

Louisa nodded, a spark of something gleaming in her eye. "I remember."

"Olive wanted to really make people pay attention. I was hanging round Kew by then. I knew Mac and Jim, and I was always there, badgering them to teach me about the plants and let me help out. When Olive found out, it gave her an idea."

Louisa was staring at Ivy, obviously beginning to put two and two together. "The orchid house?"

"No," Ivy almost shouted. "No, never. I'd never destroy plants like that. I'm still not sure who did that, to be honest. I think someone overheard Olive's plan and thought they'd get in there first."

"Then the tea pavilion?"

Ivy felt hot shame flood her. "The tea pavilion."

"Oh, Ivy."

Win was looking baffled.

"What? You need to explain, darlings. Don't forget, I was down in Dover back then, happily bumbling along with Archie—no clue about the Suffragettes or any of this business."

"We hid some paraffin in the crypt at St. Anne's," Ivy said. "And when it got dark, we sneaked in and got it—we used it to soak pads of fabric.

Apparently that's the best way to make sure a fire catches. It was bell-ringing practice and one of the ringers was a Suffragette. She rang the bells extra loud to make sure no one heard us. I took Olive and another woman, Lilian, into the Gardens and I led them through to the pavilion. They scattered the pads around and then set the pavilion alight. I was horrified, you have to believe me. I didn't realize how brutal it was going to be, that it would burn so fast or so hot."

"Did you burn your arm?" Louisa said. "Is that what the scar's from?"

Ivy pushed up her sleeve to show the burn that she kept hidden. Louisa must have noticed it one day when they were getting dressed in the break room. It had faded to pink now, rather than the livid red it once was, but the skin was puckered and shiny, and it would never go away. Ivy thought of it as a mark of her shame for being involved in such a terrible deed.

"I deserved it," she said.

Win was looking at her, eyes narrowed. "No," she said. "No you didn't, darling."

"I shouldn't have done it."

"Probably not, but you were young. And you thought you were doing the right thing for women you respected."

"And remember how it was back then, Ivy?" Louisa put in. "Things were hot, fevered, almost out of control. Emily Davison died just a few weeks later, remember? It was so shocking."

Win nodded. "Oh, I remember how awful that was. That poor woman falling under the horse like that."

"It was dreadful," Louisa agreed. "We were fighting so hard and getting nowhere and people were becoming more and more desperate." She shook her head and looked at Ivy. "Burning the tea pavilion was wrong, there's no doubt about it. But I understand why it happened and it wasn't your fault."

Ivy breathed out slowly. Off the hook again. "Should I tell Mac?"

"No!" Louisa and Win shouted together.

"I don't think so, Ivy. Not this time," Louisa added.

"But I feel so awful."

"He was dreadfully upset about the orchids and the tea pavilion. Remember we had to hide our badges, that first day? It's taken him all this time to accept us, and to accept our involvement with the Suffragettes, Ivy. Don't put this on him."

"I should be punished, though. I should make amends for what I did."

"Not by telling Mac."

Win looked thoughtful. "I agree with Louisa," she said. "Darling, I see why you want to confess, but I really feel, in this instance, it wouldn't be helpful. It might make you feel better, but I'm not sure it would make Mac feel better."

"What can I do?"

"My Archie always used to say that when you did something wrong, you had to make it right."

"I can't rebuild the pavilion," Ivy said.

"No. But I'm sure there's another way to make amends. Heavens above, you've been working in Kew long enough—your efforts in the Gardens should be enough."

"It's not enough," Ivy muttered.

"Then we'll come up with something else."

"Really?"

Louisa nodded, agreeing with Win. "Really. For now at least, let's keep this secret between the three of us Kew Gardens Girls. No one else needs to know."

Ivy nodded. "All right," she said. "I'll keep it secret. For now."

Chapter 31

March 1917

Ivy was feeling glum. There was still no news of Jim, and as her baby's arrival grew closer, she became sadder, feeling sure that her little one would never meet his or her daddy. She was being well looked after, with Win and Louisa caring for her at home, Mac fussing over her at work, and the Suffragettes arriving with food for her, or bootees for the baby, or just funny chatter to keep her mind off where Jim could be.

Mac had stopped her doing anything too physical, which had annoyed Ivy at first, until she realized how much better she felt after a day doing less rigorous tasks. And with the weather still freezing, there wasn't much to do anyway. Today, Louisa and the others were preparing the vegetable beds—they'd expanded again—while Win divided the tulips that were coming up in big clumps and Mac pruned the wisteria. Ivy had been in the greenhouse, preparing some seedlings, but there wasn't much for her to do, so now she'd come to her letter garden. It had been looking a bit sad over winter, but to Ivy's delight, things were beginning to grow again. She had some daffodils coming through, there were hyacinths that had flowered at Christmas, and more were coming into bloom now—blue as she'd hoped, meaning constancy of love. She'd prepared a patch for Louisa's lilies to grow when the frost had passed, and in the corner, the poppies that she'd grown from the tiny black seeds Jim had sent the last time she'd heard from him were beginning to flower—earlier than Ivy had expected. Their bright colors filled her with joy and she understood how the flowers popping up across the bleak battlefields gave the soldiers hope. Where there had been nothing, soon there would be color. She stroked her belly as the baby turned somersaults inside. It was just as where there had been nothing but grief, now there was new life.

Mac had brought a bench into her little garden and she sat now, taking a rest and thinking about what was to come. She thought she was ready for the baby's arrival. She'd now told everyone who needed to know. Jim's mother had been first shocked, then emotional and pleased, grasping Ivy to her chest and promising to help in any way she could. She'd even asked her to move in, but Ivy was happy at Win's and couldn't imagine living with parents who weren't hers and brothers she hadn't grown up with. Her own mother had been trickier. She'd broken the news while they walked to a Federation meeting together, hoping that being out in public would temper her mother's reaction.

"I'm going to have a baby," she'd said.

Her mother had stopped walking and looked at her, resignation in her face. "Oh, Ivy. Will you get wed?"

Ivy bit her lip. "It's Jim's baby, Mum. Of course it's Jim's baby."

"But Jim is in France. Or . . ."

Ivy had swallowed a sob. "I know that."

"So no wedding?"

"No wedding."

"What about the money? It ain't cheap bringing up kids on your own, and Lord knows I know it's not easy."

"Mum, it's going to be all right. I've got people helping. Win's said I can stay as long as I want, and Lou's stepping in—she's already calling herself Aunt Louisa—and Mac's been wonderful."

Her mother had eyed her doubtfully. "Really?"

"It's not what I'd have chosen, but it's what's happening and I'm going to have to make the best of it."

Just at that moment, the baby had decided to do some twirls and Ivy put her hand on her belly.

"Is it kicking?"

She took her mum's hand and put it on the spot where the baby was wriggling. "Feel it?"

Her mother's face broke into a wide smile. "A baby is always a gift."

"Especially now," Ivy said. "When Jim could be . . ."

Her mum nodded. "Especially now."

They carried on walking, Ivy feeling grateful that her mother had taken things so well.

"Been sick?" her mum asked.

"As a dog."

"Thought so, You've got that gray look about you. You're having a girl."

"A girl?" Ivy said. "I keep imagining a little boy, like Jim."

Her mum screwed her nose up, looking Ivy up and down. "Nope. That's a girl, mark my words. Your hair's flat, you're covered in spots and you look worn out. Girls steal their mother's looks."

Ivy had rolled her eyes. No one knew how to insult her like her mother. "Thanks."

"You'll see."

She couldn't say her mother was enthusiastic, but she had accepted she was going to be a grandmother and she was being fairly helpful, offering tips for the birth, and how to feed, and when to put the baby to sleep and when to wake it up. Mostly her advice was accompanied with thinly veiled insults, but it was fairly helpful all the same.

So she was all set. The crib was in her bedroom at Win's, the clothes were in her wardrobe, and she'd seen a doctor. She just had a few weeks to go until she met her son or daughter.

"Boy or girl?" she whispered as she rubbed her belly. "Boy or girl?"

"I think it's a boy," a voice said.

Ivy froze, her hand still on her stomach, hardly able to believe what she was hearing. Not wanting to ruin the illusion, she looked up slowly, and there, peering at her through the poppies, was Jim.

Jim. Her Jim.

She blinked. She must be tired if she was seeing things.

But no, the man was still there. He was wearing a uniform and he was holding a walking stick. He had his hair shorter than she'd ever seen it, and he had a big scar down one side of his head and across his cheek. But he was smiling.

"Ivy," he said.

She stood up, barely breathing. "Jim?"

"It's me."

In two strides he was across the garden, which was fortunate because Ivy was suddenly so dizzy she thought she might fall over if it wasn't for Jim's strong arms around her and his mouth on hers and his hands caressing her swollen stomach. She was crying and he was crying and they were kissing and laughing and sobbing all at once.

"It's really you." Ivy wept. "It's you. My Jim."

"It's me. I'm here."

"I thought you were dead. I thought I'd never see you again. I thought our baby would never know you."

Jim kissed the tears from her face and pushed the hair back from her forehead and kissed her again and then very gently he bent down and kissed her belly.

"Hello, baby," he said.

Ivy ran her fingers over his shorn hair and touched the pink scar on his head.

"What happened?" she said. "What happened to you?"

They sat on the bench, Jim's arm around Ivy and her nestled into his chest, not even minding how scratchy his uniform was.

Jim stared into the distance.

"We went over the top," he began. His voice sounded odd, like it was full of tears, angry and sad all at once. "Ivy, I have never been so frightened in all my life. Never. It was like being in someone else's body. My head was screaming at me not to climb that ladder, not to run toward the guns, but my body kept moving. I knew if I stopped, then our officers would shoot me. We had no choice. We had to go when we heard that whistle."

He paused.

"Whistles are like funeral bells out there. You hear one on the wind and you know that's it for hundreds of lads, just like that."

Ivy laced her fingers into his but she didn't speak. She understood that he had to talk, to get it out. Maybe he'd never speak of this again, but for now, he needed to explain the things he'd seen and what he'd done.

"We were running across no-man's-land," Jim went on. "The mud was awful. Sucking, great lakes of it. One lad next to me slipped and he was gone, under the surface, and then there were people running over where he'd been. I couldn't stop, couldn't help him up."

"No, of course not."

"We were trying to run, and my ears were ringing. I could hear shouts but it was though they were a long way away. Everything seemed to be in slow motion. I saw another lad—my mate, George—up ahead of me. He was there and he turned round to shout something at me, and then his head was gone."

His voice broke.

"He stayed upright, Ivy. For a second, George was still standing there even though his head had been blown off. Then he dropped into the mud and he was gone. I still see it sometimes, when I shut my eyes. His face as he turned to me and how it exploded as the bullet hit him."

Ivy felt a tear trickle down her cheek. No one should see horrors like that. No one.

"Then suddenly, we'd reached the Germans. One loomed up at me out of the smoke and I had my gun out, and I was thinking, 'This is it, this is the moment I kill someone.' I didn't even mind, you know? Because I'd seen what they'd done to George and I was so angry, I wanted to hurt them like they'd hurt him.

"But then I looked into his eyes—this German—and he looked like me. He was the same. Same age. Same hair. He was just like me, Ivy. And I couldn't pull the trigger. We just stood there for a second gazing at each other, guns drawn but neither of us shooting. And then a shell exploded."

Ivy winced. "What happened then?"

Jim shrugged. "I don't know. I don't remember anything until I woke up in a field hospital. They didn't know who I was. Apparently me—and the German—had been blown clear and they found us both in the mud a day later. Our uniforms were in tatters, my jacket was so torn that they didn't even know if I was British at first. I'm lucky it was our boys who found me, Ivy."

"What happened to the German?"

Jim swallowed. "He died. He got an infection and he died, before I woke up. They didn't know his name so they couldn't tell anyone. His parents will be wondering what's happened to him and they will never find out."

"How long were you unconscious?"

"A few days, and then in and out for about a week. I couldn't remember anything, but apparently I was rambling in English so they knew I was a Tommy."

"Thank God," Ivy breathed.

"I was in the field hospital for a fortnight, and then I was transferred to another hospital somewhere near the coast, and eventually to a convalescent home in Surrey."

"Why didn't anyone tell us?" Ivy said. "Your mum's been beside herself."

Jim grimaced. "I got hit on the head." He traced his scar, self-consciously. "They had to do surgery, to take the shell casing out. When I woke up at first, I didn't know my name or where I was from."

Ivy shuddered, thinking of Jim's head studded with pieces of a weapon.

"Even when I was in Surrey, and healing well, it took a while for my memory to return. For a while I could only remember that my name was Jim—no surname."

"And then you remembered?"

"Well, that's where things got a bit strange," Jim said. "A chap called Walter Boniface came to visit me. He said he was from the War Office and they thought I might be James Dobson."

"How did he know?"

Jim shrugged. "No idea. But as soon as he said my name, things started coming back to me. I remembered you and my family."

"When was this?" Ivy was trying to understand what had happened.

"Just last week. I wanted to get the nurses to contact you, but Mr. Boniface said he wanted to check a couple of things first. Then another fella turned up and said he'd arranged for me to be discharged and he'd got a car waiting."

"A car?" Ivy was astonished. "Who was he?"

"An MP. He was really posh and very important. One of those people who just gets things done, you know the type? One of the nurses said she recognized him from the papers. His name was Marcus Francis-Evans and he said he was doing a favor for a friend."

Ivy shook her head. "This doesn't make sense."

Jim grinned, his familiar wonky grin that she'd not seen for so long. "I know. But I don't care, because I'm here and I'm with you and you're having a baby."

He put his hand on her stomach and Ivy had a sudden thought.

"Did you know? About the baby? Did you get the baby's breath I sent?"

"No," he said sadly. "That was clever. No, Mr. Francis-Evans told me."

"What?" Ivy was even more bewildered. "How on earth did he know?"

Jim clearly didn't care. He kissed her again.

"Show me the garden," he said. "Show me what you grew with the seeds I sent."

Hand in hand, they wandered around the little patch of earth that Ivy had transformed with his letters.

"I was hoping those hyacinths would be blue," he said, delighted as they looked at them. "And I can't believe those poppies have bloomed already."

"So early," Ivy agreed. "Maybe they knew you were coming home."

She told him that she'd given some of his poppy seeds to Win as a way of easing the pain of Archie's death and he smiled.

"She sounds like a real character."

"Oh, she is." A thought occurred to Ivy. "I wonder if she had anything to do with those posh chaps who tracked you down? She knows all sorts of people."

"Maybe," Jim said. "She's never even met me, though."

"We'll ask her. She's been so good to me, Jim. Her and Louisa."

She showed him the patch of ground where Louisa was going to plant her lilies in memory of her lost baby, and he smiled.

"You're a good woman, Ivy Adams."

"I've learned from the good women I've got around me," she said.

She looped her arm through Jim's and he leaned on her. He'd broken his leg in the blast and though it was mended, it still ached after a while.

"I'm going to miss them, though," she said. "The seeds. I've got nothing else to plant."

"Ahh, perhaps not." Jim limped across to the bench where he'd left his bag and dug around inside for a while.

"Got it," he said, triumphantly holding something between his fingertips.

Ivy squinted at it. "What's that?"

"It's an acorn. I found it on the battlefield and I was going to send it to you. It was in my boot, for safekeeping, and somehow it survived the blast better than my uniform. Do you want to plant it? I thought it could grow here at Kew, strong and tall, and be a fitting memorial to all the men that we've lost."

"Yes," said Ivy, a wonderful idea coming to her all at once. "Let's plant it. But not here."

"Where?"

"Follow me."

Taking his hand, she led him out of her letter garden and across the lawns to where a pile of darkened ashes marked the spot where the tea pavilion once stood.

"Here," she said.

"Why here?"

"Ashes are a good fertilizer." She took a breath. "And I'm making amends."

Jim frowned. "What for?"

Ivy didn't answer. "I can't bend down," she said, gesturing to her stomach. "Can you do it?"

Jim crouched on the ground, brushed away the frozen ashes with his hand, and dug a small hole. Then he dropped the acorn into it and covered it up again.

"There you go," he said.

Ivy offered him her arm. "I think we should go and see Mac," she said. "He's going to be thrilled to see you. And as we walk, I'll tell you why I wanted to plant the tree right here."

She held out her arm. Jim took it and they started to walk—slowly because Ivy was heavy and her belly was cumbersome, and Jim's leg was hurting—toward the main building.

"In 1913, things were really bad at home . . ." Ivy began.

Chapter 32

One week later

"I suppose," said Jim, "we should get married."

They were in the lounge at Win's flat, having just devoured the most delicious Sunday roast thanks to Bernie. He had arrived at Kew unexpectedly just a few days before, weighed down with a chicken sent by Matthew, a bag of potatoes, a cauliflower, a cabbage and six bottles of beer made with Matthew's hops.

He'd burst into the break room, a couple of days after Jim had arrived, startling Louisa and Mac, who were in there, heads bowed over an order form for fruit bushes, and Ivy, who wasn't doing anything useful but just liked to come to work anyway.

"Is he back?" he'd said. "Is Jim back?"

Ivy had struggled to her feet. "He's back."

"Where is he?"

"At his mum and dad's."

"And is he all right? Is he hurt?"

"Bit battered and he's got a cracking scar, but yes, he's fine."

Bernie breathed out in relief and dropped his bags so he could hug Ivy. "I'm so glad."

She hugged him back and then released him, looking at him through narrowed eyes. "How did you know?"

"What?"

"That he was back? Louisa has written to you, but she only posted the letter yesterday."

Bernie shrugged. "Lucky guess?" he ventured.

"Bernie, did you do this? Did you get those men to find him and bring him home?"

A flush rose up Bernie's neck. "I did write to a few old friends, just to see if they could help."

"I thought it was Win, but when I asked her, she knew nothing." Ivy was delighted. "It was you."

Louisa looked interested. "Who did you write to?"

"A chap I knew at school called Wally."

"Walter Boniface," Ivy said. "He found out Jim was in hospital and couldn't remember his name and went to visit him."

Bernie grinned. "He always loved a puzzle, old Wally did. Good at crosswords, too."

"And what about Marcus Francis-Evans?"

Louisa blinked. "He's in the cabinet, isn't he? Did you go to school with him, too?"

"No, not me. His son went to St. Richard's, though I didn't have much to do with him. He was a very musical boy and I didn't get involved in the choir or orchestra."

"But he remembered you well enough to do you such a big favor?" Ivy was impressed.

Bernie looked at his feet. "I asked Vivienne to ask him."

Louisa and Ivy both stared at him in shock. Mac, oblivious to why they were surprised, simply shrugged his shoulders and carried on with his order form.

"You asked Vivienne?"

"I wrote a letter to Francis-Evans and asked him to help, then I enclosed it in a letter to Vivienne."

"What did you say?" Ivy understood how difficult that must have been for Bernie.

"I just wrote that I bore her no ill will and asked her to help."

"Did she reply?"

He gave a small smile. "In a very Vivi way. She sent me a postcard from Worthing—that's the closest town to school—and scrawled on the back that she'd sent my letter on and she hoped I was well."

Louisa chuckled. "Oh, for an ounce of her self-confidence."

"I like you much better without it," Bernie said. "Wally told me he'd found a man he thought could be Jim, and when I told him Francis-Evans knew about it, too, he got him involved. I got a letter yesterday telling me Jim was on his way home."

Ivy threw her arms round Bernie. "You magical, special, smashing man," she said. "I can't believe you did this for us."

"You looked after me when I needed it," he said simply. "I was just returning the favor."

Matthew had given Bernie a few days off from the farm to catch up with Jim and have a break while things were quieter over winter. He was staying with Mac and his family, and now they were all gathered at Win's having had a celebration meal—cooked by Louisa, of course. Win rarely ventured into her kitchen. "I'm not built for cooking, darlings," she always said.

"I'm sorry?" Ivy said to Jim now. "What did you say?"

"I said we should get married."

She looked at him, his cheeks already rounder and with more color, thanks to a week of eating meals made by his mum. His scar still livid across his head and face but his eyes full of love and hope. And she laughed.

"No." She chuckled. "We can't get married."

Jim made a face. "Why not?"

Ivy sat back against the sofa, so her huge pregnant abdomen rose up, and she pointed at her belly button. "Because of this. I doubt any vicar in London would offer to marry me in this state."

"Darlings, I could ask around," Win said. "Someone's bound to know someone who would do the honors. Perhaps for a small fee?"

But Bernie gave a small cough. "I think I may be able to help there, too."

"With a fee?" Win looked doubtful as she glanced at Bernie's weather-beaten face, his slightly too-long hair and his battered clothes.

He laughed. "With a vicar."

Jim sat up straighter. "Really?"

"Really. Remember when I was hiding in St. Anne's? I got to know Reverend Miller rather well. We often chatted when I was tending the graves. I always suspected he knew I was hiding out in the crypt, but he never said so. That was one of the reasons I wanted to help him out by looking after the churchyard."

"St. Anne's?" Ivy gasped. "That would be perfect."

Mac shook his head. "You're really something, Bernard Yorke."

Bernie laughed. "I just believe in helping other people whenever you can."

"Well, you most definitely do that."

"What do you say, Ivy?" Jim turned to her. "Do you want to marry me, in St. Anne's at Kew Green?"

Ivy could hardly believe how quickly despair had turned to happiness. She never wanted to feel as bleak as she had when she thought Jim was dead, ever again. She wanted him close to her, and the baby, forever. She smiled at him.

"I do."

Jim whooped and Louisa and Mac cheered, and Win started to cry.

"I'm so happy for you, darling," Win said when Ivy looked at her, concerned. "We're going to have the most wonderful wedding."

"You need a dress," Louisa said, looking excited. "Do you have anything that could do?"

Ivy grimaced. "Nothing that would fit."

"Would you believe, I've still got my old wedding dress," Lou said. "No idea why I've hung on to it for all this time, given how awful my marriage was. I wonder if we could alter it so it fits you?"

"You'd need a lot of extra fabric to fit over this thing," Ivy said, prodding her belly.

"I've got mine, too," Win said. "Why don't we put them together somehow? The Suffragettes will help. Henrietta is very clever with a needle."

Bernie got up.

"I'm going to speak to Reverend Miller right now," he said. "Shall we say, a week from Friday?"

"I think perhaps we should do it a bit sooner than that," Ivy said as the baby kicked her hard, taking her breath away. "I think this little one's in a hurry to arrive."

"This Friday?"

"Perfect."

"Hang on," Mac said, standing up, too. "I'll come with you. I'm going to go and see what we've got in the food stores at the Gardens. See if we can't come up with a good meal for after the ceremony."

He and Bernie disappeared out the door.

"Louisa, let's find my dress and see what we can do with it," Win said. She and Louisa went into her bedroom and Ivy and Jim were left alone.

"Are you sure?" Jim said. "I don't want to push you into anything. I know the last week's been a bit of a whirlwind."

Ivy thought she'd never been surer of anything in her whole life.

"I can't think of anything I'd rather do than marry you, Jim Dobson," she said.

And she felt just the same when Friday arrived and she, Louisa, Win and Bernie were standing outside the door of St. Anne's. The bells were ringing loudly, but instead of making Ivy feel guilty, as the sound always used to, it filled her with joy and hope for the future.

Inside the church were her mother and her siblings. Her dad might show up at some point, but Ivy found she wasn't bothered either way; she had a new family now. Jim's parents and his brothers were there, too, along with Louisa's Teddy, all the gardeners from Kew, and the Suffragettes—Win had been right; Henrietta had done a wonderful job creating a dress for Ivy to wear. Perhaps it wasn't quite what she'd have chosen, but considering there was a war on and she was hardly easy to dress, it was a triumph. Ivy smoothed the silky skirt over her stomach and admired the way it swirled round her legs.

"Ready?" said Louisa.

"Ready."

Bernie held out his arm and Ivy took it. "Then let's go and get you wed."

It was a wonderful ceremony. The singing sounded more joyful than Ivy had ever heard it before, Reverend Miller was sweet, Jim looked so handsome in a new, clean uniform, and one of the Suffragettes—or maybe it was Louisa—coughed so loudly over the part when Ivy was supposed to promise to obey that she was fairly sure no one, least of all Reverend Miller, heard her leave that bit out.

And now, she was Mrs. Ivy Dobson and soon they would be a family. Jim was going to move into Win's flat with her for a while—Win had been adamant that they should stay and Ivy was sure that while Win was looking forward to the baby's arrival, she was also afraid of being on her own. This way they could care for each other, like a real family.

"Shall we head on over to the Gardens?" Mac said, as they filed out of the church. "I've got a surprise for you."

Ivy and Jim exchanged a glance—they weren't expecting any more surprises.

But when they all reached the Gardens, there waiting for them was a photographer.

"I thought we should have a memento of this special day," Mac said. "This is Henry—an old friend of mine. He's a dab hand with photography."

Ivy kissed Mac on the cheek.

"Thank you," she said. "This is a lovely idea."

They all lined up for a photograph. Ivy and Jim in the middle, Bernie to Ivy's side and Win to the side of him. Louisa next to Jim, with Mac by her side.

"Watch the birdie," Henry cried, and the flash went off with a *snap*.

"Could we have one more?" Ivy asked.

"You and Jim?"

She blushed. "Actually, I was wondering if I could have one with Win and Louisa."

Henry chuckled. "Of course," he said. "Get together."

Arm in arm, Ivy, Louisa and Win grinned at the camera. They were the Kew Gardens Girls, brought together by this wonderful place and held together forever by the bonds of friendship. Ivy felt her baby kick and thought one day she could show him or her this photograph and tell them all about her friends and the times they shared at Kew. Things may not always have been easy and who knew what the future held? When the next challenge came their way, they would face it together.

Author's Note

This story is based on real-life events mixed with some imagination. The Suffragettes did vandalize the orchid house and burn down the tea pavilion at Kew in February 1913. Two women—Olive Wharry and Lilian Lenton—were imprisoned for the arson attack in March 1913, though neither served a long sentence.

Female gardeners worked at Kew during the First World War when the men were serving in the armed forces. They were given lighter duties at first but eventually proved their worth and did everything the male gardeners did. We know from records that they were paid the same as the men, but the fight put up by Louisa and the other women in the story to receive equal salaries is fictional.

Acknowledgments

A big thank-you has to go to everyone at Kew Gardens, who welcomed me with open arms, allowed me to root around in the archive and answered all my questions. Thanks also to my agent, Felicity Trew, who is a constant support.

Books are nothing without good editors, so I owe thanks to Phoebe Morgan, Sam Eades, Ashley Di Dio and Tara Singh Carlson. And thank you to all my readers, who always bring new insight to my stories.

The
Kew
Gardens
Girls

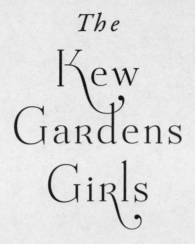

POSY LOVELL

❦

READING LIST

DISCUSSION GUIDE

A CONVERSATION
WITH POSY LOVELL

BOOK
ENDS

PUTNAM
—EST. 1838—

Reading List

To find out more about Kew Gardens and its history, I recommend *The History of the Royal Botanic Gardens Kew* by Ray Desmond and *The Story of Kew Gardens in Photographs* by Lynn Parker and Kiri Ross-Jones.

Some of the books that helped inspire me while I was writing this story were *The Country Diary of an Edwardian Lady* by Edith Holden, on which I based Ivy's journal, and *My Growing Garden* by J. Horace McFarland, which I drew on for Bernie's fictional textbook, *A Year in My Garden*.

To learn more about the Suffragettes, I recommend *My Own Story* by Emmeline Pankhurst and *The Suffragettes in Pictures* by Diane Atkinson.

For an evocative account of the Gardens in the early twentieth century, *Kew Gardens* by Virginia Woolf is the perfect read.

Discussion Guide

1. How do you think World War I affected Louisa, Ivy, Bernie and Win? In what aspects could that change have been for the better or worse?

2. Were you surprised to find that women had differing perspectives on how to support their country during the war? Which perspectives did you agree or disagree with?

3. *The Kew Gardens Girls* sheds light on the Suffragettes movement during World War I but also the politics on the home front surrounding the war. Did you learn something new about this time period during your read? If so, what?

4. The women of Kew each suffered losses and terrible heartaches but found strength in one another. Which friendship was your favorite, and why?

5. Were you surprised by how Louisa reacted when she was told Bernie's secret? If you were Louisa, would you have reacted the same or differently?

6. As time progresses during the war, Ivy and Jim's relationship grows but is also faced with hardships. What was your favorite moment between them, and why?

7. Discuss the different issues that the Kew Gardens girls faced that are still relevant today. Which ones resonated with you the most?

8. Win is a late addition to Kew Gardens but quickly becomes an important figure in the novel. What good qualities do you think she added to the group? Was there a defining moment that showed you her true character?

9. What do you think it means to be a Kew Gardens girl?

10. What were your thoughts about the ending? If you could go beyond the last page, where do you see each character's path leading?

A Conversation with Posy Lovell about *The Kew Gardens Girls*

***What was the inspiration behind* The Kew Gardens Girls?**

I love history, but I often find it's largely written by men. Often finding out what the women were doing during a certain time gives me inspiration for a new story, and this was no different. I loved discovering that the women gardeners at Kew were paid the same as men—something women are still fighting for in many sectors even now, one hundred years later. That discovery grew into an idea for the novel.

While this story is a work of fiction, the foundation is inspired by real-life events during World War I. What research did you perform in order to craft this story?

I'd never written about World War I before, so I had to do some reading about the war itself and women's roles during the time. I also got the chance to spend a day in the archives at Kew, reading all the letters of application written by women who wanted to be gardeners in 1915. It was fascinating.

Are any of these characters based on real people?

None of the main characters are based on real people, but Emmeline Pankhurst was of course a prominent Suffragette, and her daughter Sylvia—whom Ivy works with in the East End of London—did as she does in the story and formed a breakaway group. The story of the Pankhurst women is fascinating and worth checking out, if you're interested in the history of women's suffrage.

While Louisa and Ivy are both Suffragettes, their initial beliefs on how best to support their country and their cause differ. What was it like crafting these opposing viewpoints? What research went into that writing process?

I am a huge admirer of Emmeline Pankhurst, so I was disappointed to discover that she was responsible for the white feather campaign, which I think was ill-judged, unempathetic, and often downright nasty. I realized I wouldn't be the only person who thought that way—and equally, there would be people who disliked her approach to campaigning but approved of her patriotism. I decided a good way to present these opposing views would be for two friends—Ivy and Louisa—to hold them passionately.

At the center of this novel are courageous, inspiring women, but we also are introduced to Bernie, a man with an unpopular mind-set about the war. Why did you decide to add this interesting perspective into the story?

I've always thought that conscientious objectors were very brave in their own way. I wanted to explore the strength of feeling that would make someone refuse to fight, even though they knew others were dying on the battlefields. I found that when I was writing Bernie's chapters, I was completely on his side, but when I switched viewpoints to Louisa, I saw the issue differently again. I'm still not sure who I agree with!

What was your favorite scene in the novel, and why?

It's really sad, but I like the scene when Win gets the telegram about her beloved Archie from the Front, and Ivy and Louisa take her home and look after her. I think it shows the strength of their friendship, despite their different backgrounds.

Did you always know where Ivy and Jim's relationship would lead as you were crafting their story? Was there one moment in particular that you enjoyed writing the most?

I adore Ivy and Jim together. Their romance was always going to be an important part of the story, but it took on a life of its own and grew. I especially enjoyed learning about the language of flowers and using it to keep Ivy and Jim in touch when he was sent to fight in France.

What was the biggest obstacle you faced while writing The Kew Gardens Girls?

Learning about plants! We are really lucky to have a small garden in our house in London, but I don't know much about gardening. I knew that the experts at Kew would read my manuscript and check it for errors so I spent ages making sure that I wasn't putting plants in the wrong place, or having them bloom at the wrong time of year or in the wrong color.

In The Kew Gardens Girls, *the most powerful dynamics occur within female friendships. What do you believe are the key ingredients to these successful friendships?*

Support and having each other's backs, even when things are tough or you don't agree about something.

What do you want readers to take away from The Kew Gardens Girls?

That by coming together and taking action, you can achieve anything. The women—and Bernie—had huge issues to overcome, and alone they wouldn't have stood a chance, but together they triumphed. We're always stronger together.

Photograph of the author © Harriet Buckingham

Posy Lovell is a pseudonym for British author and journalist Kerry Barrett. Born in Edinburgh, she moved to London as a child with her family. She has a passion for uncovering the role of women in the past. Kerry lives in London with her family, and *The Kew Gardens Girls* is her American debut.

Visit Posy Lovell Online

Kerrybarrett.co.uk

KerryBarrettWrites

KerryBean73

KerryBean73